Only Ever YOURS

USA TODAY BESTSELLING AUTHOR

NIKKI ASH

Needing someone by your side, to help you up when you fall, to be your strength when you're weak doesn't make you a damsel.

It makes you human.

Playlist

Skin- Sabrina Carpenter

Break My Heart- Dua Lipa

I Won't Give Up- Jason Mraz

Marry Me- Jason Derulo

How to Love- Lil Wayne

The Way- Ariana Grande feat. Mac Miller

Stickwitu- The Pussycat Dolls

Body On Me- Nelly

Stay With Me- Sam Smith

Anyone- Justin Bieber

Without Me- Halsey

To those who know they've found the one,

the moment they've found the one.

One

ISAAC

"I CALL DIBS ON THE BRUNETTE."

I follow my friend's line of vision over to the two women who are eyeing Noah and me and groan. One has bleached blond hair with way too much makeup and fake tits, while the other has natural auburn hair, less makeup, and breasts that look like they're the perfect handfuls. "You're a dick. You know I prefer the brunettes."

Noah downs the last of his whiskey and chuckles. "True, but I'm sick of blondes. I'm ready for something different." He grabs the bottle from behind the counter, since the bartender is a friend of ours and doesn't give a shit, and pours himself another glass, bringing it to his lips and downing it in one go. "Besides, I'm wondering if the saying is true: blondes have more fun. And there's only one way to test that theory out." He nods toward the brunette. "Fuck her and see if she's more or less fun."

I shake my head and laugh, questioning how the hell I'm even friends with this guy.

When he refills his glass again, I side-eye him. "You okay?"

"Yeah, I'm good."

"You know I'm not going to just let you have her, right?" I tell him, referring to the brunette neither of us knows.

He laughs and says, "Of course not," no doubt remembering the first time we met. We were both at this same bar, drinking with some mutual friends, when a sexy brunette approached. We both had eyes for her, but it was me she went home with. The next night, we were out again, and a blonde approached. I told him he could have her because I'm only into brunettes. She ended up being a dud and so Noah and I spent the next couple hours bullshitting while we watched the game. When I mentioned I was going boating the next day, and he told me he'd never been on a boat, I offered for him to join me and we've been hanging out ever since.

When I glance over and lock eyes with the brunette, I hit her with my signature smirk. She smiles shyly, raising her hand to wave at me, and I know I've got her hooked.

"Damn it," Noah grumbles, as the women saunter toward us, the brunette keeping her eyes on me. "You always get what you want, don't you?"

I shrug, owning my place in this world. There isn't much I don't have, and anything I want, I can't imagine not being able to get. My dad raised me to go after what I want, to not stop until it's mine, and I use that approach in all aspects of my life.

"If you wanted her, you should've taken the initiative," I point out as the women approach and the brunette stops in front of me. "You said you wanted her, but I acted." I grin smugly. "Let that be a lesson learned." I throw an arm around the brunette. "What are you drinking, beautiful?"

She tells me what she wants, and I'm calling the bartender over to make it, when Noah's phone buzzes on the bar top.

"I gotta take this," he mumbles, grabbing it and walking away.

I order drinks for both ladies and am finding out their names, when Noah comes back over, a frown marring his features.

"What's wrong?" I ask, forgetting about the women.

"My mom," he chokes out. "She's been sick for a long time. They just called and said she might not make it through the night."

His words make me feel like a shitty friend. I never even knew his mom was sick. Noah is a quiet guy, and I never push. We hang out, drink, go boating, pick up women. But we don't really talk.

"Shit, man, I'm sorry. What do you need?"

He shakes his head. "I have to go."

He takes off toward the exit and I follow after him. "Wait, I can go with you. You've been drinking..."

"I'll take a cab. I need to do this alone, but thanks."

When he gets to the sidewalk, he hails a cab and jumps in without looking back. Unsure if I should force my way in or let him have his space, I text him, letting him know I'm here if he needs anything. He doesn't text back, even though it shows he read it.

No longer in the mood to get laid, I go back in to pay our tab and then take off to my place. I live in a condo my dad owns a couple blocks away from the bar and campus. When I get inside, I text Noah again. I've heard him talk about his mom a few times, saying they're close, but he's never mentioned his dad, so I'm assuming it's just the two of them.

I change out of my clothes and into a T-shirt and sweats, then grab my phone to call my parents. Hearing Noah's mom is sick and could die any time has me wanting to talk to my own.

A couple years ago, my mom was diagnosed with cancer and for a while we were worried she wasn't going to make it, but thankfully she pulled through and is now cancer free.

My mom answers on the first ring. "Isaac, is everything okay?"

I chuckle at her worried tone. It's pretty late on a Friday night, so she's assuming something is wrong. She isn't far off...

"I'm okay. I just wanted to say hello... and to tell you that I love you."

I can hear her smile through the phone. "Oh, *meu amor*, I love you too." *Meu amor* means sweetheart in Portuguese, which is my mom's native language. She doesn't speak it often, especially since my dad is Armenian and can't speak a lick of Portuguese, but she's been calling me by that nickname since as far back as I can remember.

"I can't wait to see you," she continues. "You're sure you're okay having us stay with you?"

"Of course." I glance around the condo that has been my home the past four years. Most kids would live on campus, but my dad insisted if I was going away to school, I would be living where it's safe—in a building he can monitor. I can't complain since it's a nice place with a kickass view. It's also walking distance from the marina where the boat my parents got me for my high school graduation is docked.

The place is pretty clean, but I'm going to need to bring someone in to make sure it's to my mom's standards. The woman is a neat freak.

"Your dad and I will be arriving on Thursday. We're both so proud of you. I can't believe you're graduating. Is there any chance the jobs you've been looking into are close to home?"

"Maybe. I'm keeping my options open."

When I told my parents I wanted to go to college instead of going to work for the family business right out of high school, I expected my dad to be upset, but I should've known better. He patted me on the back and told me he would support whatever I decided to do, even if it meant never going to work for him.

Over the last few years, I've interned at a few different companies and have found my passion is numbers, but what I want to do with them yet, I'm not sure. I'm also considering extending my schooling and getting my MBA.

"So, any reason why you called tonight... aside from wanting to say hello?"

"And that I love you," I add, remembering my reason for calling her.

She laughs softly. "What's going on, Isaac?"

My dad grumbles something in the background, I'm sure

asking my mom for the phone to make sure I'm okay. I'm one of the lucky ones who actually gets along with his parents. Don't get me wrong, my dad is a hard-ass, but we're close, and I've never wanted for anything. I have enough money in my bank account that if I wanted to, I could get on my boat and sail for years without having to work or worry about money. But that's not what I want to do... I want to find my place in this world. I've considered going to work with my dad, but I'm just not sure if it's the future I want for myself.

"Isaac," my dad says, shaking me from my thoughts. He must've taken the phone from my mom. "What's wrong, Son?" he asks in a no-nonsense tone. My dad is a fixer, and if there's something wrong, he'll do everything in his power to fix it.

"Hey, Dad. Sorry, everything's okay with me. It's actually my friend, Noah. His mom is sick and it doesn't look like she's going to make it through the night."

"Is there anything we can do?"

My parents have never met Noah, since the times I've visited home for the holidays, he's had to work, and when they've come here, he hasn't been able to join us, but they know about him and how close we've gotten over the last six months. I don't have a lot of friends, but he's become a close one.

"I don't think so. He's with her now."

We talk for a few minutes, until my phone beeps in my ear. When I pull it away and see it's from Noah, I say good night to my parents and let them know I'll keep them updated. We hang up and I pull up the text.

Noah: She's dead.

I text back, asking where he is, offering to go to him, but the text goes unread.

For the next few days, I call and text him, but my messages all go unanswered. I go by his place and bang on his door, but he doesn't answer. I know he's grieving, but I hate that he's not letting me in.

On Thursday, the day before my graduation, I'm calling Noah for the millionth time, when my phone rings. I'm expecting it to be my parents, since they called a few hours ago to let me know they're on their way, and they're only a couple hours from me. So, I'm confused when my dad's attorney's name appears on my screen.

"Frank, how are you?"

Frank Abelman has been my dad's best friend since they were kids, and his attorney since the minute he passed the bar. He's also the closest thing I have to an uncle, since my dad's brother passed away when I was younger and my mom's family lives in Brazil. She met my dad shortly after she came here on scholarship to attend college and never returned. Her parents were against them being together and pretty much disowned my mom.

"Isaac, where are you?" The sound of his voice has my blood turning cold.

"I'm at home. What's wrong?" He never calls me unless there's a reason. He's a busy man, and while he's like family, he isn't really a family man. Not like my dad.

"There's been..." I hear him swallow thickly over the phone. "Your parents... They're gone."

Two

ISAAC

GONE. MY PARENTS ARE GONE.

It's been five days since Frank delivered the news and I still can't wrap my head around it. One minute, we were making plans for my graduation weekend and the next I was planning a funeral.

Pink tulips. My mom's favorite.

Two empty caskets because their bodies were unsalvageable.

"Someone ran them off the road and their car caught fire and blew up. We don't know who did this. It's being investigated as we speak."

As I lay a rose over each of their caskets, in front of their friends and family and my father's work associates, my body is still numb, my heart shredded. It wasn't supposed to be like this. Growing up, I knew my dad's world was dangerous. My mom and I never went anywhere without a guard, and my dad always had men with him. He was threatened many times, but it always felt like he was untouchable, invincible.

Guess he wasn't.

The day drags on. The priest finishes speaking and then there's a celebration of life afterward. Everyone gives me their condolences, but my head is too hazy to even recall who half these people are.

Finally, it's over, and Frank asks me to go with him to discuss some things.

"Can it wait? It's been a long day."

"Sure," he says, tight-lipped. "Will you be staying in your family's home?"

"No, I'm going back to my place. I can't be here."

Everywhere I look, the house reminds me of my parents, of my childhood. The corner store is where my mom and I used to ride our bikes to buy candy. The park is where we would go for walks and have picnics. I went to school here, grew up here, with my parents by my side every step of the way. I can still hear my dad cheering on the sidelines at my football games at the field in town. My mom whistling as I walked across the stage at my high school graduation. I need time to breathe, time to get my shit together, and I can't do it here with every memory pulling me down.

"I understand," he says, "but we should talk soon."

He hugs me and then we part ways. Not wanting to be in this city any longer, I take off straight back to my place, using the two-hour drive to get lost in myself.

When I get home, I take a hot shower and then get dressed. I'm rummaging through my mail when I see an envelope addressed to me with my mom's handwriting.

It's postmarked seven days ago—before she was killed.

I tear it open and inside is a handwritten letter. She loves to write, has several pen pals all over the world, and once in a while she would write to me. She says there's nothing more personal in a technologically-filled world than writing a letter by hand to someone.

My dearest Isaac, the letter begins, but I can't read anymore because tears—the first that have escaped since my parents died—well in my eyes, blurring my vision. I swipe them away, needing to read my mother's final words.

My dearest Isaac,

It's been a little while since I've written to you. Next week you're graduating from college and I'm so proud of you. You've grown up into a strong, smart man, who I'm honored to call my son.

As I read the letter, sobs begin to rack my body, and tears, hot and heavy, spill down my cheeks. She goes on to tell me how much she loves me and looks forward to one day meeting the woman who will capture my heart. That she can't wait to become a grandmother. How she's so thankful to have found my father and to have been able to have me.

Every word I read makes me cry harder, drops of liquid hitting the paper and smearing the ink. And when she ends her letter, she writes something that hits me hard.

I know you're excited to make your own path, but I must confess I hope one day you find your way back home. I miss you, meu amor, and I will always be here waiting for you.

To some, her words might sound like a guilt trip, but knowing my mom, it was her way of making sure I knew I always had a place to go. That no matter where I ended up, where she and my dad were, was my home.

The letter ends with her signature hugs and kisses. I read through it again, and then a third time, wishing her words would come alive and I could hear them straight from her mouth.

But they don't. They stay silent, merely ink on a page. And when it hits me that never again for as long as I live will I see my parents, hear their voices, receive a letter or a phone call from them, I slide down the wall I was leaning on and cry, until at some point, the tears dry up and my head throbs so hard, I lie on the cold wood floor and close my eyes, praying when I wake up this will all be nothing more than a nightmare.

Frank: We need to talk.

IT'S BEEN DAYS, OR MAYBE WEEKS, SINCE I'VE SAID goodbye to my parents, yet it still feels like it was yesterday. I haven't left my condo since I arrived. I can't remember the last time I ate or drank anything, or hell, even showered. It all feels like a fucking blur. Frank has called and texted several times, but I keep ignoring him. Whatever he has to say, I don't want to hear it unless he's going to tell me my parents are still alive.

The phone rings, his name appearing, and I click end, only for it to ring again.

"How many fucking times are you going to call?"

"As many as it takes," he says. "Your father left a will and we need to go over it, sooner rather than later. There are things we need to discuss. Decisions that need to be made."

Shit, I didn't even think about any of that.

"Fine. I'll be there soon."

We hang up and, in a hazy state of fog, I pack a suitcase, unsure how long it's going to take. I'm driving north on Campus Road, when the bar Noah and I frequent catches my eye. Fuck, how long has it been since we've spoken? Days? Weeks? I don't even know what day today is.

At the next light, I make a quick U-turn and head to his place, wanting to check on him before I leave. I'm not sure how long I'll be gone and the last time I heard from him he'd lost his mom. He doesn't even know mine are gone as well. I tried to call him to tell him what happened, but he wouldn't answer my calls, and I wasn't in a place to be there for him when I could barely take care of myself.

When I get to his apartment, I knock a few times and then try the knob to see if it's unlocked. Surprisingly, especially since he lives in such a shitty area, it opens.

"Noah, you here?" I call out. When nobody answers, I walk farther in. The living room is empty and so is the kitchen. But his bedroom isn't.

I find him sitting on the edge of his bed, a bottle of whiskey in his hand. With red-rimmed, glassy eyes and a look of despair, his gaze meets mine. He looks like shit—rightfully so.

"What the fuck are you doing here?" he mutters, raising the bottle to his lips and taking a long swig.

I pry the bottle from his hand. "I was trying to get a hold of you. My parents... they were killed a few days after your mom passed away."

Noah's lids slowly shut and his head drops, shaking from side to side. "I'm sorry. Life's a bitch."

I nod, even though he can't see me, because he's right. It is. "I have to go home. Handle a bunch of shit. Why don't you come with me? It'll be a change of scenery." I can use the company, and based on the way he looks, he probably shouldn't be alone.

He releases a harsh breath and his eyes ascend to meet mine. "You want me to go with you?"

"Yeah."

He glances around his bedroom. "All right, let's go. It's not like I have anything left for me here."

After he packs a bag, we throw it into my trunk and get on the road. It's only two hours to Crystal Harbor, where I grew up, and the ride is quick, both of us lost in our own thoughts.

When we pull up to my family home, where Frank insisted we meet, I look over at Noah, who's staring at the monstrosity of a house with wide eyes. To most, the place looks ostentatious with its marble fountains and rose gardens and colonial-style pillars holding up the second floor wraparound porch, giving it an aerial view of the hundreds of acres it sits on, but to me it's just home. At least it was when my parents were alive. My dad built this home for my mom for their ten-year anniversary. Every detail came from love, and now, I don't think I can even go in. And I definitely have no desire to stay—or live—here.

"I don't think you ever told me," Noah says. "What did your dad do for a living?"

"He was a real estate developer... amongst other things."

Frank walks outside to greet me as I turn the car off and get out, Noah following my lead.

"Isaac, thank you for coming. I know this is hard for you."

I make introductions and then we follow Frank into the house. The smell of my mother's floral perfume hits my nostrils and it takes everything in me not to break apart, but I push it down, not wanting to lose it again. I can lament in my misery later when I'm alone.

"It seems your father never got around to updating his will," Frank says once we've had a seat in my dad's office. I keep my eyes on Frank, unable to look around at anything that's my dad's. It's too hard, hurts too much.

"What do you mean?" I ask.

"His will was created *before* you made your decision to go to college and take a different route..."

He doesn't have to explain further because I know what

this means without him saying another word. My dad would've given me the damn world if he could, and until I left for college, his dream was for me to join the family business, to work alongside him and one day take over, so it makes sense he would make sure, in his death, I'm taken care of.

"Since you were his only child, he left everything to you," Frank says. "His homes, his companies, his assets... Everything that was his is now yours."

I nod in understanding. My life is no longer mine. I'm no longer a college graduate seeking employment. I'm Isaac Petrosian, real estate developer and vigilante.

Three

ISAAC

TWELVE YEARS LATER

"FUCK!" I POUND MY FIST ON THE TOP of the desk and stand, pissed as hell. "Brad was supposed to sign off on the permits, so what the hell is the problem?"

Noah doesn't even flinch, used to my outbursts. It comes with the territory when you're running one of the largest real estate development companies in the country and have enemies standing on the sidelines waiting at every turn to see you fail.

He hands me the paperwork. "He *was* on board... But there's been some new developments."

I skim the papers, my anger rising with every word I read on the page. "Are you kidding me? The ERM has deemed fifteen acres a goddamned wetland?" I drop the papers onto the desk and pace the floor. The hundred-acre parcel of land was approved to be turned into an industrial park. When my father purchased it over fifteen years ago, it only had one acre of wetland and since then, Brad, the mayor of Crystal Harbor, and I came to an agreement. I would build the community a new park and he would look the other way while I had that acre bulldozed over. Now, days before we're scheduled to clear the land, he's pulling this bullshit? The ERM—environmental resource management—is only called out when someone calls the county and makes a damn complaint, and Brad damn sure knows better than to do that. This makes no sense and I'm going to get to the bottom of it.

"Let's go." I snag my jacket from behind my chair and shrug it on, grabbing my keys and pocketing my phone.

Ten minutes later, we enter the town of Crystal Harbor. Situated just inside the Marion county limits, about twenty years ago, it was voted on and declared its own town, separate from Chester Creek, the city I live in. The population is six thousand and everyone knows everyone.

Aside from when I'm doing business, I try to stay out of this damn town as much as possible. It's been over a decade since my parents died, but it still hurts to be here. Instead of living in town, I renovated the marina my dad left me. I updated the docks and warehouses and erected a three-story building. The first two floors belong to Petrosian Enterprises. The third is where I built the condo I live in.

I offered to build Noah one as well, especially since I owed him for moving here with me and helping me handle my shit, but he likes his space and privacy, and instead, chose to build a home on the edge of town on several acres off the beaten path.

The second I pull up to the parcel of land, I already know someone's been here. There are trail marks across the grass and dirt. I step out of the truck and Noah joins me.

"Flags and stakes," he points out, grabbing one out of the ground and throwing it to the side.

"Somebody called the county." I pull a stake and throw it.

We walk over to the post holding the permit board and it's been red tagged.

"Who do you think reported you to the ERM if not the mayor?"

I don't even have to think about it. "Pruitt. He's been gunning for the property, trying to push me to sell it. He wants to build a golf course on it and is pissed I'm going to stick an industrial park in his back yard." I grin, loving how pissed I make him. Even if it means he's making shit more difficult for me.

Noah laughs. "You're a dick."

I shrug, owning it.

"Let's go. I need to find Mr. Mayor and have a talk with him."

We're on our way back to the office when Noah points to the country club. "Isn't that Daddy Pruitt?"

I glance over and sure enough, Clint Pruitt is getting out of his cherry red Corvette and handing the keys to the valet. Crystal Harbor Country Club is the go-to place to dine and mingle for all the wealthy, pretentious assholes who live here, so of course he's here. I have a membership, but only for times like this.

After the valet grabs my keys, we head inside and are quickly seated. I glance around, looking for the dickhead, but I don't see him anywhere. While Noah and I eat lunch, a few people stop at our table to talk to me. I might not live in this town, but I damn near own most of it.

Just as we're finishing up our lunch, I see Clint walking over to the table next to me to speak to someone. Before he can make it there, I step into his line of vision, causing him to scowl.

"Clint, it's been a while."

"Not long enough," he mutters. "What the hell do you

want?"

"I thought maybe we could have a chat about my property over on Sycamore. Someone called it into the county."

I study his features closely to see if they reveal it was him, but he remains impassive. He's either not responsible, or he's doing a good job at hiding that he is. My guess is the latter. It wasn't too long ago he threw his own business partner to the wolves, sending him to jail for fifteen years for tax evasion and money laundering while he walked away scot-free. You can't do that without being a damn good liar.

"I don't know what you're talking about," he says, attempting to walk around me.

I step to the side as well, blocking him. "You better hope not," I warn, plastering a fake smile on my face. "Because if it is you who's fucking with me, you're going to regret it."

He blanches, but quickly schools his features. "Are you threatening me?"

I move closer to him, invading his personal space. "You know me better than that, old man. I don't threaten; I take action."

Without waiting for him to respond, I walk past him and out the door, finding Noah already standing next to my vehicle, waiting for me. When we arrive back at the marina, I call my secretary to join us as I stalk straight to my office.

"Mr. Petrosian," she says when she enters. Every time she calls me that, my heart sinks slightly in my chest. Now in her late sixties, Elouise Garner was my father's secretary for over twenty years and agreed to stay on as mine when I took over twelve years ago. I don't think I'll ever get used to hearing her call me Mr. Petrosian. It should be him who's here, not me...

"Find out where the mayor is so I can pay him a surprise visit."

"Yes, sir." She nods and then disappears.

"On a positive note, I just got word the shipment that came in went smoothly," Noah remarks once she's gone. "The merchandise is being delivered to the buyers as we speak."

"Good. At least one thing is going right."

My phone dings with an incoming text and when I see who it is, I groan.

"Rea?" Noah guesses.

"Yeah, she isn't getting the hint that it's over."

"Well, you were together for a while." He shrugs.

"A few months, and it's been over for just as long." I click on her name and block her. Maybe now she'll get the hint. At the very least, I won't have to read any more of her bullshit texts begging me to give her another chance. If she loved me like she claimed, she wouldn't have been texting another man behind my back.

"When are you going to finally realize that most women are conniving manipulators?"

"Not all," I point out, dropping my phone back onto my desk. "My mom wasn't."

Noah rolls his eyes, no doubt sick of hearing my shit, but I don't care. My parents had the kind of marriage I want. They weren't just in love. They were best friends. The other half to each other's souls. And I'm not going to stop looking until I find someone like that. And I'm sure as hell not going to settle for anything less. Noah might be okay being a bachelor for life, but I'm not. I thought I'd be married with kids by now, but at thirty-four, I'm still single and alone.

"She's out there," I tell him, walking over to the bay window that showcases the view of the marina and docks below. "And when I find her, I'll make her mine and never let her go."

"Mr. Petrosian," Elouise cuts in. "The mayor will be at the annual Crystal Harbor Dance for a Cause gala on Friday night. Would you like me to purchase tickets for you?"

Just fucking great. I eye Noah, silently asking if he's going to join me, but he's already shaking his head. "I'm heading to California tomorrow to meet with a new buyer," he reminds me. "And then to the East Coast to look at those properties you asked me to check out."

Shit, he's right. He scheduled that trip months ago.

"Get me two tickets and call Fairy Tales to arrange a date for me, please," I say to Elouise.

She nods and then exits.

"Well, damn." Noah smirks. "Never thought I'd see the day *you* would be using Fairy Tales."

"That's because I prefer to date a woman who isn't getting paid to be with me."

He chuckles. "And I prefer to pay a woman so she fucks me how I want it." He shrugs. "To each their own." He stands and walks toward the door. "I'll see you when I get back."

Four

CAMILLA

BANG. BANG. BANG. BANG.

The sudden pounding on my front door jolts me awake, and I grab my phone to see what time it is: eight o'clock. Jesus, I've been asleep for less than two hours.

"Camilla! I know you're in there!" the building manager yells through the door. "Open up! Your rent is late, again!"

As I throw my sheets off me and grab a pair of shorts and a hoodie to cover my body, I groan in annoyance with myself. I knew this was coming. It's the first of the month, which means rent was due last week... and I haven't paid yet. Hell, I haven't paid last month's either.

I unlock the deadbolt, the knob lock, and push the chain to the side, then open the door slightly, refusing to let the sleazeball in. He's suggested, on more than one occasion, what I can do in lieu of paying my back rent and that is so not happening.

"Gordan."

"Camilla." His beady eyes drag down my body, and even though I'm fully dressed, I still feel exposed in the dirtiest way possible. The guy is beyond gross and should be arrested for harassment. I'm sure I'm not the only woman he propositions when he comes around and makes threats about the back rent. "Do you have any money for me?" His hair is greasy and I can smell the weed permeating his skin. His teeth are a buttery shade of yellow, and I'm forced to hold back my gag.

"Give me a second." I shut the door in his face and go to my purse, pulling out all the bills I can find. I count it all up, but it's nowhere near enough to pay one month's worth of rent, let alone two. Between the electric, water, and my cell phone—that I only keep paid so my dad can get ahold of me—and the money I've sent to my dad, I'm broke.

I'm working forty hours a week, but because it took me months to find a job, during which time my measly savings were depleted, I'm behind on everything. I've tried to find a second job, but nobody will hire me. I've been blacklisted everywhere within a forty-mile radius of that stupid town. I've cut back on everything possible, but I just can't seem to get caught up no matter what I do.

I count the money again, hoping maybe some bills will magically appear, but of course they don't. I sigh in exhaustion, knowing I can't continue like this. Something has to change.

Losing his patience, Gordan bangs on my door again. I drop the money back into my purse since it's pointless to give it to him. I'm going to be kicked out soon anyway, so I might as well keep the money I have to eat with.

"I don't have it," I tell him when I swing the door back open.

"You know what this means, right?" he says, stepping into my doorway.

I close the door almost all the way to make it clear he's not welcome. "It means I need a little more time."

"If last month and this month aren't paid by next week, you're out. Understand?"

"Yep." I slam the door and then press my back to it, scrubbing my face with my palms, unsure how the hell I'm going to come up with the money by next week. It doesn't take a mathematician to know it's impossible without robbing a bank.

Since I don't have any internet on my phone, and I have the day off, I make a plan to go to the library to look for a second job. It sucks because it's Friday and that's the busiest night at the bar, but the bar has been slow, so the other girls who've been there longer get the good shifts before me. I quickly shower and get dressed, and am about to head out, when there's another knock on my door. Since it's unlike Gordan to visit twice in one day, I figure it's Yasmin, my neighbor and only friend.

I open the door and find her standing there with a big smile on her face. "Good morning." Her voice is chipper, *too chipper*, but since she extends her hand with a venti cup of coffee from Starbucks, I ignore it, taking the caffeinated beverage from her. I haven't had Starbucks in God knows how long. That shit is for the rich... and I'm far from it.

I inhale the sweet aroma and then take a slow sip, savoring the taste of peppermint mocha hitting my senses. It doesn't matter that it's May, peppermint mocha can be drunk all year because it's that good.

Once I've taken another couple sips, I glance at Yasmin. "Why did you buy me this?"

There's only one reason someone as poor as us buys someone a seven-dollar cup of coffee: to kiss one's ass before asking for a favor.

"Can't I just buy my favorite friend a delicious cup of coffee?" She plops onto my gray microfiber couch—one of the few things I was allowed to take with me when I was forced to leave my home. "Oh, I got you this too." She hands me a brown bag.

When I open it up, I gasp. "Banana loaf?" That single piece of bread is like four dollars! "What the hell do you want?" I sit in my reading chair and break a piece of the bread off, popping it into my mouth. Mmm... so delicious and moist. The sweet taste of the banana and cinnamon...

Yasmin shakes her head. "You're right, I do have a favor to ask."

"I knew it." I side-eye her playfully. "Let me enjoy my coffee and bread first at least."

She giggles, her green eyes lighting up with mirth. "You're such a coffee addict."

"Not coffee, Starbucks. If you had brought me Dunkin', I would've kicked your ass out."

"True," she says with a laugh before sobering. "I saw Gordan come by."

So much for enjoying my food and beverage. "Yeah, I'm a little behind on rent... But I'm going to find a second job."

"I think I have a temporary... and *possibly* permanent solution to your problem."

"Is this your segue into your favor?"

"Kind of..." She bites down on her bottom lip nervously. "But it will also help you... kind of a win-win."

"Just spit it out." I take another sip of my drink, sighing at the minty flavor hitting my senses. It reminds me of Christmas, my favorite holiday. There's nothing she could ask me to do that would ruin what I'm feeling right now.

"I need you to go on a date for me."

Except for that.

"No way," I choke out, pounding my chest as my hot drink skates down the wrong tube, making me cough and splutter.

"Camilla, please, just let me explain before you say no."

"No." I shake my head. "And I've already drunk half the coffee, so black, black, no trade backs."

She snorts out a laugh. "You're so crazy. Please, just listen."

"No," I repeat. "That escort gig is your thing, and I'm not getting roped into it."

I met Yasmin at Azul Lounge when the owner took pity and hired me. We worked together for a couple months before she received an offer to work for Fairy Tales Escorts. It's a high-end escort service that many of the wealthy men in and around Crystal Harbor use. It's not sleazy like some services, and sex isn't always part of the deal—unless the woman agrees beforehand—but I can't imagine having to go on a date with a man I don't like and fake chemistry between us.

"It pays a grand for the evening."

Whoa... "Say what?"

She smirks knowingly. "Now I've gotten your attention."

"You get paid a thousand dollars to go out with a man for a few hours?"

"More depending on what I agree to."

"I thought you said you don't have sex with them." I give her a stern look.

"I don—" I raise a single brow, daring her ass to lie to me. "Fine... I have a few times, but it's not that bad. I know it sounds slutty, but it's just sex and the money is well worth it."

"How worth it?" Call me curious.

"Triple what you make for a night out."

Holy Jesus, mother of God! "Why the hell are you still living at your mom's place if you're raking in that much dough?" She works several nights a week.

"You know my dream is to open up my own yoga studio downtown. And I don't want to have to take out a loan. Most businesses fail their first year because they don't bring in enough revenue to stay afloat and I want to make sure I lower my chances of that happening."

I smile at my friend, proud of her... and a bit envious. There was a time I had a similar dream, only mine was to open up a small boutique that sells all types of things like women's clothing and shoes, perfume, and makeup—all the latest trends—but now, it's nothing more than a fantasy. "That's awesome. You can totally do it."

"Thanks. I have a long way to go, hence me living with my mom, her nasty boyfriend, and their roommate, but I'll get there."

"So why do you need me to go out for you?"

She clears her throat and, if I'm not mistaken, blushes. "I met this guy..."

Oh no... Nothing good ever comes from that. I know it firsthand.

"His name is Todd and we hit it off. He asked me out and I really want to see where it goes... But Lucinda called me into work since I told her I would be available. I don't want to cancel on him. It will look bad and—"

"And what if it does work out? Are you going to quit your job?"

Yasmin flinches, as if she didn't even think about that. "I guess... I'll just see where it goes and then go from there. Maybe it won't even turn into anything, but it's just been so long since I've been asked out." Her lips curve down into a frown and I move from my chair over to the couch next to her, setting my cup down and taking her hand in mine.

"I'm proud of you for moving forward." Her last relationship ended badly. I didn't know her then, but she confided in me how terrible it was. Thankfully, she got out of the shitty situation alive and moved in with her mom and has gotten her life back together.

"Thank you," she murmurs. "He was really sweet. I met him downtown when I was window shopping storefronts for my yoga studio. He asked me to join him for coffee and we spent hours talking, then he asked me out." The look of hope in her eyes is my undoing.

"I'll do it."

Her brows kiss her hairline. "You will?"

"Yeah. What the hell...? I need the money and you deserve to go out on a real date."

Yasmin engulfs me in a bear hug. "Thank you so much! There's only one catch..."

Oh boy, here we go...

"He has to think you're me."

"Yasmin!"

"It's not that big of a deal. All the girls use fake names. I'm Jasmine."

"Like the Disney princess?" I groan at her cliché choice of name.

"Yeah, it's close to my name, so it's easy to remember."

"Okay, so I'm Jasmine for the night. I take it Lucinda doesn't know about this?"

"No way, she'd kill me. Luckily, from the information she sent to me, this guy has never used Fairy Tales before and he made it clear it's only a one-time thing. So, you'll go on the date for me, make an easy grand, and I won't have to cancel on Todd."

"Why did you say this could be a permanent solution?" I can't possibly take over for her permanently. She has to make a living, and this is her only source of income.

"Lucinda mentioned they're hiring. I know the only reason you won't apply is because the thought of going on a date with a stranger makes you uncomfortable, but once you see it's really not that bad, you might be more comfortable and apply. And with how much it pays, you'll have no problem paying your bills. Maybe you can even go back to school without taking out any loans."

Everything she's saying makes complete sense, but I still can't imagine ever being okay with going out with a man I have zero chemistry with, and I definitely can't fathom having sex with a stranger.

"We'll see. Let's just get through tonight and pray neither of us gets caught."

"We won't," she insists. "He's expecting a brown-haired, green-eyed woman, and we have similar features. As long as you go by Jasmine, what can go wrong?"

"Famous last words," I mutter.

"WHAT DO YOU THINK?" I TWIRL AROUND IN MY BLACK shimmery Saint Laurent off-the-shoulder evening gown and matching heels Yasmin lent to me from Fairy Tales. Since the women are expected to play the part, they're given clothes to wear that go with the situation. Based off this dress, I'm guessing we're going somewhere formal, maybe to dinner or a show...

Yasmin glances over at me from applying her eyeliner and grins. "You look perfect. Like a fairy tale princess." Her phone chimes with an incoming text. "It's the call service. The driver is here to pick me... *you* up."

Suddenly, a pack of butterflies attacks my belly. I'm really going to do this. I haven't been on a date in almost a year, and now I'm about to go on one with a wealthy man who's expecting a professional escort.

"Stop," she says. "I can see it written all over your face. You're freaking out. Just pretend like it's a blind date. These men only want a woman to have on their arm. I'd be surprised if he says more than two words to you the entire night. Enjoy yourself. Eat the expensive food, drink the expensive alcohol."

"I'm not even twenty-one!"

She waves me off. "You will be in a couple weeks. Besides, you're me, and I'm twenty-seven."

"Oh, God. This is going to go so badly," I groan.

"It's going to go perfectly," she says slowly, placing her hands on my shoulders. "Take a deep breath."

I do as she says, inhaling and then exhaling slowly.

"There. Now go. You don't want to keep him waiting."

I nod once and take another deep breath. "Okay, do I need your phone for anything?"

"Nope. At the end of the night, the driver will drop you back off here. Once you're home, text me and let me know how it went and then I'll check in with Lucinda and she'll never know any different."

"All right." I wrap my arms around her. "Good luck on your date."

"Thanks. You too."

Grabbing the clutch Yasmin lent me, I toss my phone inside of it in case of an emergency—like if this guy turns out to be a creep and I need to call for an Uber—along with my keys and head downstairs.

I spot the black limo, which stands out like a sore thumb in the poverty-stricken neighborhood we live in, and saunter over with my head held high, reminding myself I'm going to make enough to pay almost an entire month's rent in one night by doing this.

I expect the driver to get out and greet me, so I'm a bit taken aback when the back door opens and a man, dressed to the nines in a sexy black tux complete with a bowtie, steps out. Even in the dark of the night, I can make out his features: chiseled jaw with neatly trimmed stubble covering his face. His brown hair is short but messy in that sexy sort of way only men can get away with, and as I walk closer, I notice he's sporting a tattoo. It's a simple, elegant scrawl going vertically down his neck, maybe a quote of some sort. On some people it might make them look hard, or even trashy, but on him, it only adds to the appeal. I briefly wonder if he has more ink hidden underneath his attire.

When I reach him, he extends his hand, silently asking for

mine, which I give freely. Only a few inches from him, it's clear he's much older than me but has aged well. His eyes, a light brown—look like warm drizzled caramel when the light hits them—meet mine, and his mouth curls into a smile that nearly takes my breath away. His lips are supple and pink and his teeth are white and straight. He's masculine, but also kind of... pretty. He looks like he could be on a Calvin Klein ad or on the cover of a business magazine.

"I'm Isaac," he says, bringing my hand up to his mouth and placing a gentle kiss to the top of it. "Thank you for joining me this evening and on short notice."

My heart flutters in my chest like the wings of a hummingbird during flight and my skin prickles with goose bumps, and the apex of my legs—holy shit, it's like the moment a man touches you in just the right spot. I'm all hot and bothered and worked up, yet all he's done is kissed the top of my damn hand and murmured a few words to me.

"And you are?" he prompts when I say nothing in response.

Shit! Who am I? The way he's staring at me is making it hard to think. When his thumb massages a circle across my knuckles, the sensory overload becomes too much, and I abruptly jerk my hand away, needing to break the connection. His brow furrows, causing lines across his forehead to appear, making him look several years older, but he doesn't question me. Instead, he raises a single brow, which confuses me, until I remember he just asked me for my name.

My name... I'm... Jesus, why can't I remember my name? His gaze sears into me, and I worry I'm going to have a panic attack, right here, in the middle of the parking lot.

"You *are* from Fairy Tales, right?" he asks, glancing around.

Fairy Tales... Oh! Yes! Fairy Tales.

"I'm a princess," I blurt out, then cringe when I realize I just said my thoughts out loud. "I mean..." I clear my throat. "I'm Jasmine, like the princess."

The corner of his lips curves into a sexy smirk. "It's nice to meet you, Jasmine, like the princess. Shall we?"

I nod, afraid of saying anything else stupid, and slide into the limo. When he edges in and closes the door behind him, the air feels as though it's been sucked out and it's hard to breathe. And then, when he reaches across me to grab a bottle of champagne and the smell of his cologne hits me—an earthy, cedar scent—I know I'm screwed. Because this man is what dreams are made of. And me? I can't afford to dream right now. Reality is hard enough as it is.

Five

ISAAC

SOFT WAVES OF BROWN HAIR

and honey-colored highlights flow down her back. Emerald eyes that when the light inside the limo hits them just right remind me of *home*. Her breasts are round and perky and her lips are plump with a bit of shine to them. Her makeup is light and pretty, reflecting the fairy-tale princess persona she mentioned, which contradicts the dark, sinful dress she's wearing. She's got curves that make me want to ask for a chance to explore every dip and swell—no road map needed. I'd rather learn my own way around every inch of her.

She said her name is Jasmine, but I don't buy it. She probably uses a fake name to match the escort service's fairy-tale theme. That's okay because

I have every intention of finding out her real name along with everything else there is to know about her. I can't remember the last time a woman, just from looks alone, had me wanting to know more. And when she spoke nervously as she blatantly checked me out, it only heightened my curiosity.

Who is this woman and how do I make her mine?

I pour her a glass of champagne, hoping it will help calm her nerves. She takes it, smiling uncertainly, as she crosses her legs, exposing a good portion of her tanned, creamy thigh through the wide slit that runs up the outside of her leg, ending at almost her hip. Her dress is the perfect mix of sexy and classy.

We sit in silence for a few minutes, drinking our champagne, before she finally speaks up. "Is there anything I need to know for tonight?" Her voice cracks slightly and not for the first time I wonder why she's so nervous. She does this for a living, so she should be comfortable, right? This is my first time paying for a date, but she's a professional.

"It's a typical charity function. We'll drink, eat, maybe dance a little, there'll be some auctions, I'm sure…" My goal was to corner the mayor since he's avoiding me, find out what the hell is going on, and then dip out before dinner is served, but now I'm planning to milk this date as long as possible. Give myself some time to get to know this woman. I know she's being paid to go out with me, but that doesn't mean I can't get to know her for real.

She nods, gnawing on her bottom lip, and then downs half of her glass in one swallow. I watch her as she looks out the window, staring at the dark city that's lit up with little shops and stores as we drive through town. She looks lost in thought and it makes me wonder what she's thinking about.

From all the times Noah's used this agency, I was expecting an overly sexual, promiscuous woman, who would purr like a kitten and be all over me like a lioness. Noah's mentioned on more than one occasion how straightforward the women are. It's why he prefers them—they know the score and get paid enough to not ask questions. But this woman seems different... almost shy. If she hadn't confirmed who she was, I would've assumed I picked up the wrong woman.

Unable to take the silence any longer, I ask her if she's okay.

She twists around to face me, her eyes locking with mine. "Why wouldn't I be okay?" she asks, her voice coming out breathy.

"You seem nervous."

Her eyes widen, but she quickly schools her features. "I'm sorry." I expect her to elaborate, but she doesn't, which confuses the hell out of me. This is her job, yet she's acting like she's on a first date and isn't sure what to think.

We pull up to the front of the country club where the gala is being held and I swear I hear her gasp as the driver opens the door for us.

I exit the limo first and offer my hand to help her out. When her hand lands on mine, I feel her trembling. What the hell is going on here? In my line of business, it's imperative to be able to read people, and what I'm gathering from her silent cues is that she's scared. But of what?

Instead of going inside, I pull her around the corner, away from prying eyes, and gently push her against the wall. One of my hands lands next to her face and the other goes to the curve of her hip. "I don't know you, but I can tell when something's wrong, and there's something you're not telling me. This is your chance to be honest before we go in there. Because everyone in this town knows everyone and if there's something you're hiding, they're going to know."

She swallows thickly and closes her eyes as if she's at war with herself. Finally, after several long beats, she speaks. "I used to live here... in this town. I haven't been back in a while and it's making me nervous." She opens her eyes and her gaze locks with mine. "I'm sorry. You're paying for this date and you deserve better. I'll get myself together. I promise."

She lifts her chin and squares her shoulders as if doing so will help give her the strength she needs to proceed. As I watch her put on a brave face, my feelings toward her shift. I can't explain it, but all I want to do is take her in my arms and protect her from whatever it is she's afraid of. I know firsthand what it's like to be in this town, filled with its memories, but it feels as though there's something more going on with her. She's worried about ruining our date, but my only concern is what— or who—has her trembling. I barely even know this woman, but for some reason, I feel protective of her, and if I find out who it is that's making her feel like this, I can guarantee there will be hell to pay.

"I need to meet with the mayor, but once I do, we can go," I assure her. "And if at any point someone does something to upset you, let me know."

She nods, and for the first time, seems to relax slightly. With a small ghost of a smile, she stands taller and links her arm with mine. "Thank you."

We bypass the red carpet circus show and head straight in. I'm stopped several times by business associates and politicians I've done business with. Jasmine stays quiet with her arm hooked in mine, and nobody asks about her. That's not my usual style—treating a woman like a trophy on my arm—but

I figure she prefers it over being the center of attention. With everyone we come across, I watch to see if anyone even so much as looks at her the wrong way, but from what I can tell nobody does.

When we get to the bar, I order a scotch on the rocks and she asks for a bottle of water. "Not much of a drinker?" Most women would enjoy the fact that their drinks are being paid for and order something expensive.

"Not really." She opens the bottle and brings it to her lips. I watch, mesmerized, as she tilts her head back, exposing her slim neck, and swallows the water. Thoughts of kissing my way down the column of her slim throat have my dick swelling in my pants, and I have to look away so I don't end up with a half-chub right here.

I glance around the room, looking for Brad, but don't see him. The music has started, but the dance floor is still empty.

"Would you like to dance?" I ask, hoping maybe it will help calm her nerves.

She looks out at the dance floor, torn, but then nods. I empty my glass in one gulp and take her half-drunk bottle from her, setting it on the counter.

I guide us to the side of the floor and take her in my arms, pulling her toward me until our bodies are almost flush against each other. Entwining our fingers together, I bring her hands up and place them around my neck. She's stiff at first, but after a few minutes, she releases a sigh and her body sags in what feels like relief.

I can't help but watch her as we sway to the music. She's like a mystery hidden in a locked box and I want to figure out how to find the key so I can work it out. When she notices me staring, her cheeks flush a light pink, making her look young. The email said she's twenty-seven, but I'm not so sure about that.

"This is nice," she murmurs softly.

"Yeah, it is," I agree, unable to take my eyes off of her.

Her hands tighten slightly around my nape and she gently lays the side of her face against my chest, surprising me. Even with her tall heels, she only comes up to my chin. Without them on, she's probably five-six, maybe five-seven. Average height for a woman, but since I'm tall at six-four, it makes her appear shorter.

With her head against my chest, I can smell her perfume. It's soft and delicate—fits her perfectly. Out of the corner of my eye, I see the mayor. I should end the dance so I can catch him, but with Jasmine in my arms, I don't. I can't move from this spot. I don't know if it's the way I can feel her heart beating against mine, or how she's finally relaxed, her hands no longer shaking, but on this dance floor, with her in my arms, everything else fades away, and the only thing I want to do is dance with her.

One song blends into another and then another, and before I know it, we've danced until they pause the music and announce that they're opening the doors for the auction and the dinner.

Jasmine lifts her head and smiles shyly. "Thank you for the dance."

"It was my pleasure."

I take her hand in mine and guide us through the throng of people who are all shuffling through the doors like a herd of cattle. When we enter the main room, it's open and the tables are spread out. Along the outer walls are tables with items for the silent auctions. We find our seats on the seating chart and have a seat at the table. I glance around for the mayor but don't see him anywhere.

Two other couples join our table and introduce themselves. I don't know them personally, but I've heard of both men. We spend the four-course dinner flitting from topic to topic. The men mostly discuss business while the women talk about their kids and some charity shit they're organizing. Jasmine mostly smiles and nods, but every once in a while she contributes little nuances that reveal more and more about her. I learn she loves to stay busy. She hates to work out but loves to do yoga. She was in college but had to leave suddenly. She never gives too much, but every piece she does reveal, I stow away like a puzzle I'll put together later once I have all the pieces.

At one point, a woman makes a joke that has Jasmine throwing her head back in laughter. The melodic, carefree sound damn near knocks the wind from my lungs. Her eyes, filled with mirth, meet mine, and for the first time she shows me a genuine smile, and holy shit, is it a sight to behold.

"What?" she asks when she catches me staring at her. "Is something wrong?" Her brows furrow and her smile falters.

"Nothing's wrong. You just have a beautiful smile."

Her cheeks flush pink, and her smile slowly expands until it's back to the way it was, and my only thought, as I stare at her mouth, is that I would do anything to ensure she always smiles like that.

When dinner is over, a speech is made by none other than the mayor. Of course I can't speak to him while he's up there, so after we've had dessert and it's announced the auctions will close in thirty minutes, I suggest we walk around so we can check them out.

The first table has several items to bid on, like first edition books and antiques, but none of them interest me, so I move us to the next table. This one is filled with trips.

"Is that you?" Jasmine asks, pointing to the four-day at sea on a yacht donated by Isaac Petrosian with Petrosian Enterprises.

"It is." Elouise must've donated it in my honor in exchange for the last-minute tickets. "You ever been on a yacht?"

Her mouth twitches in thought, and I zero in on her heart-shaped lips, wondering what it would feel like to kiss her. "I've been on a cruise once. My mom loved to go on them. She and my dad used to go on them a lot, but they only took me once when they said I was old enough." Her face falls slightly before she quickly catches herself. "Anyway... a cruise, yes, but never a yacht. My dad is more of a skiing and vacationing in the mountains kind of man."

Interesting... She lives in one of the most poverty-stricken areas in the city, yet her parents sound like they have money. Another puzzle piece...

"I'm with your dad. It's why I love my yacht. It's spacious and comfortable and can house quite a few people if I want to invite anyone, but it's usually just me and sometimes Noah. There's nothing more enjoyable than spending a few days out in the Pacific Ocean away from everyone and everything."

"That sounds nice," she says, her lips quirking into a small smile. "Who's Noah?"

"He's my right-hand man. I own a few businesses and he helps me run them."

"What businesses?" she asks curiously.

"A real estate development company for one. I also import heavy machinery for construction and mining companies. I own the marina over off Ocean Ave just outside of town."

Her eyes widen slightly in recognition. It would be hard to live in this area and not know my marina. It's the biggest one in the state and is privately owned. Nobody within a hundred-mile radius can import or export anything without going through me.

We move down the line and I fill out a few of the auctions. When we get to the end, I see Brad talking to none other than Clint Pruitt and his asshole offspring.

"The person I need to speak to is over there," I tell Jasmine, nodding toward the men standing in the corner, bullshitting.

Because my hand is on the small of her back, I feel her stiffen on the spot. But before I can question her and find out if one of those men are who has her scared—and if one of them is, I'll make him regret the day he was born—she mutters, "I need to use the restroom, I'll be back," and scurries off, leaving me standing alone.

Six

ISAAC

AS JASMINE DISAPPEARS through the crowd, I consider going after her, but I really need to speak with Brad, and the fact he's standing with Clint is even more convenient.

"Gentlemen," I announce, making my presence known. Brad flinches and Clint grumbles under his breath. James—Clint's son—glares. "I'm glad I could catch you together. There seems to be a problem with the property over on Sycamore." I glance from Clint over to Brad. "It seems someone called the ERM on it. Clint, here, says he has no clue. Do you know anything about that?"

Without hesitation, Brad shakes his head. "I told you we had a deal."

"I know what you said, but the ERM being

called and deeming fifteen acres as wetland tends to send mixed messages."

"It wasn't me," Brad insists. "I was just telling Clint about your plans to make a community center and park..." I watch him closely as he rambles on about the agreement we came to. I've done enough business with him over the years to know when he's lying, and unless he's gotten better at it, he's not. Which means either Clint or someone else is trying to fuck with me.

"I can ask around," Brad offers.

"Thanks," I tell him. "The industrial park is happening, even if I have to alter my plans slightly. But if we can't figure this out, the first thing to go will be the community center and park." My eyes roam over his shoulder and land on Jasmine, who's standing by the bar, her eyes darting around nervously. I glance at Brad once more, ignoring the presence of Clint and his son. "I have someone looking for me. We'll get together soon."

Without giving any of them another glance, I walk past them and over to Jasmine, whose eyes meet mine. Her shoulders drop slightly and a poor excuse for a smile graces her lips, making me long for the real one she showed me earlier.

When I reach her, I cage her in against the bar, resting my hands on either side of it against the edge. "You find the bathroom okay?"

"I did. Did you find your guy?"

"Yeah. They still have the auction, but I don't need to be here for that. I did what I came to do. You want to get out of here?" Maybe I can convince her to go somewhere with me so we can talk and get to know each other better.

She gnaws on the corner of her lip, contemplating for several long seconds. "I don't think that's a good idea," she finally says, her lips turned down in a frown. "I just..." She releases a harsh breath. "Tonight was a mistake."

I don't know what she means by that, but I don't bother asking, because I know, even after only spending a short time with her, she has no intention of telling me anything. It doesn't matter if there's evident chemistry between us, she's got shit in her closet she's not ready to let out yet. She's going to need more time to open up to me, and that's okay because I have all the time in the world.

"It's okay," I tell her, backing up and giving her her space. "Thank you for accompanying me tonight."

Her eyes descend to the floor and she nods once. "I'm sorry..."

"You have nothing to be sorry for. You were hired to escort me tonight and you did just that." I pinch her chin gently to raise her face so she'll look at me again. "Let's get you home. It's nearly midnight. Wouldn't want you turning into a pumpkin." I wink playfully, and the cutest fucking giggle escapes past her lips, showing me more of the real her.

The ride to her place is filled with high tensioned silence. More than once I catch her peeking at me through her lashes, almost as if she wants to say something, but she remains quiet. When the driver pulls up, I get out first so I can help her out. And with a chaste kiss to her cheek, I thank her again for accompanying me and then wait until she's inside her building before getting inside the car to go home.

After getting changed, I head into my study and pour myself three fingers of scotch before sitting down at my desk and waking my computer up. I'm logging in when a picture frame on the corner of my desk catches my eye. I pick it up and stare at it for several seconds, the organ in my chest clenching in pain. The picture is of my parents, taken the day of their twentieth anniversary. Dad surprised her with a vow renewal ceremony and a party afterward. It was a few months before they died, and although a lot of those months were a blur after they passed away, I can still remember that day like it was yesterday, when I asked my dad why they were getting married again.

"*Because when you love someone the way I love your mom, you want to show them.*"

"*But you did show her by marrying her the first time.*"

"*And today, I'm going to show her all over again.*" He waggles his brows, and I fake gag at the thought of my dad showing my mom how much he loves her. My parents have always been affectionate with each other for as long as I can remember.

There's a knock on the door and Frank pokes his head in. "The priest is ready for you."

"*Thank you,*" Dad says with a smile on his face. "*Let's go, Son.*" Dad pats my shoulder tenderly. "*I have a woman to marry... again.*"

I glance over at the calendar. The anniversary of my parents' death is coming up next week. They would've been married for thirty-seven years. As much as I hate that I lost both of them at the same time, there's something tragically romantic about the fact they died together.

My father used to tell me on several occasions when my mom was sick, he couldn't imagine living without her. When shit was bad and we weren't sure if she was going to make it, a few times I wondered if he would find a way to take his own life.

I think about my conversation with my dad that day. I've dated plenty of women, but not one of them made me want to marry them once, let alone twice. And while I've asked women out, I never felt the need to be persistent.

Jasmine's face flashes in my head. It's too soon to have any *real* feelings toward her, I don't even know her, but I can't deny there was something there. With every frown, every sigh, every time she tensed up, I wanted to comfort her, find out what was wrong, and fix it. When she danced in my arms with her head against my chest, it felt right. When she smiled, it was as if my world brightened. And when I watched her walk into her building, I wanted to pull her into my arms and beg her not to leave.

An incoming call on my computer breaks through my thoughts. I click accept and Noah's face appears on the screen.

"Hey, how's California?"

"Overcrowded with assholes," he drawls. "I sent you over the numbers for the property in Sacramento."

"Thanks, I'll pull it up now." When I reach over to set the picture frame down, it knocks my cup of pens over, sending the frame and pens to the ground. The glass frame shatters across my floor, and I curse under my breath as an onslaught of emotions hits me hard.

"What the hell was that?"

"A picture frame broke," I choke out.

He eyes me speculatively for a long moment. "What's going on?"

"The anniversary of my parents' death is coming up." I take a large swig of my scotch.

"I'm sorry, man. Anything I can do?"

"No, but thanks."

He nods. "How'd it go tonight with Brad?"

"Not much happened. Brad denied having anything to do with the ERM being called out. Clint was there and didn't say shit. I put some pressure on Brad to fix it, so hopefully he's smart and does."

An email pings and appears on the top of my screen; it's an invoice from Fairy Tales.

"Have you ever gone out with a Jasmine from that escort service?" I ask Noah, changing the subject.

He thinks about it for a moment before he shakes his head. "I don't think so, why? Is that who you went out with tonight?"

"Yeah."

I try to come across nonchalant, but of course the fucker can see right through me and smirks. "How'd it go?"

"Not so good," I say with a chuckle. "I think I'm going to request her again."

"What? Why?"

"There was just something about her... I think she might be the one."

Noah barks out a laugh and I click end on the call before he can comment. We never went over the information he sent me, but I'll deal with it tomorrow. Tonight, I have an escort to book.

Seven

CAMILLA

ISAAC PETROSIAN. OWNER OF
the multimillion-dollar real estate development
company that was left to him by his late father, Samuel
Petrosian, several years ago after his and his wife's sudden
death. I was young, only nine years old, but I remember my
father talking about it. They were driving somewhere
and were driven off the road. Their car flipped and
caught fire, both killed before anyone could make
it to them.

The news hit the town and it was said Samuel
had enemies due to illegal dealings. Samuel and
my father were business rivals—both real estate
developers competing to own the city—but I also
remember them getting along. A few times when
Isaac was away at college, his parents came over for

dinner. His mom was sweet and would bring me gifts. When they died, my parents attended the funeral.

Of course the man I ended up on a fake date with is one of the wealthiest, most notorious men in Chester Creek, and where does he take me? To a charity function at the country club my parents belonged to. I practically grew up there, playing at the pool with my friends during summer, attending tennis and golf lessons. We'd have brunch there every Sunday after church, until my mom passed away—then the church and brunch stopped.

This city is too damn small, and it's why I need to get out of here somehow. I'll never be able to have a fresh start as long as I'm stuck here. But how can I leave, knowing my dad is here and can't go anywhere?

I push the thought aside as I secure my items into a locker and then sign in with the front lobby officer. Once I fill out the notification to visit form, I step to the side to wait for a visiting room to become available. It's Saturday morning, so there are several people waiting, some complaining about how busy it is, but I'm used to the process since I've been coming here every Saturday for the last four months—after waiting five weeks to be approved.

I wait patiently for my name to be called, and once it is, I step through the metal detector and follow the officer to the videoed visiting room.

The moment I see my father, he stands and envelops me in a strong hug. "There's my girl," he mutters into my hair, every word filled with emotion. The hug ends too soon and we take a seat across from each other at the table.

"You look good." He reaches across the table and pats my hand. "How are you?"

"I'm okay. You?"

His eyes scrutinize me, knowing I'm lying, and he sighs in sadness. "Camilla, please don't lie to me. It's bad enough I only get to see you once a week for an hour. I can't stand the thought of not knowing what's going on with you."

I bite my tongue, not wanting to bring up the irony in his words. *It goes both ways, Dad.* He wants me to talk to him, yet on several occasions he hid shit from me. Important shit. Starting with my mom being sick. I only knew she was dying when she was literally on her death bed. And then, instead of telling me he was being investigated for tax evasion and money laundering, he chose to hide it from me. I didn't know my dad was in trouble until I had reporters banging on my door wanting a statement.

"I'm okay," I repeat, this time making it a point to perk

up. He doesn't need to know my rent is way overdue and if I don't figure something out, I'm going to be thrown out on my ass. When I woke up, I expected Yasmin to tell me I screwed her over and she was fired, but instead, I was shocked to find an email notifying me that Yasmin had sent me a thousand dollars—which helps, but isn't enough to cover all that I owe.

"Cam, please," Dad insists. He's stubborn and won't stop asking until I give him something.

"I've been thinking about going back to school," I lie. "It's too late to apply for a loan, so I was wondering if maybe you have any money stashed away." It's doubtful he does, but anything would help, and I can always pay him back.

The second a frown tugs on his lips, I regret bringing up the subject of money. Since the day he was sentenced to fifteen years in a federal prison, along with losing every asset he owned, money has been a tough subject for him. It nearly killed him when we had to use my trust to pay for his legal representation—who in the end didn't do shit and is partly the reason why he's sitting in prison. I can't prove it, but I would bet my life he was paid off to throw my dad's case.

"I wish I did, sweetheart, but they took every last cent. If I had anything, I would give it to you."

I know he would and I hate that now he's going to be

stressed out over knowing he couldn't give me what I need.

"It's all good." I plaster a smile on my face. "I can take out a loan next semester. It's no big deal."

His lips flatten and he closes his eyes, shaking his head before he reopens them. "I'm so sorry, Cam... I—"

"Stop. Our time is limited. Tell me, how are you? It looks like you've been working out."

Dad chuckles softly, and just like that the conversation takes a positive turn and we spend the rest of our time together chatting away, pretending like we're not sitting in a visiting room that's being recorded.

When our time is up, I hug him, tell him I love him and I'll see him next week, and then head out. With all the stops, it's a two-hour bus ride back to Chester Creek. I use the time to check out the job listings in the newspaper. I find a few places hiring, but of course when I call and give them my name, they tell me they'll take my number and get back to me.

I'm feeling utterly defeated when I walk down the hall toward my apartment and find Yasmin standing outside my door with a prominent frown on her face.

"What's wrong?" I ask, instantly concerned. Then I notice what she has in her hand—another cup of Starbucks coffee. Oh, shit.

"We need to talk."

"This feels a lot like déjà vu," I mutter, snatching the coffee out of her hand and taking a sip.

"That's because it kind of is," she says as we sit on my couch. "I need you to go out with Isaac again."

"Nope, no way, not happening."

"Camilla, please," Yasmin begs. "He's requested me... *you*... personally. If you don't go, I'll be caught and lose my job."

"He requested me?" What in the actual hell? Why would he do that?

"Yep, he emailed last night after he dropped you off."

"It doesn't make any sense. The date went horribly. I was a mess, completely unprofessional. He spent more time asking if I was okay than enjoying himself. Why in the world would he go out of his way to request me?"

Yasmin shrugs. "I don't know, but he requested me to attend a business dinner with him."

When I groan, remembering how awkward the date was thanks to me, Yasmin mistakes my reason and asks, "Was he super pervy?" She scrunches her nose up in disgust.

"No, actually..." My cheeks heat against my will, and Yasmin, of course, catches it.

"Ohhh, he was hot, wasn't he?"

There's no point in denying it. "So freaking hot. He's a bit older, but you can tell, even with him fully dressed in his tux, he's built. Messy just-fucked hair, a tattoo running down the side of his neck with a quote that reads, 'Against all odds.' Oh, and did I mention he's Isaac Petrosian?" When Yasmin squints her eyes, having no clue who he is, I explain. "He's one of the largest real estate developers on the West Coast, hell, probably in the country. He's worth millions."

Not that I give a shit about money. I've dated men with money, was engaged to one, and they do nothing for me. If anything, after watching the way money shattered my father and his livelihood, it's more like a turnoff. Greed has the capability of rotting someone from the inside out.

But Isaac seemed different, like he didn't feel the need to flaunt that he was probably the wealthiest man at the event last night. Don't get me wrong, he carried himself with confidence and ease, but his *I don't give a fuck attitude* seemed more from him really not caring what people thought and less from the fact he could probably buy them all out.

And I won't even mention to her the sparks that flew between us when we were dancing. The way he held me in his arms. For those few moments, it didn't feel like two strangers on a first date. When I was in his arms, it felt like I'd known him my entire life, like we just fit...

"He sounds like a catch and a half," Yasmin says, snapping me from my thoughts.

"Exactly, so why the hell is he requesting my bumbling, awkward ass?"

She laughs. "Umm, maybe because you're a total knockout and have the personality to match."

"Not last night... I was in rough shape."

"Well, he must've seen something you didn't." She shrugs. "On the bright side, it's another grand in your pocket."

That's definitely a plus but... "I can't take your money again. It should be you going on the date, not me."

She shakes her head. "No way. I put you in this situation in the first place. I have commitments four other nights, and I'm seeing Todd again." Hearts dance in her eyes and a smile spreads across her cheeks.

"I'm judging by your face-splitting grin, your date with Todd went well?"

"It was amazing," she gushes. "He was a complete gentleman. He took me to dinner at Pioneer's and then we went for a walk downtown and got ice cream for dessert."

She spends the next several minutes telling me about her date and how she's falling hard and fast for this guy. She's completely smitten with him and is looking forward to seeing him tomorrow night.

"Did you tell him what you do for a living?"

Her face falls. "No, but I did tell Lucinda to take sex off my profile."

"That's a good idea, but you're going to have to tell him soon, you know? Sooner the better..."

"I know." She sighs. "It's just something that's hard to explain, and I can't quit. I need the money. I think I'm going to start looking for a new job, though, if things between us get serious."

"Good luck with that," I grumble.

"Haven't found anything yet?"

"Sure, lots of places are hiring... until I tell them I'm Camilla Hutchinson. I swear I've been blacklisted from everywhere besides Azul's." And that's only because Yasmin got me the job.

"I'm sorry, hon. Have you thought about working at Fairy Tales? It pays way better and you could work less, giving you more time for school once you go back."

I release a harsh breath, wishing it were that easy. "Yas, you didn't see me last night on that date. Hot mess would be putting it nicely. I was a complete basket case. I can't imagine doing that four nights a week with four different men."

"It couldn't have been that bad if this Isaac guy wanted to jump back on the Camilla train."

"Or there's something wrong with him. Maybe he's a serial killer or a rapist." Although I would be seriously shocked if he was, because when I was with Isaac, he made me feel safe. Once he found out Crystal Harbor held bad memories for me, he made sure to keep anyone from asking questions. Even when we were eating dinner and conversing with the other couples, if someone asked a question that was too personal, he would cut in and either answer or change the subject.

Then again, I was with my ex for almost a year and he was a complete tool, so what does that say about my instincts and taste in men?

"All guys are fully vetted," Yasmin says with a laugh. "Lucinda doesn't mess around with our safety. There's nothing wrong with Isaac. You're just being paranoid."

"Yeah, okay. They also said there was nothing wrong with Ted Bundy... until they found all the bodies."

Eight

CAMILLA

AS I STEP OUT OF MY BUILDING

and walk toward the man leaning against the side of a limo, a foreboding sense of déjà vu comes over me. He's dressed similarly to the other night, only now he's in a suit instead of a tux. His hair is still messy and the stubble on his face is a few days old, giving him that *I don't give a fuck* vibe. With his arms crossed over his chest, his suit jacket stretches taut across his body, and a chunky watch dons his wrist.

He drips masculinity. His confidence is sexy, and the way he drags his eyes slowly down my body, starting with my eyes and descending to my heeled feet, isn't creepy like Gordan. It's different, as if he's simply appreciating what's in front of him, like one might look at a precious piece of art.

As I approach him, I send up a silent prayer that tonight goes a little better than the other night. This time I at least know what to expect, so my nerves are calmer, and since Isaac knows how I feel about Crystal Harbor, I'm hoping he wouldn't book me for another date if he plans to spend his night there.

With the perfect mixture of swagger and nonchalance, he pushes off the side of the vehicle and steps toward me, meeting me a few feet away from the limo.

"Jasmine," he says, dipping his head to give me a kiss on my cheek. As the fake name rolls off his tongue, a weird sense of unease washes through me, making me wish I could be honest with him, so I could hear him say my real name when he speaks to me. The masculine scent of his cologne hits my senses, wrapping around me like a cozy blanket on a cold night. And when his warm lips press against my cheek, chills race up my spine, forcing me to outwardly shiver.

He chuckles softly, knowing how much he's affecting me, and instead of backing away, he brings his mouth up to my ear. "You smell even more delectable tonight. Like vanilla with a hint of strawberry." He audibly inhales, running his nose along my jawline before he steps back, his eyes roaming my body once more, this time with heat in his gaze. "And you look absolutely breathtaking."

I'm in a short, lacy, maroon dress that shows off my curves, paired with black heels with the signature red sole—both Yasmin's since anything I owned of value was consigned months ago.

"Thank you," I say, internally cringing at how breathless I sound. I shouldn't be this affected by a man I don't even know—especially after the shit I went through with my ex—but there's something about him that draws me in, making my head foggy, and my hormones kick into overdrive.

Isaac opens the door for me, grasping my hand softly to help me inside, then follows suit, sliding in behind me before closing us in the limo. Music is playing softly in the overhead speakers, and the privacy partition is up.

"How was your weekend?" he asks a few minutes into the drive. I glance outside and take a breath of relief when I see the vehicle head north, away from Crystal Harbor.

"It was good. I worked Saturday and was off Sunday."

His body outwardly tenses, his jaw tightening, and I freeze, realizing I almost slipped up. Luckily, I didn't mention where I was working, so his reaction must be due to him thinking I was escorting men while I was working.

"Did you have a good weekend?" I ask, quickly putting the attention back on him.

After a few seconds, a sigh escapes his lips and his body and face soften. "I did. I worked Saturday and spent Sunday on my boat."

"I went to the beach Sunday morning to watch the boats."

"Where?"

"Chester Creek Beach. It was crowded and got hot too quickly, so I only stayed for a couple hours." In Washington, there's more rain than sun during the summer, so when it's actually sunny out people tend to take advantage of it.

"I was there as well. I docked at Wallen Island and did some fishing. It was very relaxing and my boat provided plenty of shade." His brown eyes meet my green and a breathtakingly beautiful smile spreads across his face. "Had I known you were there, I would've invited you to join me."

Unsure what the hell to say to that, I simply smile back and ask, "What's the name of your boat? Maybe I saw it." I love people watching, and when I go to the beach, I always find the names on the boats and create stories in my head about where the names came from.

"Only Ever Yours."

"Sounds romantic... Care to share who *she* is?" I flutter my eyelashes playfully, but quickly stop when a frown appears on his face.

"It's named after my parents. They passed away several years ago. My mom had those words engraved on the inside of their wedding rings in Portuguese, which is her native language, for their twentieth anniversary. They were the most in-love couple I've ever seen," he says, a small smile breaking through his sadness.

My heart sinks, remembering how his parents died. "I'm sorry." I lay my hand on his, which is resting on his lap. "I lost my mom to cancer and that was hard enough, I can't imagine losing both my parents..." *And in such a sudden, violent way*, I think but don't say out loud.

"Losing someone we love is never easy, but I'm thankful I got so many years with them. They were the two people I looked up to the most, showing me every day what love looks like. I hope one day the name of my boat will have a deeper meaning."

His eyes, filled with heated intensity, connect with mine, at the same time he threads our fingers together, causing butterflies to explode in my belly. After several seconds, I avert my gaze and slide my hand out of his—remembering where I am and why—to break the connection that's sizzling between us. But he's not having it, because the second my face begins to turn, he catches my chin and forces me to look at him.

"Your eyes are beautiful," he says softly. "That shade of green reminds me of the home my father built for my mom. It was a two-story colonial sitting on hundreds of acres of land. When it would rain, the grass would turn a bright green. I hated the rain because I couldn't play outside, and when I would complain to my mom, she would tell me that rain is Mother Nature's way of pressing the refresh button. That's what your eyes remind me of... a fresh start."

Be. Still. My heart.

I swallow thickly, stunned by his words, and say the first thing that comes to mind to change the subject. "Is there anything I need to know about tonight?"

At the charity function, he made it a point to refrain from introducing me to anyone, focusing on the person he was speaking to—for which I was grateful—but at dinner, it will be more intimate—then again, Yasmin did tell me that most men prefer a trophy date... a pretty woman to be seen and not heard. But something tells me that's not Isaac's style and I need to stop trying to lump him into the same category as my ex.

"I have to be honest with you," he says. "There's no business meeting tonight. I wanted to see you again and this was the only way. The second you stepped out of the limo Friday night I wanted to see you again. I couldn't stop thinking about you all weekend."

Well, okay then. I guess that explains him booking me that same night.

"I tried to book you for Saturday and Sunday, but I was told you were working..." He raises a questioning brow and I swallow down my nerves.

"She probably just meant unavailable," I mutter, hating that I'm lying to him. But what else can I do? I can't risk telling him the truth and him getting mad and going to Lucinda. Yasmin could lose her job.

Thankfully the limo pulls up to the front of a restaurant I've never heard of and the driver opens the door for us. Isaac nods at him and, with his hand resting on my lower back, walks us inside to the hostess stand.

"Two for Petrosian," he tells the young woman, who taps away on the iPad. "Yes, sir. We have a table for you right this—"

"I heard the rumors, but I didn't believe them," a voice I would recognize anywhere says from behind us, cutting off the hostess. I stiffen and Isaac's hand glides around my back, squeezing my hip in what feels like a protective gesture as he turns us around to face none other than James Pruitt... my ex-fiancé.

"So, it's true, then," James says with a sleazy smirk, his arm thrown over some six-foot-tall plastic Barbie look-alike. "Isaac Petrosian is slumming it."

My cheeks heat with embarrassment and anger as Isaac pulls me closer to him, kissing the side of my temple before he speaks. "Christopher's is owned by a good friend of mine. Tonight is the grand opening and I'm here to support him. If that's considered slumming it, what are you doing here?"

Oh, God... I close my eyes, wishing the floor would swallow me up. He thinks James is referring to his choice of eating establishments, not his date.

James's brows dip in confusion, and then once the pieces all click together, he barks out a laugh that's equivalent to a fork scraping across a plate, while I pray he doesn't say what I think is coming next. I glance around the area, planning my escape, but Isaac's hold on me is so tight, there's no way I'm getting away.

"That's not what I meant," James says once he's finally stopped laughing. "I was talking about *her*." He nods toward me like I'm barely worth his time. "Surely, even *you* could do better than that," he sneers. "Hell, with the blood money you have, I imagine you could *pay* for better. But hey, if you want my sloppy seconds, have at it."

And. Kill. Me. Now.

"What the fuck did you just say?" Isaac's voice is low and growly, dripping with menace. He releases me, just barely, and steps toward James.

"I'm talking about you and my ex-fiancée," James says, looking smug. "Camilla."

"Who the fuck is Camilla?" Isaac asks, confused.

Before James can answer him, I cut in, unable to watch this train wreck any longer. If anyone is going to tell Isaac who I am, it's going to be me—and definitely not my asshole ex. "I am," I say, turning to face Isaac and giving James my back. "Can we go somewhere and talk, please?"

"Wait a second," James says, clearly not done with destroying my life. "You didn't know her name? Who the hell did you think she was?"

"It's none of your business," I bark out, done with his shit. "Go away."

"No," James says with a snicker. "What games are you playing?" He looks at Isaac. "You're somewhat of a smart man. Don't you look into who you're dating? She's Camilla Hutchinson. Daniel Hutchinson's daughter." He doesn't bother to explain who my dad is because everyone knows who he is, especially those in the real estate industry—and there's no way Isaac got to where he is in this world without doing his research.

"Don't you dare speak my father's name!" I yell, getting into James's face. "Don't talk about him. Don't think about him." I shove against his chest, every ounce of bottled up anger pouring out of me. "You and your lying piece of shit father are the reason he is where he is! And one day someone is going to fuck you over the way you did him."

Hot tears prick my eyes and, not wanting to give James the satisfaction of seeing them, I storm past him, pushing him to the side as I flee the restaurant.

I get to the front where the valet is, and I'm looking for a cab to jump into, when a strong pair of hands grip my shoulders from behind, spinning me around.

"I don't take well to being made a fool, especially when it comes to those asshole Pruitts," Isaac says with a glare. "So, you're going to need to tell me what's going on. Right fucking now."

His reminder of my lies—and getting caught—stops me in my tracks. Isaac not only deserves to know the truth, but the future of Yasmin's job is now in his hands.

"James was right," I admit, swiping a tear that's fallen despite me begging myself not to cry. "I'm Camilla Hutchinson. James and I dated for a while, and last year, when I was home for spring break, he proposed." Of course, I had no idea he was cheating on me the entire time. "In August, James ended our engagement. I didn't know why, and I didn't really care." That was the first sign I knew I never really loved him. "Shortly after, the IRS came after them, and Clint threw my dad to the wolves, framing him for tax evasion amongst other things. I realized James ended it because he wanted to make sure all ties were cut between our families."

I exhale a sharp breath. "I'm sure you know everything that comes after since it was splashed all over the news and social media. My dad is now serving fifteen years in prison while Clint and his son are walking free."

Suddenly feeling mentally exhausted, I walk over to the bench behind us and have a seat. Isaac follows, staying quiet so I can finish my story. "I'm sure you also know my dad lost everything... which means I did too. After I moved home to be by my dad's side during the trial, I lost my scholarship for school, and then lost my home when they confiscated it. I moved into the building I live in, which ironically, is owned by the Pruitts' real estate company."

I roll my eyes. I had no idea they purchased it and eventually plan to renovate and charge triple. It wasn't until I was late the first time, Gordan mentioned the owner isn't giving any second chances because he wants everyone out.

"I realized quickly, when I was looking for a job, I was blacklisted everywhere thanks to Clint and James. And even those who didn't know them would see my last name and put two and two together. It sucks living in a small city where everybody knows everybody, but I can't move because my dad is in the federal prison here, and even if he wasn't, I can't afford to."

I shake my head, realizing I'm rambling on. "Sorry, back to the name change... I met Yasmin, with a Y, after I moved into the building. She got me a job at Azul's and then left shortly after to work at Fairy Tales since they pay better. Recently she met a guy that she fell for, and her date with you was on the same night he asked her out. She needed an out and I needed the money, so I went in her place. She goes by Jasmine, like the princess. We figured it would be a one-time thing since I was a hot mess during our date, but then you requested me again. And now... here we are."

Isaac nods, his eyes never leaving mine, and then he says something I'm not expecting. "I'm glad she couldn't make it." He takes my hand in his. "I enjoyed our date, hot mess and all."

I find myself smiling, despite how badly this night has turned out, once again. "I did too." And now comes the hard part… "I need to ask you a huge favor."

"Yeah?"

"Can you please not tell Lucinda about what happened? I can give you the money back for both dates, as a matter of fact, I insist." With the drama I've caused, I should be paying him instead of the other way around. "But Yasmin needs this job and if Lucinda finds out, she'll be fired."

"You're not giving me any money back," Isaac insists, "and I'll tell you what… I won't rat on your friend under one condition: you agree to go out with me again."

"Excuse me?" I stand, yanking my hand from him. Maybe it's after watching everything my father went through, and losing my choices and rights along the way, but what he says doesn't sit right with me at all. "Did you seriously just blackmail me?" I don't wait for him to answer. "Maybe in your world that's how things work, but not in mine. And the way to start a relationship or whatever it is you're asking me for, is *not* by blackmailing me into it." The sad thing is, had he just asked me out, I would've said yes because I'm that attracted to him.

Without allowing him another word, I stalk back toward the restaurant to find someone to call me a cab. I hear Isaac calling after me, but I don't turn around. Luck must be on my side—for once—because just as his voice gets closer, a cab pulls up and I jump in without asking if it's available. I make sure, as the car drives away, not to give another glance to Isaac. I already dated and was engaged to a man who played games, and I'll never do that again—even if the chemistry between us is sizzling hot.

The driver grumbles when I give him my address since it's in the bad part of town, but thankfully keeps driving. After paying him, I get out and walk upstairs. I'm going to need to tell Yasmin what happened, but right now all I want is a hot shower and some ice cream.

When I get to my apartment, I find a notice on my door. Fucking James. I have no doubt he's behind this shit. I unlock my door and go inside, pulling out my phone so I can text Yasmin.

Me: Can you get me that job at Fairy Tales?

Yas: I'll call her in the morning. Are you texting me while on your date?

Me: No... Long story. Come over in the morning.

Yas: Will do.

Nine

ISAAC

"HOW'S IT GOING?" I ASK NOAH

as I type an email to Lucinda requesting Jasmine again. I fucked up tonight with Camilla. I should've just said I wouldn't rat on her friend and then asked her out, but instead, the shrewd businessman in me came out and I blackmailed her like a dumbass. I didn't even realize what I was doing until she threw it back in my face and ran. I messed up and now I need to make it right, and since I can't just show up at her place— well, I could, but that probably wouldn't get me any points in her book—although, now that I think about it, booking her probably isn't the best way to get her attention either.

Shit... I cancel the email and glance back at the rectangle with Noah's face in it.

"Are you listening to any fucking thing I'm saying?"

"Sorry, I'm a bit distracted. Did you send the numbers over to me?"

"Yeah. They're all in the email."

"Thanks, I'll look them over in the morning when I have a clear head."

He eyes me for a long moment. "What's going on, Isaac?"

"I met the one," I tell him, not even bothering to sugarcoat it.

"The who?" He knows what I mean, but he's being a dick.

"The woman I'm going to marry."

His brows hit his forehead. "When? I've only been gone for like a week... Wait a fucking second. Are you talking about the escort? Isaac..." He groans.

"She's not an escort. It's a long story, but yes, her. She's an unexpected surprise. Kind of a hot mess..." I say with a chuckle, using her words. "But a beautiful hot mess."

Noah stares at me through the screen like I've lost my mind, and I guess to someone like him, who has no desire to find love or settle down, it might seem like I have. But to me, it feels right. Now I just need to figure out how to make shit right with her again.

"I don't even know what to say," Noah remarks, sounding

exhausted from what I've told him. "Try not to marry her before I get home."

I bark out a laugh because he's not joking. He knows how I feel, and I've told him on several occasions, if I found the woman I want to spend my life with, I wouldn't hold back. My parents' time with each other was brought to an end years too early, and I won't sit back and let life pass me by. I learned from what happened to them, nothing in this life is guaranteed—including our time.

"Don't forget Saturday we have a shipment coming in. I won't be back until Monday."

"Got it." I jot it down so I don't forget. "Anything else?"

"Nope." He looks at me with concern and I wait for him to say what's on his mind. "I know you like this woman..."

"I do. A lot."

Noah sighs. "Just be careful."

"Always."

"I'M SORRY, BUT SHE NO LONGER WORKS HERE."

"You sure?"

"Yep, she quit."

She told me the other night she was working here. It's only been a couple days. What the hell happened in such a short amount of time to make her quit her job, especially since she needs the money?

"All right, thanks."

I exit Azul's and get back in my car. I figured stopping by her work was a little better than showing up at her place, but since I don't have her phone number, she's leaving me no choice.

I pull up to her complex and walk inside. The building has ten floors and each floor houses over twenty apartments. After asking several people passing by if they know Camilla Hutchinson, I quickly realize I'm not going to find her here unless I get lucky and catch her coming or going. This woman has me in knots and I need to find her so we can talk. After I ask a few more people, I head home and call my friend Lance. He's a PI and can find anything out about anyone. He tells me to give him twenty-four hours, and I thank him. Hopefully by this time tomorrow I'll be with Camilla, apologizing for the way I handled shit.

ALMOST TWENTY-FOUR HOURS ON THE DOT, JUST AS

he promised, he sends me a text with an address for her and a current location: **Rainy Days. She's currently there with a few people drinking.**

I consider which way to go about this. I could wait until she's home and show up at her place, or I can head over to Rainy Days since it's only about a ten-minute drive from my place. The sensible thing to do would be to wait until she's home... Rainy Days it is.

Thirty minutes later, I walk into the overcrowded and foul-smelling place and have a seat at the bar. I order a scotch on the rocks and glance around in search of Camilla. As if drawn to her, my eyes find her almost instantly. She's dressed in a flowy navy blue top, the back missing, a pair of short white shorts that show off her creamy thighs, and high heels that look tall and pointy enough to be considered weapons. She's dancing with a bunch of people, but one guy in particular is close... too close.

I drink my shitty excuse for a scotch and watch, mesmerized by the way Camilla sways her hips and ignores the guy who keeps creeping around her. He whispers something into her ear and she shrugs, slightly cringing. It's obvious she isn't feeling this guy, but she's too polite to say something.

Creeper walks over and orders two Jack and Cokes,

throwing a twenty on the bar top when the bartender hands them to him. My eyes stay on him as he then takes them over to the table, and after glancing around, reaches into his pocket and drops something into one of the drinks. Motherfucker. I stand, ready to go over and fuck his drugging ass up, when Camilla sidles up next to him. I was so busy watching him, I didn't see her join him.

It all happens in slow motion yet so damn fast. I'm pushing my way through the crowd, trying to make it over to her, shouting her name over the music. But it's too loud, the music is thumping too hard, and I'm too far away. He hands her the spiked drink and she downs the entire thing in one gulp.

Fuck!

When she sees me, her eyes go wide in shock, but I don't have time to explain. I stalk past her and over to Druggy Creeper and, grabbing him by the collar of his shirt, push him against the wall.

"What the fuck did you put in her drink?"

His eyes bug out. "I don't know—"

"I saw you." I pull him forward and then slam him against the hard surface. "You have three seconds to tell me what you gave her before I make a single call and ensure you disappear and are never found again."

I faintly hear several people shouting around me, but I ignore it all, focusing on the guy in front of me. It takes an ungodly amount of restraint not to kill him right here on the spot, but I remind myself that won't help Camilla—and you never kill anyone with witnesses.

"It's just a little GHB," he says, shaking in fear.

"*Just* a little GHB?" I bark. "It's not just a little anything when she doesn't know about it."

I reach into his pocket and pull out his wallet, grabbing his license and scanning it before I pocket it. "I now have your info, including where you live. And I promise you, one day, when you least expect it, you'll be paid a visit. Better watch your back, *Rusty*." I cock my arm back and punch him straight in his face, making his head snap to the side. He hits the ground, but I don't stay a second longer.

"We need to go," I tell Camilla, who's staring at me in shock and confusion.

"What's going on? What are you doing here?"

"That asshole drugged your drink, and since you downed it like a shot before I could stop you from drinking it, in a few minutes, it's going to hit your system hard, making you feel disoriented. Have you ever taken GHB?"

"No," she gasps, covering her mouth in fear. "I've never done drugs. What's going to happen to me?" Her voice cracks. She's scared of the unknown, but I won't let anything happen to her.

"I can't believe that asshole!" a woman yells, stumbling over her own two feet. She's clearly drunk, and based on the way she wraps her arms around Camilla, must be her friend.

"Who are you?" I ask the woman.

"I'm Yasmin," she slurs. "I'm so sorry, Camilla. I never should've brought you here. You didn't want to go and now that piece of shit drugged you."

"I'm okay," Camilla assures her since it's only been about five minutes and the drug hasn't kicked in yet. I need to get her out of here before it does.

"C'mon," Yasmin slurs. "Let's get you home. I'll call us a cab."

"No, you won't," I step in. "I'm going to take you home and then I'm taking her with me to keep an eye on her."

"Like hell you are," the woman hisses. "Who are you anyway?"

"Isaac Petrosian."

Her eyes go wide, no doubt recognizing my name. "Okay, but that doesn't mean you're taking Cam with you anywhere."

"I... I don't think I feel so good," Camilla murmurs. "I feel kind of hot." She attempts to lift her top up, not thinking about the fact that we're in a bar filled with people.

"Not here," I tell her, scooping her into my arms and glancing at Yasmin. "I'm taking Camilla back to my place where I can make sure she's okay. You're too drunk to handle it if something happens to her. Now, I need to get her out of here before the drug hits her hard. You coming or not?" Camilla is my only priority, but since Yasmin's her friend, I'd rather not leave her here.

Her mouth opens and closes several times before she nods. "Fine, but if something happens to her..."

"*Nothing* is going to happen to her on my watch. Let's go."

While I carry Camilla to my truck, she fans herself, saying she's hot and wants to take her clothes off. Her eyes are growing heavy and I know it's only a matter of time before she becomes lethargic.

The ride to Yasmin's place is quick. Even shit-faced drunk, she's worried about leaving her friend with me, so I give her my phone number and address before I make sure she gets inside safe, and then leave.

Camilla's eyes are closed and she's moaning incoherently as I carry her to the elevator in my building and then into my place. She tries to talk, apologizing for everything that's happened, and then tries to kiss me, but I shush her, laying her in my bed. I grab her a bottle of water and help her drink it and then go about taking her heels off. I leave her shorts and shirt on, and then pull the blanket over her.

"Isaac," she slurs, grabbing me by my shirt when I stand to get changed. "I... Something feels...wrong." Her eyes, filled with fear and confusion, flutter open and closed, and my heart squeezes behind my chest.

"It's okay," I tell her, kneeling next to the bed. "I'm here and I'm going to make sure you're okay. You were drugged, and you have to wait for it to get through your system. Just close your eyes and sleep, sweetheart." She nods slowly and her eyes close. When her breathing evens out, I know she's asleep.

I stand and kiss her forehead, then change into some comfortable clothes before I grab my laptop and have a seat in the bed next to her. It's only eleven and there's no way I'll be sleeping tonight. Drugs like GHB can have a variety of side effects, and until I know she's safe and it's out of her system, I'll be watching her closely.

As I stare at her sleeping soundly, her chest rising and falling, I can't help thinking, despite the reason she's here, how perfect she looks in my bed. If it were up to me, she would never leave. That shitty apartment complex she lives in is no place for her. She should be here, with me, where I can love her and spoil her and make sure she's always taken care of.

I laugh to myself, fully aware of how crazy I sound. But I don't care. There's no doubt in my mind Camilla is the one for me. Now I just have to get her on board.

Ten

CAMILLA

AS I PRY MY EYES OPEN, WHITE
light filters in through the windows, nearly blinding me and forcing my eyes to quickly shut. Pounding, deep inside my skull, like someone has taken up drumming in my head, has me rolling over into a fetal position.

Buzz. Buzz. Buzz. Buzz.

The sound of a phone going off has me reaching around for my phone. I peel one eye open and find a slew of texts from Yasmin asking if I'm okay. I quickly type back that I am, so she doesn't worry, then drop my phone onto the bed, closing my eyes.

What the hell happened last night?

After a few minutes, the pain decreases slightly

and I try again. This time, when I open my eyes, I gasp in shock, having no idea where I am. The room, a deep bluish gray, is large and filled with expensive-looking mahogany furniture. The paintings of the beach and ocean on the walls give nothing away, and neither does the view of the intercoastal outside.

I sit up and my head throbs, a woozy feeling overtaking me. I stay still, waiting for the room to stop spinning, and once it does, I climb out of the bed so I can figure out where I am and how I got here. The first thing I notice on the nightstand is a bottle of water and a pack of pain pills.

After I pop the pills into my mouth, I chug the bottle of water, not realizing how dehydrated I am until the water and pills slide down my dry throat. Then, sitting back on the bed, I open the note and begin to read:

> Camilla,
> Please don't be scared. Last night I found you at Rainy Days where a man (who will one day pay) drugged you. I made sure Yasmin got home safe, and then, so that I could care for you, brought you back to my place, where you are now...

With his words, everything from the last forty-eight hours

comes flying back to me.

Getting hired by Lucinda and going on a date with an asshole who tried to hit on me.

Punching said asshole and getting fired.

Yasmin coming home and crying that she told Todd about her job and he dumped her.

Telling her I've been fired from Fairy Tales.

Begging the manager of Azul's to hire me back and him refusing, deciding to make the moment a life fucking lesson.

Yasmin insisting we go out and forget all our problems.

Meeting some douchebags who wouldn't leave us alone.

Agreeing to him buying me a drink so he'd go away.

Downing the drink so I could do as Yasmin insisted and forget all my problems.

I scrub my palms over my face, remembering Isaac showing up and telling me I'd been drugged, which was the last thing I remember. I can't even imagine what would've happened had Isaac not been there. I could've been kidnapped or raped or murdered. Oh my God! I could've been kidnapped and then raped and then murdered! What the hell was I thinking accepting a drink from a man I don't know? I know better than that. That's club rules 101. You never accept a drink from a man you don't know.

My phone buzzes, so I grab it and see it's Yasmin calling.

"Hello."

"Hey," she says softly. "I needed to hear from you that you're okay."

"I'm okay. I'm at Isaac's..."

"I know. I tried to take you home, but he insisted and I was drunk..." She sniffles into the phone. "I'm so sorry."

"It's okay. It was a shitty night, but we're both okay and safe."

"Are you coming home?"

"Yeah." I glance at the note. "I'm just waking up. Isaac isn't here, but he left me a note. I'm going to read it and then get going. I need to look for a job." I sigh in exhaustion, knowing there's no way I'm going anywhere but to my bed today. My entire body feels like it's been run over by a semi, and all my energy has been depleted.

"You were drugged," Yasmin says. "You need to rest. You can job search tomorrow."

"You're right. Are you working today?" I can barely remember what today is.

"Yeah. Text me once you're home so I know you made it okay."

"Will do."

We hang up and I start reading the note over again from the beginning.

Camilla,

Please don't be scared. Last night I found you at Rainy Days where a man (who will one day pay) drugged you. I made sure Yasmin got home safe, and then, so that I could care for you, brought you back to my place, where you are now. I watched over you and was hoping to be here when you woke up, but I have to go to my office. I'm not sure when I'll be back, but please make yourself at home. I must admit, despite the circumstances, I really liked seeing you in my bed. Actually, I more than liked it. There's food in the fridge and a list of places you can order in from. Just give them my name and they'll add it to my account. If you want to relax, my bathroom has a large tub, and down the hall on the left, I have a library if you enjoy reading. I have Netflix and all that shit on the TV if you want to watch something. If you want to leave, I *understand, but I hope when I get home, you're still here because I'd really love it if you'd stay.*

Xo Isaac

Holy shit. I read the note again just to make sure I'm not seeing things. He wants me to stay? For how long? He probably just means today, right? His offer is tempting, and a part of me wants nothing more than to stay and wait for him to get home. Before James messed things up and then Isaac pissed me off with his blackmail stunt, there was evident chemistry between us. But the other part of me, who remembers how much of a fool I've made of myself, wants to cut my losses and leave without doing any more damage. *Yet*, he did make it clear in his note he'd love it if I'd stay, and this *was* written after everything that's happened.

Feeling as if my bladder is going to burst, I set the note down, climb out of the bed, and pad into the bathroom. There's a double sink to the left, a gigantic spa tub that could fit like four people on the right, and farther in is the shower—it can probably fit more people in it than the tub—and the toilet, which has its own door for privacy. I'm not a stranger to the finer things in life, but this bathroom is like what you see on that old MTV show *Cribs*.

As I relieve myself, staring at the tub with candles

surrounding it and a bottle of bubble bath on the edge, I figure having a bath while I decide whether to stay or go won't hurt. But then my stomach rumbles, reminding me I haven't eaten since yesterday, so I put the bath on hold and go in search of something to eat. The rest of Isaac's place is just as gorgeous as his bedroom and bathroom. Gray walls and dark wood floors run throughout the place with different pieces of art hanging in various spots. It's a typical bachelor pad, but it's clear Isaac has good taste—or his interior designer does.

When I get to the main area of the house, it's an open floor plan with a beautiful state of the art kitchen, a dining room with a table that seats six, and a living room that has an open view of the marina thanks to the wall-to-wall glass windows.

Keeping it easy, I find the coffee and brew myself a cup while I make some toast. I cut up some strawberries I find in the fridge and add a bit of whipped cream to the top. It's been a while since I've been able to have extras like whipped cream. There was a time when I would've taken items like that for granted... now it's a luxury I can't afford.

Once my breakfast is ready, I take my plate and coffee into the library Isaac mentioned in his note. With mahogany floor-to-ceiling bookshelves filled with books, and a comfy looking couch and reading chair, this room is without a doubt my favorite so far. I set my mug and plate on the end table and then go about searching for a book to read. It seems Isaac has a bit of everything from *Knowing the Stock Market*, to Edmund Spenser's *The Faerie Queen*. I settle on *The Scarlet Letter*, a novel I haven't read since high school. I can't remember the last time I felt this content, this relaxed. I know what's waiting for me outside, but for a little while, I'm going to pretend like none of it exists.

I'm several chapters in when I finish eating, once again addicted to the story of Hester Prynne. The bath is calling to me—more so the need to get out of my clothes from last night and scrub myself clean—so I take Hester with me and, after filling the entire tub with hot, soapy bubbles and lighting the candles, get in. It's been way too long since I've had the luxury of soaking in a bath, and I don't think I'll ever take such a thing for granted again.

I have my head resting back and my eyes closed, simply enjoying the water, when I hear the door creak open. My eyes pop open and standing in the doorway is Isaac. He's dressed in a business suit—today it's gray—and his face is freshly shaven. Our eyes meet and the electrical current that courses through me, from just his look alone, is enough to make my entire body shiver.

Quickly remembering I'm naked in his bathtub, I glance down, thankful the bubbles are mostly covering me.

"You stayed," he says, a small smile gracing his lips.

"You asked me to."

He steps farther into the room, his gaze staying trained on my face, not once descending. "You look beautiful like this. How are you feeling?" He shrugs off his jacket and tosses it onto the counter. For a second I wonder if he's going to join me in the bath—and the idea of him doing so only seems to turn me on—but then he rolls up his sleeves, exposing his muscular forearms and... holy fuck, tattoos. The man has a sleeve of tattoos on his right forearm and I swear my lady parts just wept in desire.

"My head hurts and my body is really sore," I tell him truthfully. He kneels next to the tub and takes my hand in his, kissing the tops of my knuckles. "But it could've been a lot worse. Thank you for saving me."

His lips flatten in a line and he nods. "I'm just glad I was there." He rises and kisses my forehead, the simple, sweet gesture causing a pack of butterflies to attack my chest, then walks around behind me, opening the closet. "All morning while I was in my meeting, I imagined you like this."

I glance behind me and see him open a stool and set it

down. He grabs a cup from under the sink and then has a seat behind me. As he turns the water on and fills the cup, I wonder what he's doing, until he lifts it to my head and gently pours it over my hair, making sure none of it goes into my eyes, and that's when it clicks; he's washing my hair.

Unsure what to make of this, I just go with it, since it's already happening.

"I could barely focus," he adds. "They were talking numbers and I couldn't keep up." He takes the bottle of shampoo and squirts some into his palm, then goes about massaging my scalp. His strong hands thread through the strands of my hair while his fingers deftly massage every inch of my head, and I moan in pleasure, not caring that he can hear me.

"I just kept thinking about you, in my bed, in my home. I wondered if you stayed or left, and if you were here, I kept picturing you just like this, naked and in my bathtub, but my imagination didn't do you justice." He takes the cup and rinses out my hair. I tilt my head back, making it easier for him, thoroughly enjoying this surprise pampering.

When he's done, he leans forward and presses a soft kiss to my shoulder, sending my heart racing. "I knew it," he whispers into my ear. "The first time I saw you walk toward me, and now, seeing you in my bed, in my bath, it confirms it."

"Confirms what?" I breathe.

He grasps my chin between his fingers and tilts my head to the side to look at him. "You're the one... You're meant to be mine."

"Isaac..." I gasp. "I—" We've only just met, have barely been on a single date... How can he possibly know that?

"Shh... I know. It's too soon to know that," he says as if reading my mind. "But I do, and soon you will too." His eyes land on my lips, and I know he's going to kiss me. I should stop him. I hardly know him. Yet, I do nothing as his mouth comes down onto mine, his supple lips curling around my own.

His tongue pushes past my parted lips, and I find myself moaning into his mouth. He tastes like mint and bad decisions, and still, I have no intention of stopping wherever this is going. The kiss is soft and gentle yet filled with heat and promise.

Wanting more of him, I twist around so I can deepen the kiss. Water splashes around me, no doubt wetting the floor and probably Isaac, but neither of us cares enough to stop. His fingers grip the back of my nape tightly, possessively, as mine find the front of his shirt and pull him toward me, needing to be closer to him.

Isaac meets me halfway, kneeling while I lift onto my knees, ignoring the fact I'm completely naked and there's no way the bubbles are covering me in this position. We kiss like this, tasting, coaxing, learning each other, until Isaac ends the kiss. His gaze sears into mine, filled with passion and hunger, but he makes no move to go any further, only staring at me as his chest rises and falls in quick succession. He's affected as much as I am.

"What's wrong?" I ask, wondering why he's not still kissing me.

"Not a goddamned thing." He presses his lips to mine one more time before he pulls back again. "Stay with me."

"Tonight?"

"Tonight... tomorrow... forever."

I giggle at how crazy he is, but he's not laughing. "I can't stay here forever."

"Let's start with tonight," he says, placing a kiss to the corner of my mouth.

"Tonight," I agree, completely mesmerized by him.

The most gorgeous grin spreads across his face, and my heart contracts behind my ribcage. The way he's looking at me right now, like my spending the night is the sole reason for his happiness, makes me want to agree to anything he wants, just so I can see him smile at me like that over and over again.

Eleven

ISAAC

CAMILLA'S HERE. IN MY HOME,

in my clothes, sitting on my couch looking through menus so we can decide what to order. When I got a call from my secretary that a contract I was waiting on was ready to be signed, and the owner was chomping at the bit to sign, I had no choice but to go in and handle it. It took everything in me to leave Camilla, but since it was after nine in the morning, I knew she was safe.

All morning, I wondered if she was still here, considered running up to check on her, but one thing led to another, and the next thing I knew it was after two in the afternoon. The first chance I got, I locked up the office and headed back upstairs, hoping like hell she was still here.

And she was. Naked in my tub.

"How about pizza?" Camilla says, dipping her head under my arm and snuggling into my side.

I wrap my arm around her, loving how comfortable she is with me.

After I washed her hair and helped her out of the bath, I was a little worried she would retreat, but she didn't. I gave her some clothes and then space to get dressed, while I threw a load into the washer and came out to the kitchen to figure out what to order for lunch.

I heard her feet padding across my wood floor and then her arms encircled around my waist from behind. "Thank you," she whispered, resting her head against my back. "I can't remember the last time I felt taken care of."

"Sounds good." I take the menus from her and give her a kiss on her forehead. "What do you want on it?"

"I'm a cheese girl, but you can order half with whatever you want." I stow that information away, like I do with everything I learn about her.

"I'll order the pizza and you pick the movie." I lift her chin and kiss her softly, still in shock at how quickly we went from her running away from me to me being able to kiss her, and how natural it all is. "Chick flick or action?"

"Why can't it be both?" she says. "Like *Mr. and Mrs. Smith* or

Gone in 60 Seconds."

"You got a thing for Angelina Jolie?"

"She's hot. She's definitely in my top five elevator passes."

"Your what?"

She laughs. "You know, the people you'd fuck in an elevator if you got the chance." My thoughts go straight to fucking Camilla in my elevator... Against the wall, bent over...

"Earth to Isaac?" She waves her hand in front of my face.

"Huh?"

"I asked who yours are."

"You."

She snorts. "Who else?"

"You." I grab the back of her nape and bring her face to mine. "You're the only person who came to mind." She swallows slowly, and then her tongue darts across her bottom lip, her eyes on mine. "I've wanted you since the moment I first saw you. You're the only person who's been on my mind, and you're the only person I want in that elevator."

She sighs into me, and I dip my head, sucking her bottom lip into my mouth. I nibble on it lightly before I suck the other one in. Her hands come up and wrap around my neck, and I pull her closer, pressing my mouth to hers. She kisses me back, her hands gliding down my shirt-covered chest.

"Fuck, Cam..." I groan, pulling back slightly and resting my forehead against hers. "My dad told me it would be like this, but I didn't get it... not until now."

"Didn't get what?" she breathes, out of breath from our kiss. "What did he tell you?"

"When he met my mom, he knew right away that she was the one. On their twentieth anniversary they renewed their vows and I asked him how he knew she was the one so quickly, and he said, 'When you meet the woman you want to spend your life with, it'll feel different. You'll be drawn to her. She'll take up room in your head and in your heart and you'll do everything in your power to make sure she knows how much she means to you. You won't need hours or even days or weeks to know it. Right then and there you'll just know'."

Camilla's eyes widen. "You really think I'm the one?"

"Yeah," I tell her honestly, "I do. I know we don't know each other, but—"

She presses her fingers over my mouth and smiles softly. "I get it... because I feel the same way about you."

Fuck. Me. This woman.

"Order the pizza and I'll pick out a super romantic action flick." She leans over to grab the remote from the coffee table and my shirt slides up, exposing the bottom of her ass. "Are you naked under there?" I nod toward my shirt.

She blushes slightly. "I didn't want to put on my dirty underwear. They're in the washer with my clothes."

"I left you boxers with a shirt."

"What? I didn't see them." Her cheeks turn a beautiful shade of crimson and I chuckle at how fucking adorable she is.

"They were on the bed. Not that I'm complaining..." I eye my shirt, loving that underneath she's bare and exposed. "I'm one hundred percent on board with you going panty-less."

I waggle my brows and she groans, smacking my chest playfully. I'm damn close to attacking her right here on the couch, but her stomach growls loudly, reminding me I need to order the food.

I dial the number on the menu, and while I'm waiting for them to answer, walk back to the bedroom to grab the boxers Camilla didn't see. They're on the bed, under a pillow that was thrown over them. After I place the order, I walk back out to the living room, to find Camilla still on the couch and flicking through the movies.

"Look what I found." I twirl the boxers around my finger. "They were under a pillow." I extend my hand like I'm going to give them to her, but quickly pull back before she can grab them.

She glares, but the hint of a smile on her tells me she isn't really mad. "Give me."

I sit on the couch next to her and hold them away while she gets on her knees and tries to grab them from me. When she reaches across me, her shirt rises again, exposing most of her ass, and I can't help latching onto her hips and placing her on my lap. My hand that's not holding the boxers gives one perfect globe a squeeze.

"Isaac, give me the boxers," she demands through a laugh.

"But I like you like this." I peck her lips. "Knowing there's nothing under here." In this position, she's straddling my lap, and even though the shirt is covering her, knowing her bare cunt is underneath is a fucking turn-on.

"It's hardly fair." She pouts. "I'm in only a shirt and you're completely dressed."

That gives me an idea...

"Let's play a game. Two truths and a lie. If you guess my lie, I'll give you the boxers."

Her brows furrow in contemplation. "Fine, but if you don't guess mine, you have to take an article of clothing off."

"Sweetheart, you want my clothes off? Just tell me. I'll gladly take off anything you want."

She snorts a laugh. "You go first, so I can get the boxers."

I think for a few seconds about what will stump her. "Okay, I majored in history in college, I lost my virginity in college, and my favorite breakfast food is pancakes."

She scrunches her nose up. "This is hard. Pancakes are delicious, so I feel like that can be the truth, but what if you did it on purpose to throw me off? I can't imagine you majoring in history, more like business or something to work with your dad. And losing your virginity in college? No way, unless you didn't grow into this face and body until after high school."

I chuckle at her rambling thoughts. "So, which is the lie?"

"You sure two of them are truths?"

"Yep, and one is a lie."

She huffs. "Okay... I'm going with...The lie is that you lost your virginity in college."

"Wrong. The lie is that my favorite breakfast food is pancakes. They're good, but my favorite breakfast food is waffles with whipped cream and chocolate chips."

"Ugh. Really? You lost your virginity in college?" She groans.

"Yep. Freshman year with Lucie Palomino. What about you?" I ask, hoping she'll tell me so I can learn about her.

"Sophomore year of college," she mutters, "with James."

"James, really?" As if I didn't already hate that asshole as it is, the thought of him getting something as precious as

Camilla's virginity makes me want to disassemble his and his father's entire business.

"Yep, he's the only guy I've slept with."

"Why him?" I know why he would want her, but I just can't picture her giving him the time of day.

"We grew up together. It was always a running joke that one day we would get married. He asked me out a few times, but I always said no. I wasn't really into guys too much in high school and he was a couple years ahead of me. The summer before my sophomore year of college I was home visiting and we spent some time together. When I went back, he came to see me a few times and we started dating. He invited me to Hawaii for spring break and proposed. It felt right at the time." Her eyes descend in what looks like shame or maybe regret, and I tilt her chin up so she'll look at me.

"What happened?"

"Aside from him ending things just before he and his father framed my dad? When I came back, I found out he'd been cheating on me with several women."

"He's a piece of shit."

She nods in agreement, then changes the subject. "So, history, huh?"

I laugh at the confusion on her face. "I love history. You

know what they say... In order to change the future, you have to learn from the past. I planned to teach it. Even considered getting my masters and one day teaching at a university."

"What happened?"

"My parents died and my dad left me everything, including his businesses."

She nods in understanding. "Do you ever wish you'd taken a different direction?"

"Life's too short for regrets. My dad would've understood had I chosen not to follow in his footsteps, but it was all I had left of him. Every day when I'm doing what he used to do, I feel closer to him. Like a part of him is with me."

"I met them," she says. "Your parents. It was years ago, but I think you were away at college. They came over quite a few times for dinner. Your mom was so sweet and would bring me little gifts."

I smile, loving that even though it was a long time ago, my mom met Camilla. I know she would love her now.

"They struggled to have kids. Took them a while to have me and after that, she never got pregnant again. Because I was their only child, they spoiled me."

Camilla smiles softly. "Same with me. My mom couldn't carry a baby, so they hired someone to carry me. Mom said it was hard to watch someone else carrying her baby, so they only did it once. I was given everything I could ever want or need—materialistic as well as love and attention."

"I'm sorry about your mom," I tell her, already knowing the story. "I met her a few times at various social engagements and she was very nice."

Her eyes fill with emotion. "She was the best."

We're both quiet for a few moments, lost in our own heads and loss, before Camilla says, "My turn."

"All right, hit me with 'em."

She taps her chin a few times, thinking about what to say. "Okay, let's see... I want to open a high-end fashion boutique one day, my favorite color is pink, and I have a tattoo in a spot that can only be seen when I'm naked."

My hands, which are resting low on her hips, tighten at the mention of her last possible truth. "Your lie is that your favorite color is pink." I don't even have to think about it.

"How are you so confident?"

"Easy, the second you brought up fashion, I remembered your dad mentioning once at a business dinner, his daughter was attending fashion school."

"And what about the tattoo?" She raises a single brow. "How do you know that's not the lie?"

"It could be." I drag my eyes down her body. "But I'm really fucking hoping it's the truth."

When she huffs, I know I'm right.

"I'm going to need to see this tattoo... now."

"No way." She shakes her head, then squeals when I quickly lift her and flip her onto the couch on her back.

"Where is it?" I ask, pretending to search for it.

"Nope, I'm not showing you," she says stubbornly, crossing her legs to deny me access. "You'll have to earn it."

"How?"

"You want something from me, you have to give me something."

"Name it."

"Give me the boxers."

"Fine." I reach back and grab them, holding them up.

"Now put them on me," she says with a twinkle of mischief in her eye.

I find the holes and push them up her smooth legs, making it a point to run my fingers along her flesh. I expect her to take over once they're above her knees, but instead, she lifts her shirt, exposing her neatly-trimmed pussy and... a fucking tattoo just below her hipbone.

Forgetting about the boxers, I slide to the side of her, so

my face is parallel with her hip. "When did you get this?" I ask, running my fingers along the ink.

"A few months ago." When I raise a brow, silently asking her to explain, she continues, "It was a month after my dad was sentenced to prison. I had lost everything, and what I didn't lose, I sold because we needed the money. I couldn't afford the apartment he was renting, so I moved into the one I'm in now. I was job searching, but nobody would hire me. I felt defeated, like I was at my lowest."

She sighs and her eyes gloss over. "I was downtown and stopped inside the art gallery to take a break. There was a painting on one of the walls of the most beautiful tree blowing in the wind. The way it was painted, you could almost feel the pressure on the tree. It was titled, 'Bent, not broken,' and it just... called to me. I felt like I was the tree, so close to breaking. One more gust of wind and I would snap.

"After I left, I was walking by the front of a tattoo shop and the tattoo artist was outside smoking a cigarette. He asked if I wanted to get something. I was about to tell him no, that there was nothing of meaning I'd want tattooed on me permanently, when the image of the painting came to mind."

And so she got the words, *bent, not broken*, along with a small colorful tree swaying in the wind, tattooed just below her hipbone. This woman, still so young, has been through some serious life-changing shit, yet she remains so strong.

I trace the ink one more time, then press a kiss to the words. Goose bumps prickle her skin, and her thighs tighten. When I glance up at her, she's staring down at me with lust in her eyes. With my gaze never leaving hers, I press my lips to the tree, darting my tongue out to lick across her flesh.

She sucks her bottom lip into her mouth and groans softly, so I do it again, this time licking my way down her bikini line. I told myself I was going to go slow with her, so I stop there, planting one last kiss to her skin. But then, like the little minx she is, she slightly parts her legs, silently conveying what she wants.

I'm about to say fuck it and spread her lips, so I can lick her until she comes, when the intercom buzzes. Since I live on the top floor of the building, I put in an intercom to notify me when someone is here, so I can let them up.

"Pizza's here."

She pouts as I drag my boxers the rest of the way up her thighs. I climb over her, stopping when I'm on top of her to kiss her.

"To be continued."

Twelve

CAMILLA

"ADMIT IT…"

Isaac shakes his head, clicking off the TV.

"Admit it!" I poke him in the ribs and a small smile peeks out. "*The Bodyguard* was not just a chick flick."

"I'm not admitting shit." He pouts playfully, crossing his arms over his chest.

"Really? You're that much of a *man*, you can't admit when you're wrong?"

He laughs and pounces on me, his arms caging me in, as my back hits the couch. "I'm very much a man." He grinds his pelvis into me, making me groan. "But I'm never too much of a man to admit when I'm wrong." The entire time we've been watching the movie, it's felt like foreplay on steroids. The hand holding, kissing, touching… at one point he even massaged my feet. But not once did he take it any further. And now, I'm wound so tight, if I don't find my release soon, I'm fearful I might implode.

His nose glides along my jawline and I shiver in anticipation. "I was wrong," he murmurs into my ear. "*The Bodyguard* was full of action."

"Thank you."

He trails kisses up my neck, then murmurs, "Stay the night." I tip my face up to give him access to my throat, and he takes advantage, kissing his way downward, while I try to think of a single reason why I need to leave. Only I can't come up with one. I need to look for a job, but that won't happen on a Friday night. I need to visit my dad tomorrow, but again, that has nothing to do with right now.

"I want you in my bed again." He lifts his face and looks into my eyes, and my heart stammers in my chest. "But this time with you aware of it." My stomach knots, remembering how close I came to something bad happening to me. It feels like every decision I've made lately is the wrong one, and now I'm afraid things are moving too fast with Isaac and me. Sure, I'm attracted to him, but what if I'm wrong about him like I was about James?

"I should probably go home."

"I could always convince you to stay." He nips at my skin, then glances up at me with a wolfish grin. He only meant it as a joke, but it reminds me...

"We never discussed your little blackmail attempt." I push him back, so I can sit up and have some space.

He sits back and at least has the decency to look regretful. "I was wrong. It's how shit works in my world. When something doesn't go my way, I find a way to make sure it does, but I never should've treated you like a business deal."

"It feels like every aspect of my life is out of my control," I tell him. "Losing my mom to cancer when I didn't even know she was sick, my dad going to prison... When he found out about the IRS investigating them, he didn't tell me. Not until he was arrested and I found out from the media."

"They were trying to protect you."

"I don't want to be protected. I want the people who love me to be upfront and honest. I've lost my home, my scholarship, I have no control over where I live..." I release a harsh breath. "I need to feel in control, and you lying about the business dinner and then blackmailing me to go out with you is the opposite of me having control. If you want something from me, ask. Don't threaten or bribe me or go behind my back."

Isaac nods and pulls me over to him, so I'm straddling his

lap.

"I like you," I admit, running my fingers through his messy hair. "But I've been burned too many times."

His jaw ticks, and his hands tighten on my hips. "I'm nothing like him."

"I hope not." I press my mouth to his and coax his lips open, slipping my tongue inside. "Take me to bed," I murmur softly.

I don't have to tell him twice. He lifts me and stands, and my legs wrap around his waist. Our kiss never breaks as he walks us to his bedroom, then drops me onto his bed. With him between my legs, and one of his hands propping him up, his warm body presses against my own. I waited months before I was with James intimately, yet after only a few days of knowing Isaac, I'm in his bed, ready to give myself over to him—and I don't feel a single ounce of shame.

Our kiss turns heated, desperate, as if we can't get enough of one another. We stay like this for several minutes, our tongues stroking, our bodies grinding, our hands exploring. But we make no move to go any further, simply enjoying each other's touch, taste, the way we feel against each other. It's like the entire world has faded away, leaving only the two of us.

Isaac pulls back, breaking the kiss, and I take a moment to appreciate him. His hair is every which way from me tugging on the strands. His lips are red and slightly puffy from our intense kissing, and his brown eyes are filled with so much adoration, my heart swells in my chest.

"You're so damn beautiful," he says, running a single finger slowly across my lips. I capture it and suck it into my mouth, biting down on it teasingly, and his gaze heats up.

Pulling it out, he drags the wet digit down the side of my neck and across my chest, until he gets to the edge of my—*his*—shirt.

"Raise your arms."

I do as he says, and in one swift move, he yanks the material over my head, leaving me in only his boxers. After he slowly rakes his gaze down my body, he dips down and takes my nipple into his mouth. He sucks on it, while his fingers pinch the other one, making me squirm in need.

I tug on his shirt, silently indicating what I want, and he releases my nipple, so he can pull his shirt off, exposing his chiseled chest and abs. His mouth comes back down on mine, and he kisses me passionately, nearly taking my breath away.

When I reach for the waistband of his shorts, wanting to feel what's inside, he breaks the kiss and slides down my body, until he's lying on his stomach between my legs.

"I was trying to touch you." I pout, annoyed he's now out

of my reach.

"And I'll let you," he says, his eyes glittering in the light coming in from outside. "But first, I'm going to need to taste you." He hooks his fingers around the elastic and pulls them down my thighs, and that's when it hits me... he wants to *taste* me.

At the thought of his mouth *there*, my legs attempt to close, but he's already between my thighs, forcing them open. I've never had a guy down there before. My ex was selfish in bed and sex was very straightforward and lacking.

But I have a feeling Isaac is nothing like James. Everything he's done since we've met has been about making me comfortable, making me feel good, making sure I'm taken care of. I can't imagine that changing in the bedroom.

And he only proves me right when he spreads my lips and licks up my slit. Stopping at my clit, he flutters his tongue up and down, causing my body to spasm. He pushes a finger, and then two into me, and because it's been several months and I've only been with one other guy, they stretch me out, forcing my butt to bow off the bed.

"Oh, God," I breathe, my body tensing up as Isaac strokes my clit with his tongue and fucks me with his fingers. It's never felt like this before. The buildup. The intensity. As if he's got a direct connection from my pussy straight to my soul.

"That's it," he coaxes. "Come for me, baby. Come all over my tongue."

He reaches up and pinches my nipple, while adding pressure to my clit and thrusting his fingers into me, and suddenly all the tension is released. My body flies over the edge and I soar through the clouds. My legs tremble and I see stars—yes, actual fucking stars—behind my eyelids.

When I pry my eyes open, I find Isaac still lying in the same spot with a knowing smirk on his face. He drags his finger up my center, and aftershocks, like a goddamn earthquake, rock through me.

"Uh-uh," I mutter, pushing his hand away from the sensitive area.

He chuckles and rolls to his side. "Just had to make sure you weren't faking it."

"That was so freaking good." I turn onto my side and face him, my eyes barely able to remain open. "Like the best orgasm I've ever had."

Isaac grins wide and pulls me toward him. "If I have it my way, I'll be the only one to ever give you any orgasms again."

Still high from my orgasm, I moan in agreement as I reach for his pants. My body might feel like Jell-O, and I could close my eyes and sleep for the next seven hours, but there's no way I'm not making sure he feels as good as I do. I'm not a selfish asshole like my ex.

But before I can reach into his pants, he lifts my hand and kisses my knuckles. "Let me grab something to clean you up."

"Not yet." I move on top of him and scoot down between his muscular thighs. "It's your turn." He's naked from the waist up, so I explore his body, trailing open-mouthed kisses along his pecs and down his torso. The spattering of hair on him tickles my nose as I work my way down his happy trail.

"Cam, you don't have to—"

His words are cut off when my hand dips into his shorts and wrap around his hard length. With my fingers barely able to fit around his thick girth, I pull the material down and free his dick. The head is purple and angry and a bit of precum is seeping out.

I wet my lips, then take him into my mouth, gliding up and down his length, as his dick thickens in response. When I release him and glance up, my eyes meeting his, his gaze is scorching hot.

Without breaking our connection, I take him all the way down my throat, swirling my tongue along his velvety-smooth flesh. I always wondered what it would be like to suck a man's dick, and I figured it wouldn't be too bad, I mean women do it every day... but I wasn't prepared to like it. Like really like it. The taste of him, the way he feels, how in control I feel.

"Cam," he growls. "I'm close..."

I consider heeding his warning, but I'm already throat deep, so I figure I might as well stay committed till the end. I pick up my pace, sucking him harder, deeper, until his dick swells in my mouth. I'm prepared to take whatever he's about to give me, but before I can, his fingers grip my hair and he pulls my mouth off him just in time, as ropes of cum jet out and land all over my breasts and his stomach.

I watch in fascination, and when he's done, I swipe a bit off his stomach with my finger and pop it into my mouth, curious. It's salty and thick and pretty freaking gross.

"What are you doing?" he asks, sounding out of breath.

"That was my first time giving head. I was wondering what cum tastes like."

His eyes go wide at my confession. "And?"

"And I'm really glad you didn't let me swallow."

Thirteen

CAMILLA

"CAM, YOUR ALARM'S GOING off."

I groan sleepily and snuggle deeper into Isaac's side. After we cleaned up, we lay down and spent hours talking until at some point my eyes closed and I passed out. His bed is comfortable, his sheets are cozy, and he smells delicious. I have no desire to move from this bed or him any time soon.

"Sweetheart," he murmurs, rolling me onto my back and kissing his way down my neck. "Is there a reason why your alarm keeps going off?"

I reach over and grab my phone to stop the incessant noise. I want to go back to sleep, but I need to get up. For one, I need to go visit with my dad, and two, I need to find a damn job.

"Yeah, I have to get going."

His kisses stop and he looks at me. "Where do you need to go?"

"Home to change, for one. Then to visit my dad."

He sits up and pulls me into his arms. "I'll take you."

I'm already shaking my head. As much as I would like Isaac to stay glued to my hip, I need to handle shit myself. Yesterday was a great escape, but lounging around and watching movies while binging on Italian food isn't my reality. "I have to go alone."

I climb out of bed and grab my clothes that are now clean, changing out of Isaac's shirt and into them. He moves to the edge of the bed, watching me. Once I'm dressed, I walk over to him and wrap my arms around his neck. "I just need a little bit of time to get myself together."

He tilts his head up and sighs. I can tell he wants to say something, but he holds back. "Can I have your number at least?"

"Of course, but it's for emergencies only, in case my dad needs to call me, so the minutes and texts are limited." I drop a kiss to his lips. "I need to get going."

"Give me a few minutes so I can take you home. You're not walking or hailing a damn cab." He palms the side of my face, his eyes volleying between my own. "I'm not letting you disappear, Cam. I meant every word I said. You're it for me."

Butterflies attack my chest, and emotion clogs my throat, so I simply nod in understanding. While Isaac takes a shower and gets dressed, I make us egg and cheese sandwiches and coffee for breakfast. I'm going to be later than usual to meet my dad, but visiting hours are all day, so it'll be fine.

A little while later Isaac walks out, freshly showered and dressed in a sharp business suit. His hair's still wet and messy, and I second-guess leaving this house and taking him back to bed so I can slowly undress him.

"Smells good," he says, kissing my cheek and taking a plate and mug. "Thank you." We sit at the breakfast bar next to each other, talking while we eat. He tells me he has an appointment this morning but will be around later if I want to do something.

"Let me see your phone." I unlock it and hand it to him. He puts his number in, then calls himself, so he has my number. "You ready to go?"

"Yep." I take our dishes to the sink, but he insists the cleaning woman who comes in a couple times a week will handle it, so I leave it so we can go.

I'm shocked when we get down to the parking garage and find Isaac drives a truck. Although, it's not just a truck. It's a beautiful sleek black on black, monster of a truck.

"What?" he asks when he catches me gawking.

"I didn't take you for a truck man."

He laughs, and the sound goes straight into my chest. "I drove you home in this truck the other night."

Huh. "I don't remember much after I was drugged..."

"You were a bit out of it," he says, opening the passenger door for me, so I can hop in. After he closes the door, he rounds the front and gets in himself. When he turns the ignition, the vehicle rumbles to life. "So, what did you imagine me driving?" he asks, smiling at me.

"Like a sports car. Something fast."

His grin widens. "I have a couple of those as well." He points in the direction of several sports cars in various colors. "But I prefer my truck. It pulls my boat and is better suited for my field of work. Driving up to jobsites in a McLaren only makes a guy look like a douche."

"You pull your yacht?" I imagined it being huge the way he explained it.

"No. The yacht stays in the water or gets shipped somewhere. But I have other boats, faster ones that I go out on when I want to have some fun."

I sigh. Boys and their toys.

When we arrive at my complex, Isaac offers to walk me up to my apartment, but I insist he leave me here. For one, I don't want him seeing my shitty place, and two, if he comes up, we may never leave.

With a kiss that's clear he's making a point to remind me what's waiting for me, he makes me promise to call him soon and then reluctantly lets me go.

He's still watching me when I step up to my building, so I wave one more time before I disappear inside. It's getting late, and I don't want to be waiting in line forever, so I need to get moving. Thankfully, the night I was drugged, Yasmin thought to grab my clutch, so I have my keys and bank card—which has barely any money on it.

When I step up to my door, ready to unlock it, I'm stopped in my place by a note on the door. I peel it off and read it several times.

No. No. No. This can't be happening... I try my key in the lock but nothing happens.

"Damn it!" I slam my hand against the door, then try to rattle it open. When it doesn't budge, I turn my back against the hard wood and slide down it, landing on my butt. Hot tears well in my eyes as I read the note again that says I've been warned several times and have been evicted. Anything of mine I wish to get will need to be done by scheduling an appointment with management.

Feeling utterly defeated, I sit on the floor and cry. It won't do or change anything, but sometimes it just feels good to cry.

"Hey," Yasmin says, sitting on the floor next to me. "I heard you from down the hall. What are you doing out here? What's wrong?" I drop my head onto her shoulder and hand her the note.

"Fuck," she mutters under her breath. "What are you going to do?"

"I don't know. For starters, try to find a job." There's no way I'm going to visit my dad in the state of mind I'm in. He would take one look at me and know something is wrong. And since he's stuck behind bars, there's nothing he can do.

"I'm so sorry," she says, squeezing my hand. "I can ask my mom if you could sleep over. My twin bed won't fit us both, but—"

"No, that's okay. I'll figure it out." Her mom is a crazy bitch and the only reason Yasmin stays is because her rent is cheap and she's saving for her yoga studio.

"Well, if you can't, I can always sneak you in." She bumps my shoulder and gives me a sad smile.

"I appreciate it."

After several minutes of her letting me cry on her shoulder, I suck it up and head to the library so I can job search. I find several places that are hiring and head to the first one. With the money I have in the bank, since I never paid my rent, I can rent a motel until I can come up with the money for another place.

I stop at the first place, but they're only hiring part-time. I fill out the application anyway since it's better than nothing and then move on to the next place. They're closed today, so I make a note to come back. The third place is a strip club, who's looking to hire a waitress.

"You sure you don't want to learn the pole?" he asks, eyeing me up and down. "You'd make better money."

"Not now," I say noncommittally, handing him my application.

He scans over it then glances up. "You worked at Azul's?"

I nod, praying he doesn't actually call the manger. I considered not putting it on my application, but since it's the only place I've actually waitressed at, I risked it.

"Arturo and I are good friends. Go way back. If he says you're good, then I'll hire you."

My heart drops into my stomach as he reaches for the phone. I should speak up, but I remain quiet, hoping Arturo takes pity on me.

He answers quickly and they talk for a few minutes before he brings me up. Whatever Arturo says must not be good because he looks at me with a frown and hangs up.

"You left him hanging."

"I did," I admit. "It was a huge mistake and I tried to make it right, but he wouldn't give me another shot. Aside from me quitting last minute, I was a good, hardworking employee. I—"

He puts his hand up, cutting me off. "You want to learn the pole, you have a job."

I sigh in defeat. "Can I think about it?"

He shrugs a shoulder. "You have until Monday."

"Thanks."

Feeling like a failure, I walk toward the edge of the city where the motels are. My phone buzzes in my pocket several times, but I just don't have it in me to check or answer the calls. If one of them is my dad, he's going to ask why I didn't show up today... but if I don't answer, he's going to worry.

I pull my phone out and sure enough it's a number I don't recognize. I answer it and my dad's voice comes through the phone. "Cam, is everything okay?"

I drop onto the bench on the sidewalk and hang my head, trying to get ahold of myself. "Hey, Dad. Everything's okay. I'm sorry I couldn't make it today." My voice cracks on the last word and I cringe, hoping he didn't catch it.

He's silent for several moments before he speaks again. "I'm worried about you."

"Please don't be."

We sit on the phone, neither of us saying a word until someone tells him it's time to get off. He must've asked to make an emergency call.

"Cam..."

"It's okay, Dad. I promise."

"I love you."

"Love you too."

The second we hang up, my face falls into my hands and I cry for the second time today, wondering when I'll catch a break. I like to think of myself as a strong person, but there's only so much a person can take before they finally break. And right now, it feels like I'm awfully close to my breaking point.

I'm crying for who knows how long when a hand lands on my shoulder, making me jump. When I look to see who it is, I find Isaac standing in front of me.

"Are you stalking me?" I half-joke.

He doesn't laugh. "You're on my docks."

I look around and realize he's right. The bench I'm sitting

on is located in front of the marina he owns. "I didn't realize these were yours."

"Most of the city is mine," he deadpans, having a seat next to me. "Since you didn't realize where you were, I'm assuming you weren't looking for me."

"No, I wasn't." I avoid looking at him, knowing my face must be a puffy and red mess from crying, but Isaac doesn't stand for it and lifts my chin, so I'm forced to meet his gaze.

"What happened? Is something wrong with your dad?"

"I didn't go see him." I sigh. "Ever wish you could rewind the day so you could start over?"

He nods and edges closer, his arm sliding behind me to comfort me. "What day would you like to start over?"

"So many..." I laugh humorlessly. "But right now, just today would be good." I rest my head against his open arm and inhale the masculine scent of his cologne.

"What would you do differently?"

"Not get out of bed. Stay wrapped in your arms all day."

He tightens his hold around me and kisses the top of my head. "What's going on, Cam?"

I start to shake my head, but he lifts my chin again, looking me dead in the eyes. "Don't tell me nothing. I can't fix it if you don't tell me."

"It's not your job to fix it."

"What did I tell you last night?" So much was said, but I try to think of what he's referring to... "You're mine, Cam," he says, not waiting for me to answer. "The one. The person I want to spend the rest of my life with, and that means whatever you're going through, so am I."

Jesus, this man. How can everything be going so wrong, yet so right at the same time? Like he's the light in my darkness.

"I get that, and I feel the connection too, but we still hardly know each other, and my burden isn't yours. Dating is supposed to be fun, not filled with baggage. I just need a little time—"

"No." He cuts me off. "I'm not giving you any time. Tell me what's wrong."

I consider lying to him. I don't want him to pity me, and I don't want to come across as some damsel in distress who needs to be saved, but as I sit here, staring out at the boats in the water, I know I need to let someone in because I'm at my lowest point. I've hit rock bottom, and I need to extend my hand and let Isaac pull me up.

"I'm homeless." When his brows furrow in confusion, I explain how I've gotten behind on my rent, and because James is trying to renovate the building and turn it into a luxury apartment complex, he's kicking out everyone he can. "All my stuff is still in there..." Not that I have much. Most of it was sold for cash, but it still sucks not having access to anything of mine. "He locked me out and I need to make an appointment to get it back."

"What were you doing all day?"

"Looking for a job. Ally Cats is hiring, but I'd have to learn—"

"The strip club?" he barks. "That's not fucking happening."

"You don't understand. My family's name has been slung through the mud. My options are limited, and I can't go back to school until August, and that's only if I can get approved for a loan."

"You're coming home with me."

"What?" I back out of his arms. "For tonight?"

"Forever. Jesus, woman, it's like you aren't listening."

"I hear you! But c'mon, you can't possibly know that you're going to want me for the rest of your life after only knowing me for like a week."

"Maybe you don't know," he says, "but I do. I want you, Cam. Today, tomorrow, forever."

"Why? Why me? I don't get it. I'm full of drama and baggage. And you must know being with me, the daughter of the man who went to prison for tax evasion and money laundering, is only going to make you look bad. You're like the perfect man and could probably have any woman you want, so why me?"

"You just don't see it," he says, cupping my face. "You've been kicked—hell, beaten down—yet you remain so strong. Your mom died of cancer, your father went to prison, and you were thrown from the only life you ever knew into a shitty situation. But not once have you complained to me. I made it clear I want you, and instead of using that to your advantage, you're at strip clubs trying to get a job."

He sighs deeply and tucks a few strands of hair behind my ear. "I know we've only just met, but I feel it, deep inside me. You're the one." He shrugs, as if it's just that simple because he says so. "I get we're on different pages right now, and I'm fine with waiting for you to catch up. We have our entire lives for you to get on the same page, but while you're doing that, you can do it from my home."

He stands and grabs my hand, pulling me up so our bodies are flush against one another. "I've been waiting my entire life for you, and now that I have you, nothing is going to stop me from taking care of you."

Fourteen

ISAAC

"WHAT DO YOU WANT TO EAT?"

Camilla looks at me like I've lost my mind,
but I ignore her. I'm not going to sit here and go back and
forth with her about her living situation. She has nowhere
to live and I have a home she can live in. It's as simple as
that. From the first day I met her, all I've wanted to
do is be with her, care for her. I didn't even know
her, but when she freaked out at the charity event
before we went in, I felt this urge to comfort and
protect her. Just like I do now. She needs me and
I want to be there for her.

"Isaac, how can you be so nonchalant about
this? Moving in together is a big deal. Have you
ever lived with anyone?"

"No, have you?" I know she hasn't, but clearly

this is how she wants to do this, so I guess I'm going to have to play along.

"Well, no, but..."

"But nothing. I know what I want. You, in my home. In my bed, in my shower—"

"This is more than sex," she says, exasperated. "This is living together."

"I know what it is." I pull her onto my lap, needing to feel her against me. She of course comes willingly, threading her fingers through my hair like I've come to learn she loves doing. "It's us sharing a space, getting to know each other, fighting over who left the clothes on the floor. It's lazy days in bed, two people coming together to create one life."

I frame her face and kiss her gently on the lips, not wanting to say what I'm about to, but knowing I need to. "If you don't want any of that, I'll understand. If I'm not the person for you, as much as it'll kill me, I won't chase you. I know what I want, how I feel, but that doesn't mean you feel the same way, and if you don't, I'll respect your decision. But regardless, if you need a place to stay, my home is open to you."

I care about her, and she needs someone to have her back—even if it's only as a friend.

She shakes her head. "I do feel the same way. I'm just scared.

These feelings have come on hard and fast, like we're soaring through the clouds, but I've hit rock bottom, so I already know how badly it hurts to fall."

"Everyone falls," I say, being honest with her. "But the difference is, you've never had me there to catch you."

Her eyes flutter closed and she lays her head on my shoulder, her soft lips pressing a kiss to the side of my neck. "Okay," she murmurs, tightening her hold on me. "I'll move in with you."

***

"What would you like to drink?" the waiter asks.

"I'll take a whiskey neat." I glance at Camilla, prompting her to order. We're at Christopher's—I figured it was the perfect place to go to celebrate Camilla agreeing to move in with me, since we never got to have dinner here the other night. Like a second chance, only this time, we'll actually succeed.

"Umm... Just water, please," she says.

The waiter nods and then disappears.

"You sure you don't want something else?" I hold up the menu. "Don't women love those fruity drinks?"

She laughs, but it sounds off. Before I can ask her what's wrong, she leans in and whispers, "Do you know how old I am?"

Her question catches me off guard. Her friend is twenty-seven, so I'm assuming she's around the same age... maybe a little younger.

"I was taught it's rude to ask a woman her age."

She laughs again, but this time it's carefree. "Maybe you should've asked before you asked me to move in." There's a twinkle in her eyes, and I have a feeling she's about to shock the hell out of me—and take pleasure in it. She has to be over eighteen since she's in college...

"My birthday is next Saturday. I'm turning twenty-one." Well, shit. She's a bit younger than I thought. "You okay with dating a younger woman?"

"It doesn't matter what your age is. It's not going to change how I feel about you." Plenty of couples have a large age gap between them. "What about you? You okay with dating an old man?"

A giggle escapes her lips. "Thirty-four is hardly old."

"How'd you know my age?"

"I might've Googled you after our date."

I pull her chair toward mine and kiss her. "I like that."

"Me Googling you?"

She scrunches her nose up in confusion and I place a kiss to the tip of it. "That you were curious enough to Google me. That I was on your mind after our date."

She's about to say something else, but her phone rings and

she pulls it out, her forehead wrinkling. "I need to take this. Order for me, please."

She stands and walks over to the terrace that overlooks downtown. She's talking softly, so I can't hear what she's saying, but her face is filled with sadness. The waiter comes over and since I have no clue what to get, I order steak and seafood for both of us.

A few minutes later, she comes over and sits back down, quiet and distant.

"Who was it?"

"My dad. I didn't make it to see him today. I found out I was evicted and didn't want to cause him more stress. We talked earlier, but he had to get off the phone, so he was calling back to check on me."

Fuck, this woman... she's so damn strong, carrying the weight of the world on her shoulders. "What time are visiting hours until?"

"Seven o'clock."

I glance at my watch. "Let's eat and then I'll drive you to see him."

"You sure? I don't want to put you out. I can—"

"Cam, you need to understand something right now. You're mine, which means whatever you're going through is mine.

Whatever you need, I'm going to make sure you have it. You are not nor will you ever be a burden to me."

Her gaze softens and her eyes gloss over, filled with emotion. "Thank you." She leans over and kisses me. "I would really like to see him. I wish you could go inside with me, so you could officially meet him. I'm going to tell him about you today. I think it'll make him feel better to know I'm not so alone anymore."

After we finish eating, we head up north so she can visit her dad. She's in there for about an hour and when she comes out, her face is puffy and her eyes are rimmed red. Because I'm not on the approved list, I'm waiting outside on the bench, dealing with work shit. When I see her heading toward me, I jump from my seat and go straight toward her. She wraps her arms around me and presses her face into my chest.

"What's wrong?" I ask, pulling back and tilting her face up.

"Nothing." She shakes her head, and I sigh in relief. "I'm just emotional. I told him about us and at first he wasn't too happy because of the age difference, but after I explained the way we feel about each other, he was understanding. But then he said..." Her cries deepen, cutting off what she's trying to say, and I'm almost positive my heart just cracked. I've seen Camilla sad, even crying, but I've yet to see her this distraught, and I don't like it one fucking bit.

"What happened?" I walk us over to the bench and sit us down with her in my lap—I'm pretty sure the woman spends more time in my lap than in her own seat—and I love it. I also love that she allows it.

"He's in there for fifteen years... maybe ten with good behavior. He got so upset, Isaac, saying he's going to miss me getting married one day and having babies." She sobs into my chest and I run my hand up and down her back, trying to comfort her. It's not the time, but her words have me thinking about our future, putting a ring on her finger, filling her with my babies. It's too soon to be thinking about all that, but I can't help it.

"I hate Clint and James," she mutters. "They framed my dad and now he's going to miss everything. Who'll walk me down the aisle one day? How will my kids know their only grandparent? He's stuck in there, while they're out here continuing to screw everyone over."

She sniffles loudly and pulls back, her eyes widening. "I'm so sorry. I wasn't trying to imply we'd—" She groans and covers her face. "I'm such a mess. I haven't moved in yet, so if you want to change your mind and run, I won't blame you."

I snort out a laugh because she kind of is a mess, but hell

if I don't love that about her. My mom used to always say my dad was her knight in shining armor, and I think a part of me would love to be that for her. "I'm not changing my mind," I tell her, kissing her softly. But I am going to have this shit with Pruitt and her dad looked into. When it all unraveled, I stayed out of it since it wasn't my business, but now that I'm with Cam, I'm going to make it my business. Clint and his spawn are shady as fuck and I wouldn't doubt they framed her dad.

We get home and Cam suggests we watch a movie. "We can, but first we have something we need to do."

She follows me to what's now our room and glances around confused. "You going somewhere?"

I laugh at how adorable she is. The woman is lost in her own world. "You're moving in." I open the top box and pull the first thing out I find. It's a picture of her and her parents.

"Is this my stuff?" she gasps, opening the box completely and digging into it.

"Yeah, I had one of my guys box everything up and bring it over here. The furniture and kitchen stuff is in my warehouse, in a storage unit, but everything else is in here for you to go through. There's plenty of room in the closet and I'll make room in the dresser."

Her head pops up in shock and awe. "We're really doing

this? I'm moving in?"

Gripping the back of her mane, I pull her into my arms. "We're definitely doing this." My mouth crashes against hers and our lips curve around each other. She tastes sweet, like the best addiction, and I know there won't ever come a time when I'll grow tired of kissing her.

She moans into my mouth, her tongue curling around my own, and presses her body into mine. I cup the swells of her ass, and she jumps up, winding her perfect legs around my waist. Our kisses become more heated as she grinds her center on me, seeking more.

With the boxes forgotten, I carry her over to my bed and lay her on the center, taking a moment to appreciate what I have in front of me. I told Camilla we have all the time in the world, but the truth is, every day I live like it's my last. When you lose both your parents as suddenly as I did, you realize the hard way how quickly life can end without a moment's notice. And I plan to spend every day spoiling the hell out of this woman.

"Isaac," she breathes, pulling me down to her. "I want you." She claws at my suit, wanting it off, and I oblige, removing all my clothes, until I'm only in my boxers. Her heated gaze silently appraises me as I climb back onto the bed to join her, and I've never been so thankful to Noah for forcing me to go to the gym every damn day until it became part of my routine.

Our mouths connect in a searing hot kiss. I told myself the first time I had her, I would go slow and learn every inch of her body, but as she drags her nails across my shoulder blades, rubbing her body against mine, I'm not sure I'll be able to go slow.

She lifts her shirt over her head, exposing her black-laced bra, then pushes her shorts down her legs, kicking them off. Her body is perfect. Her tits are plump, her stomach flat and soft, with a pink jewel dangling in her naval. "I need you inside me, now," she begs, seemingly annoyed that I keep stopping to look at her.

She wraps her arms around my neck and pulls me down to her, running her tongue across the seam of my lips before she bites down hard enough to draw blood. When I draw back, my gaze meeting hers, there's a twinkle in her eye. She wants it rough. I can sure as hell give her that.

Tugging on her bottom lip, I bite her back, and she moans in pleasure. Her legs tighten around me and she grinds her hot cunt against my dick.

"What do you want, baby?" I murmur against her lips, swiping at the drop of blood I've caused.

"I... I don't know," she breathes. "I'm just so turned on. I need you."

I chuckle softly, loving how innocent she is. "I got you."

Pulling down her bra cups, I expose her pert, rosy nipples that are begging for attention. I take one into my mouth, sucking on the pointed tip, and Camilla squirms under me. "Harder," she pleads. "Please."

I palm her breast and take the nipple back into my mouth, this time biting down on it. She groans, arching her back and thrusting her chest upward. I bite and suck on her nipple, then give the other one the same attention. Cam moans the entire time and I wonder if I could make her orgasm from nipple stimulation alone. I suck harder, testing out my theory, and she pants heavily.

"Oh my God. It feels so good."

With my lips wrapped around one of her nipples, I push her underwear to the side and dip my fingers into her, finding her soaking wet. I push two digits in and, like last time, she's tight as hell. Imagining her this tight, squeezing the fuck out of my dick, has my heart pounding against my ribcage. She might've had sex before, but it's clear he had a small dick, because she damn near feels like a virgin.

Her fingers drag through my hair, tugging on the ends, as she pushes my face against her chest, silently begging for more.

I bite down on her nipple, sucking it into my mouth, while I pump my fingers in and out of her. My thumb massages circles against her swollen clit and within seconds, she's coming hard and loud.

Needing to be inside her, I push my boxers down and yank her underwear down her legs. I sit up on my haunches, wanting to see the first time I enter her, and she surprises me when she lifts up on her elbows, glancing down.

I fist my dick, stroking it up and down, and she widens her legs, giving me access. I shift closer, lifting her hips to meet mine, and glide the head up and down her slit, watching as it glistens with her arousal.

"Don't be a damn tease," she hisses, glaring at me. "Fuck me, now."

In one swift motion, I thrust all the way in, fusing our bodies together in the most intimate way. Camilla's back hits the bed and I drop my hands onto the mattress, caging her in.

"Wrap your legs around me." I take her mouth, delving my tongue inside, and once I feel her ankles lock around me, I push in harder, making her groan in pleasure. She's warm and wet and so damn tight. As I fuck her deep, making sure to bottom out every time I pull back and drive back in, I make sure to hit her in just the right position that will send her into another climax.

I want to take her every way possible, but right now, I take her just like this, with our mouths and bodies connected. When I know I'm close, I reach between us and pinch her clit. Her head tilts up, breaking our kiss, and I nuzzle my face into her neck, sucking and biting on it as I come deep inside her.

"Wow," she breathes. I pop my head up to look at her and love what I see. She's got a tiny smile tugging on her lips and her eyes are glossed over in pure, satiated bliss.

I shift her hips up slightly and slowly pull out, my eyes staying trained on the way my cum seeps out of her. Before it can drip onto the bed, I catch it, and with a single finger, push it back into her hole, loving the way our juices feel mixed together.

"What are you—" When she realizes what I'm doing, her face flushes crimson. "Isaac, we didn't use a condom."

"Are you on birth control?"

"No." She shakes her head vehemently. "Money has been tight, and I haven't had sex in months."

"Good." I glance back down at her pussy and push the leaking seed back into her. "I'm not getting any younger. The sooner you get pregnant, the better." I can't wait to see the way she looks swollen with my baby in her.

She gasps, her eyes going wide. "You're insane, you know that, right? We just met."

"Maybe." I shrug. "But that doesn't change what I want or how I feel. Do you want kids?"

She drags her bottom lip into her mouth and nods, and that's all I need to know.

A bit of my cum escapes and hits her ass crack, and instead of dragging it back up, I press the tip of my finger to her puckered hole. She clenches her ass cheeks, and I glance up at her. "Have you ever been taken here?"

She shakes her head.

I gather more of our juices and push my finger farther into her hole, until my entire digit disappears. She drops her head to the pillow and throws her arm over her face, groaning.

"Feel good?" I ask, pulling my finger out and pushing it back in.

"Surprisingly... yes," she mutters from under her arm.

I chuckle. *So damn adorable.* "Flip over onto your stomach and don't move."

Fifteen

CAMILLA

I DO AS ISAAC SAYS, A BIT embarrassed that he was just playing with my ass, and even more embarrassed that I was enjoying it. He jumps off the bed and sprints to his bathroom, returning a minute later with a bottle in his hand.

"What's that?" I ask curiously.

"Massaging oil. I'm going to fuck your ass, and since you've never had anyone in there, it's going to hurt." My eyes bug out at his honesty. "Don't worry, you'll enjoy it. I can already tell you like it rough." He winks playfully and I turn my face down into the pillow, unable to argue. I never knew I liked it rough, until he bit my lip and then my nipples. The combination of pleasure and pain damn near had me convulsing before he even touched my pussy.

With my face hiding in the pillow, the only senses I have left are my sound and touch. I expect Isaac to go straight to my ass, so I'm confused when I feel my bra snap open and the material slide down my arms. I lift up slightly and he pulls it out from under me, leaving me completely naked. Next, I hear the top click open and a few seconds later, his hands are on my shoulders. With the slickness of the oil, he rubs my shoulders and back muscles out, loosening me up. It feels so good, my eyes flutter closed and I get lost in his expert touch.

Until his hands reach my butt and he palms each of my cheeks, massaging them for several minutes as he moves closer and closer to my ass crack. When he spreads my cheeks and droplets of warm oil land on my puckered hole, I tighten up.

"Don't do that," he murmurs. "Relax, baby."

I do as he says, as he reaches under me and props my bottom half up, lifting my ass into the air. His fingers dance across my center, and then he pushes a couple of fingers into my pussy. I groan, sensitive to his touch, but make no move to stop him.

His fingers leave me and then there's pressure at my back entrance. It can't be more than one finger, but it's tight... so tight. I don't even want to imagine what his dick will feel like in me. He must add another finger because the tightness turns to a burning.

"Fuck, Cam," he mutters. "I wish you could see the way your perfect ass sucks my fingers in."

His words make me squirm and, without thinking, my hand reaches under me to find my clit.

Isaac, so damn perceptive, doesn't miss a beat. "You touching yourself?" He reaches under me again and his fingers land on mine. "That's it. Stroke yourself. But don't make yourself come yet."

I still my fingers, knowing it won't take me long to work myself up.

Isaac goes back to my ass, pumping his fingers in and out of my tight hole, and then pulls them out completely. I sigh, missing the fullness they were creating against my pussy wall. But then he spreads my cheeks again and I feel the thick head of his dick pushing against me.

"Take a deep breath," he says. "I'll go slow."

I exhale and he pushes in. The burning I felt earlier intensifies, and I close my eyes, wondering what the hell I've gotten myself into. This man, since the first day I've met him, has this way about getting me to do whatever he wants—and right now is no different.

He keeps going, and I can feel every inch that enters me. I

keep exhaling, forcing myself to stay loose, and before I know it, he's telling me he's all the way in.

"How do you feel?" he asks, his voice tense.

I take a second to think about it. Aside from a bit of burning and pain, it doesn't actually hurt. More than anything I feel full. "I'm okay." My fingers slide across my swollen nub, and the combination of his dick in me and the sensitivity of my clit has me pushing back. "You can fuck me," I find myself saying.

He fists my hair, and I expect him to let loose, but he doesn't. He pulls out almost all the way and then slowly drives back in. Little by little, the burning turns to pleasure and before I know it, I'm grinding my pussy against my fingers while he fucks my ass.

I come first, nearly screaming out my orgasm. My body becomes languid and I drop onto my belly, unable to hold myself up any longer, glancing back, just as Isaac pulls all the way out and fists his cock. I watch as ropes of cum land all over my ass. His eyes flit over to meet mine, and our gazes lock, and it's in this moment that I know I'm in deep. What I feel for him is unlike anything I've ever felt, and I would do anything he says. The thought both excites and scares me.

I WAKE UP, FEELING PARCHED, AND GLANCE AT MY

phone. It's eleven o'clock. The darkness outside tells me it's night time, and the empty side of the bed next to me tells me Isaac isn't here. Half-asleep, I drag myself out of bed, my entire body sore from our sexual ministrations earlier.

After we showered together—where he fucked me against the wall and made me come again, I practically crashed, face first in bed. My God, the way that man dishes out orgasms... If I hadn't passed out from what I swear was orgasm overload, I would've made him take me again and again.

I stumble over the stacks of boxes, reminding me I never put anything away since we got sidetracked. I run my hand across the top of one of the boxes as I walk past them and my heart flutters in my chest. I don't know how Isaac managed to get all my stuff, but I owe him so much. For him to go out of his way to get my things, and so quickly, means the world to me.

I pad down the hall in search of him, but when I find him in his office, he's on the phone with someone. When a masculine voice speaks over the speakers, I realize he's on speakerphone. Not wanting to interrupt him, I'm about to back out of the room, when his eyes catch mine, and a smile that takes my breath away forms on his face

"You're awake," he says, ignoring whoever's on the phone. The voice on the other line comes to a halt.

"Yeah, I was thirsty. Sorry, I didn't mean to interrupt."

"You're not interrupting anything. C'mere." He nods toward his chair, backing up slightly, and I go to him without question, as if I'm a magnet, drawn to him and his force field.

When I climb into his lap, remaining quiet since he's still on the phone, I look over and see he's not on the phone, but on a video call. I try to move off him, but he clasps my hips and holds me to him. "Noah, I want you to meet Camilla, my girlfriend."

"Hey," I say shyly to the man on the other end, thankful he can only see us from the chest up, since I'm in Isaac's shirt and nothing else.

"Nice to meet you," Noah says with a half-smile. He looks to be around the same age as Isaac, with similar features, only he seems a bit edgier, rougher around the edges. Maybe it's just because he's on the computer, but he appears more closed off than Isaac.

"Noah's in Tennessee looking at some property for me," Isaac explains. "He'll be home Monday. We should all go to dinner."

"After my four-hour flight? Not happening, bro. The only thing I want to do is go home and crash."

"I could cook," I offer quickly. Isaac's done so much for me.

It's the least I can do.

"You cook, baby?" Isaac asks, nestling his face into my neck. My insides twist, wanting him right here, but I refrain, knowing his friend can hear and see everything.

"I love cooking," I admit. I just haven't had anyone to cook for in a long time, or the money to buy groceries...

"Noah?" he questions, turning his attention back to his friend. "Will you be up for a home-cooked meal? I'd love for you to meet Camilla in person."

"Sure," Noah says slowly, looking at us like we're aliens from another planet. I wonder if he knows I'm living here. "I should be home before dinner."

"Perfect. Keep me updated."

Without saying goodbye, Isaac ends the call.

"That was rude." I turn around, so I'm straddling his lap.

"What?" He raises a single brow in confusion.

"You just hung up on him."

"No, I didn't."

"You didn't even say goodbye."

He laughs. "I told him to keep me updated. Same thing."

I roll my eyes because... men. "Are you and Noah close?"

"Yeah, he's like a brother to me. We met when I was in college and hit it off. His mom died shortly before my parents, and he moved here with me to start over... has been helping me run my businesses ever since."

"Aww." I palm the sides of his face and kiss the corner of his mouth. "That's sweet. Like a bromance."

"What the hell is a bromance?" He takes my hand and kisses the inside of my wrist, causing butterflies to erupt in my belly.

"You know... like a romance between bros... bromance."

He grunts. "The only romance I want is with you." He captures my mouth and lifts me onto his desk, his strong hands palming my thighs. When he parts my legs and notices I'm still panty-less, he breaks the kiss, eyeing my bare pussy.

"Are you sore?" he asks, dragging a single finger gently down my center. "I want you, but I don't want to hurt you."

Hell yeah, I'm sore, but there's no way I'm telling him that. I want him just as bad. I spread my legs wider and grin. "I'm good. Now show me how much you want me."

"THIS IS LIKE HAVING TWO HOUSES." I STARE IN AWE around the inside of Isaac's yacht, once he's done giving me the tour. It's fifty feet of pure luxury. The exterior has comfy weatherproof seats both in the sun and in the shade, as well as a spot for people to comfortably lie out. There's even a table so you can eat in the sun. I had assumed that was it until he took me downstairs, where he showed me a damn apartment. A nice-sized living room with plush leather couches, two bedrooms—one with a king-sized bed and the other with two twins, a full-sized bathroom, and a complete working state of the art kitchen. "Who needs all of this to go on a boat?"

Isaac chuckles. "Anyone who wants to be comfortable. I've sailed down the coast in this thing for days. I told you I have a smaller boat for speed. Would you rather go on that one?"

Hmm... comfort or speed? "Does the smaller one have a bed?"

Isaac gleams, knowing exactly where I'm going with this. "Nope."

"Yacht, it is."

We head out onto the deck and Isaac goes about what I assume is undocking the boat, so we can take off. Once he's done, he walks up to the area where the steering wheel is and the boat starts to move. It's a beautiful day in the low eighties, and the water looks like black and blue glass. He slowly drives us south, through the inlet. I'm not sure where we're going, but it's not out to the ocean. With the sun shining down on us and the wind whipping my hair around, I feel like I'm able to take my first real breath of fresh air in months.

"What are you thinking about?" Isaac asks, his eyes meeting mine. I join him where he's steering the boat and wrap my arms around him from the side. He pulls me in front of him and cages me into his arms, between the wheel and his strong chest, making me feel safer than I've felt in a long time.

"How safe you make me feel," I tell him honestly. "My dad's still in prison, and I can't change that, but these past few months have been rough. Clint and James didn't stop with my dad. They blacklisted me from getting a job, from renting anywhere but that apartment complex, and once I was there, they wouldn't fix anything that was broken. I had no hot water, my freezer didn't work. They kept upping everyone's rent because they want them out. I just felt like I was drowning and then you came along..."

He kisses the side of my temple, and I sigh into his embrace. "I never wanted to be a damsel in distress, but even so, you saved me." The last words come out choked, my throat filled with emotion.

"Hey." He turns me around so I'm facing him. "You are not a damsel in distress. I told you before how strong you are. This world, this life, isn't meant for anyone to go through it alone. Needing someone by your side, to help you up when you fall, to be your strength when you're weak doesn't make you a damsel. It makes you human."

Tears burn my eyes. I'm falling so hard and fast for this man. How he's gone thirty-four years without being scooped up, I'll never understand, but I'd like to think it's because he was waiting for me—we just didn't know it.

I try to form words, but when they don't come, I wrap my arms around his waist and hug him tightly, hoping to convey how much he means to me. He places a soft kiss to the top of my head. "You're not alone anymore, Cam. I'll always be by your side."

Tears fall down my cheeks, and we stay like this for several minutes, in each other's embrace. Once I'm more collected, I glance up and find him smiling at me with tenderness in his eyes.

"So, where are we going?" I ask, clearing my throat.

"There's an island I love to get off at. We can lie out and enjoy the sun. They have an area with shops we can walk through. There are also several restaurants along the inlet we can dock and have lunch at."

"That sounds perfect."

When I glance out at the water, I want to capture the moment, but I don't have a phone with a camera. "Can I borrow your phone to take a few pictures?"

He doesn't even bat an eyelash, when he pulls his phone out of his board shorts pocket and hands it to me, relaying the code for me to get in. While he drives, I take pictures of the water, of the few islands we pass, and a few of Isaac. Then he insists we take a couple together.

"Why don't you go lie out and relax," he suggests. "It'll probably be another half-hour before we get to the island."

"I think I'll stay here with you."

He glances at me and hits me with his gorgeous smile. "All right, then let's play a game."

"You love games, huh?"

"Growing up, my parents always played them." He shrugs. "How about twenty questions?"

"Okay, I'll go first."

We spend the half-hour asking each other questions and getting to know one another. I learn a lot about him, like his favorite foods and bands, what he enjoys doing for fun, all the places he wants to travel to. The conversation with us flows, like it always seems to do, and before I know it, we're docking at the island he mentioned.

We spend the day lying out and exploring, then stop at a delicious seafood restaurant for lunch. In the afternoon, Isaac makes love to me in his bed, and then again on the front of the yacht, and one more time in the water. By the time we arrive back at his marina, I'm sun-kissed and sexed out.

"Tomorrow I have to go into the office," he says, once we're home and he's helping me put my stuff away. "I'm going to get you a real phone added to my plan and a credit card so you have money."

I freeze at his words. "I don't need any of that. I'm going to find a job."

He puts the stack of clothes down and pulls me into his arms. "I know you don't need any of that, but it's what's going to happen. I meant what I said, Cam. I'm going to take care of you. And that asshole Clint and his spawn are going to get what's coming to them."

Chills race down my spine. "You can't mess with them, Isaac. They're horrible people. Look what they did to my dad and they were best friends and business partners. Please, promise me you'll leave them alone. I don't know what I would do if something happened to you."

I cling to him tightly and he eyes me for a moment, his features softening and then hardening. "I have it in my power to fuck with them, just like they fucked with you. Trust me, they're going to pay, and nothing will happen to me." The way he speaks, it's clear he's already made up his mind and there's no point in arguing. I just have to hope he knows what he's doing because I've already lost everyone I love, and I'm not sure how I would handle losing him too.

Sixteen

ISAAC

"DON, AS ALWAYS, I APPRECIATE

doing business with you." I hang up the phone, satisfied with the way our conversation went. Fucking James thought he would get one over on me, but he's young and dumb, doesn't understand how this world works. Money talks and I have a shit ton of it, which means my voice, without saying a word, is louder than his. One call and I was able to have those wetlands overlooked. I have the green light to move forward with my industrial park and there's not a damn thing James or his father can do.

The phone rings and I groan. Elouise is sick, so I insisted she take the week off, but the fact is, with her age and the way her health is declining, it's time for her to retire. I just need to figure out how to find someone who can fill her shoes. The woman handles everything around here, and has since I was a kid.

When the phone stops and then starts again, I answer it. "Petrosian Enterprises."

"Good morning, I'm expecting a piece of equipment this week and Elouise told me she'd call to confirm, but I haven't heard from her."

Cursing under my breath, I apologize and quickly write down his information, since the phone is already ringing again.

"Damn it." I slam the phone down and am about to pick it up again, when there's a knock on my office door.

"Am I interrupting?" Camilla asks timidly. She's dressed in a bright yellow flowy top and skinny jeans, with a pair of sandals on her feet. Her hair is straight and her skin is bronzed from our time on the boat yesterday. She looks gorgeous and I wish I could say fuck it and take her home so I can get lost in her. Sure as hell beats dealing with all this shit.

"No, please come in."

She smiles softly and walks inside. "I brought you lunch." She holds up a plate that's covered in foil. When she sets it down, I get a whiff of the delicious smell. I pull the foil off and there's a hot ham and cheese sandwich. I told her yesterday it was my favorite.

The phone rings and I groan. "Thank you so much. It's kind of crazy right now. Mondays are busy anyway, but I'm without my secretary and the phones are ringing off the hook. I considered pulling someone from another department to help out, but—"

"I can help you," she says, smiling brightly.

"You can?"

"Of course I can. It's the least I can do after everything you've done for me. What else am I doing anyway? I don't have to start dinner until later. I don't know anything about what you do, but I've answered phones for my dad plenty of times."

I sigh in relief. "That would be amazing." I pick up my sandwich and take a large bite, starved. The cheese is gooey and the bread is perfectly toasted.

"Good?" she asks with a smirk when I moan in pleasure.

"So damn good."

The phone rings and Camilla stands. "You eat and I'll answer the phones. I'll have to run each one by you, but at least I can be a barrier, so you aren't bothered over everything."

"Thank you. I really appreciate it."

She saunters over and kisses my cheek before heading out. "Let me know if you need anything."

I'm not sure how many hours pass, but with the quiet from

being able to turn off my office phone, I'm able to get a shit ton of work done. Camilla doesn't once interrupt me, so I'm assuming either the phone stopped ringing or she hasn't needed to let me know. When I glance at the clock and see it's already almost three o'clock, I'm about to walk out and check on her when I hear yelling from out front.

I'm out of my seat and through my door in seconds. When I get to where Elouise's desk is, I find James and Camilla in a heated match.

"That's really fucking cute." James snickers. "Not good enough in bed so he put you to work?"

"Fuck you!" she yells, slapping him across the face. My chest fills with pride and fire—pride, that she can handle her own, and fire because I'm going to kill this fucker.

"You ever speak to my girlfriend like that again, and I'm going to make you regret it." I get in his face, creating a wall between him and Camilla. "You're not welcome here, ever."

"You think you were slick reporting me to the city because this dumb bitch was kicked out? I have—" I don't let him finish his sentence before I slug him straight in the jaw.

He stumbles back and I get in his face. "I warned you not to speak to Camilla that way, and that included speaking about her. Don't speak to her, about her, hell, don't even think about her."

"You think you can turn me in and what? You'll magically get the city to approve your park? It's not happening!" he barks, holding on to his face that's dripping with blood.

"I turned you in because you fucked with my girl. Upping the rent, not fixing shit, evicting her without proper notice. You're a piece of shit. And FYI, since you're a little behind, I already got the green light this morning for the industrial park." I grin extra wide just to fuck with him. "Now, take your ass out of my building before I kick you out."

His eyes dart between Camilla and me, glaring at the both of us. "This isn't over," he threatens.

"Yeah, it is. Now get out."

The dumbass is at least smart enough to do as I say and leave.

Once Camilla and I are alone, she turns to me with a scowl on her face. "I warned you," she says. "Why would you mess with him? Do you have any idea what he's capable of?"

I bite back a laugh, knowing she's seriously concerned, but she doesn't really know who I am and what I'm capable of. "Cam, I promised you it would be okay and I meant it." I lock the office door and take her into my arms. "I've missed you all day." I cup her face and kiss her lips.

All the tension in her body releases and she wraps her arms around me. "You're changing the subject." She mock glares. "And we've been in the same building all day."

"But it's not the same as being in the same bed or on the boat with you. I missed you." I kiss her harder, needing to taste and feel her, and she reciprocates, wrapping herself around me. I lift her into my arms and she winds her legs around my waist. The phone rings as I'm walking her back to my office, but I murmur against her mouth to ignore it.

Since the main office is locked and we're the only people on this floor, I don't bother closing my door. I lay her out across my desk, not giving a shit about anything other than being inside her.

We break our kiss only long enough to tear each other's clothes off and then our mouths connect once again. I dip my fingers into her warmth to make sure she's wet, and when I see she is, I line our bodies up and enter her roughly. Her body slides back slightly, but she grasps my arms and holds on as I fuck her hard and deep, kissing her the same way. Her orgasm hits her first, and from her tight cunt squeezing my dick, I follow immediately after.

We're both panting loudly, still kissing like horny teenagers, when the door creaks open and I pop my head up to see who the hell could possibly be here.

"Oh shit," Noah says with a laugh, making Cam jump. "My bad. I was…" He chuckles. "Next time close your door." With a sly smirk on his face, he waggles his brows and closes the door behind him.

"Oh my God." Cam groans, hiding her face in my chest. "I can't believe that's how I officially meet your best friend."

I stifle my laugh, not wanting to make it worse. "It's all good. I guess he's back." I shrug.

"Ya think?" she says with sarcasm laced in her words.

I pull out and quickly grab some tissues so I can clean her up. She takes them from me and finishes before standing.

"Noah is a self-declared bachelor for life. What he walked in on is probably tame compared to how he spends his nights. Don't worry about it." I lean forward and cage her in my arms, planting a kiss to her lips. "Thank you for helping today. I got a lot of work done. I'm going to speak to Elouise about retiring. It's time. She deserves to relax and enjoy life. She's worked hard for too many years. I'm going to look into hiring someone new. I'm sure Elouise will help train whoever it is."

"I can do it," she says, shocking me. "She can train me. I'll get to work with you, make my own money, and stay busy. I'm trying to save up to go back to school in the fall anyway."

This woman... so damn different than the women I've associated myself with.

"Cam, you're with me now. You don't have to work. Your credit card will cover anything you want." Then something hits me. "Where are you planning to go to school?" She was in school hours away from here.

"I'm going to see about attending school here. My old school is too far to visit my dad every week."

I sigh in relief. "We'll figure it out." I tuck a wayward strand behind her ear and kiss her softly. "I need to speak to Noah about a few things. Did you get whatever you need to make dinner?"

"I did," she says. "But I'm serious about working. I'm a fast learner, and you're pretty much the only person in this stupid city who will hire me."

As much as I don't want her to have to work, I can tell the idea of feeling independent is important to her, so I nod in agreement. "I'll speak to Elouise about training you."

She beams with satisfaction and wraps her arms around me. "Thank you!"

After we get dressed, she heads upstairs to start dinner while I head over to Noah's office, which is next to mine. He's on his computer when I walk in and a shit-eating grin splits across his face.

"You fucking cradle robber."

I roll my eyes and drop into the guest chair across from him. "Like you're one to talk."

"Yeah, I fuck 'em, but I don't date them."

"Actually..." I clear my throat and throw my ankle over my leg. "I moved her in."

His eyes go wide. "Jesus, Isaac, you're totally going to wife her."

"You already know I am."

He shakes his head and chuckles. "I don't even know how we're friends."

"My dad knew my mom was the one seconds after he met her and they spent over twenty years together, happy and in love, before their lives were taken. When you know, you know."

His jaw tightens and he looks like he wants to say something, but instead just nods and changes the subject. "Have you taken a look at the email I sent you?"

"I did. The parcel in Rochester looks to be the best suited for what we want to do..." We spend the next hour going over the different pieces of property he looked at, until I get a text from Camilla letting me know dinner will be ready soon.

"Let's go. Dinner awaits."

Noah laughs under his breath. "I still can't believe you're playing house with this chick. What is she? Twenty?" He means it as a joke, but he's spot-on.

"She'll be twenty-one next week." Speaking of which... "I was thinking of flying to Monte Carlo for the weekend to celebrate her birthday. You game?"

"Hot Mediterranean women and gambling? Always."

I lock up the office and we head upstairs, where I find Camilla setting the dining room table that rarely ever gets used. There's music playing on the television as background noise, and she's setting a bowl onto the table. When I get closer, the smell hits me, along with a million memories of my life before my parents died. "Did you make Lula kebabs and rice pilaf?" I mentioned to her it was one of my favorite dishes my grandma on my dad's side of the family used to make.

"I did. I hope it's good. I found a recipe online."

She leaves the room to grab the rest of the food, and I glance at Noah, grinning from ear to ear. He shakes his head and laughs under his breath. "Jesus, you're going to be wifed up by the end of the damn week."

The thought of sticking a ring on Camilla's finger doesn't scare me in the slightest, but I'm not going to rush it. I don't want to scare her or send her running, and I know she's having trouble with the fact that her dad is behind bars. With any luck—and money—my guy will be able to find out the shit the Pruitts are up to and maybe I can figure out a way to flip shit on its head.

"What would you like to drink?" Camilla asks us, when she sets more food on the table—several skewers of perfectly grilled lamb and tortillas. She must've found my grill on the terrace and used it.

"I can grab the drinks," I tell her, kissing her temple. "Have a seat. Would you like water or wine?"

"I bought sweet tea. It's in the fridge."

I pour her a glass, filled with ice, then make Noah and me each a glass of scotch. We all find our seats and dish out the food. Camilla eats quietly while Noah and I discuss some more business. When he brings up the industrial park, mentioning how pissed Clint must be that I got the green light, she freezes in her place, giving me a pleading look to heed her warning. I reach over and squeeze her thigh, silently telling her it's all good, then change the subject.

"Camilla's going to be working with us so Elouise can retire, at least until she starts back at school."

Noah nods. "What are you going to school for?"

"Fashion. I'm majoring in merchandising and business. My

dream is to open up a boutique that sells the latest trends in fashion."

"What prompted that?" he asks.

"My mom was a model. She traveled all over the world, modeling for different designers, and later, worked for a designer. When I was little, she would bring home clothes and let me play dress-up in them. I love everything about the industry. The clothes, the designs, accessories. Nothing makes a woman feel more secure and beautiful than when she's dressed for the occasion."

I watch in awe the way she lights up as she talks about fashion. It's the same way I felt when I was in college, spending my hours discussing history. I'm good at what I do, and I don't regret taking over my father's company, but listening to the passion in her voice reminds me of what I'm missing by not following my own dreams.

"Who's your mom?" Noah asks. "Do I know her?"

Camilla's face falls. "Probably not. She died from brain cancer when I was nine. Her name was Charlene Jennings, but once she married my dad, she became Charlene Hutchinson."

I can see when the name clicks for Noah, his eyes meeting mine, silently asking if I know who I have sitting at my table. Everyone in the business world knows about Daniel

Hutchinson, and how quickly he went from being one of the top real estate moguls on the west coast to being a name people only whisper about. I nod subtly, making it clear I know and not to say a word. I can tell through his gaze what he's thinking, she's out for my money. She's broke and is using me to fill her bank account while gaining back some of her family's status. But I don't believe it for a second, and nothing he says will convince me otherwise.

"I've never heard of her," he says. "And I'm sorry for your loss. I too lost my mother."

"I'm sorry," she says, her voice filled with remorse.

"So school and then opening a boutique, huh?" he says, switching gears. He comes across nonchalant, but I can tell he's about to dig now that he knows who she's related to. "Those are some lofty goals."

"They're more like dreams," she admits softly.

"What's the difference?" he asks.

"Goals are attainable. They have a deadline. Dreams are simply fantasies that give you hope for the future, that one day you'll be able to turn into a goal."

Her words leave him momentarily speechless as he looks at her, trying to figure her out. But before he can question her anymore, I steer the conversation in another direction. "Do you have any plans for your birthday next weekend?"

She turns her attention on me. "Only to visit my dad, but aside from that, I'm free."

"Good. Don't make plans. I want to take you to Monte Carlo. You can invite Yasmin, if you wish."

"Oh, you don't have to—"

"Nonsense. You only turn twenty-one once and going gambling is like a rite of passage."

"In Monte Carlo?" She laughs. "You realize we live like right next to Vegas."

Noah snorts. "Vegas is where you go to get wasted and hook up with whores. It's not where you take your girlfriend for her birthday." He shivers in mock disgust. "I'm pretty sure you're liable to get an STD from simply walking on the strip."

I laugh at what a snob my best friend is. When I met him, he was broke and the neighborhood he lived in looked like one giant STD. Now he's too good for Vegas. Not that he's wrong... it's just funny to hear him speak like that.

"Camilla," he says, standing and picking up his plate. "The food was delicious. I can't remember the last time I had a home-cooked meal. Feel free to invite me over for dinner anytime." He winks playfully and she blushes.

"Please leave it," she says, taking it from him. "I'll take care of the dishes."

"Well, in that case, I'm going to roll my fat ass home. I'll see you in the morning." He pats my shoulder and then kisses Camilla on the cheek. "It was good to meet you."

He takes off, leaving Camilla and me alone. Bringing the dishes up to the sink, we work together to rinse them off and put them into the dishwasher. While we're washing them, a song comes on that I recognize, making me stop in my place.

"What's wrong?" Camilla asks.

"Will you dance with me?"

"What?" She laughs in confusion.

"Dance with me." I grab the plate she's holding and set it on the counter, then guide us into the living room, where it's easier to hear the music. Once we're in the center of the room, I lace her fingers with mine and bring them up to my chest, wrapping my other arm around her waist and pulling her close to me.

"This was the song my parents danced to the day they renewed their vows," I murmur, locking eyes with her. "I can still remember watching them dance in the middle of the dance floor, completely head over heels in love."

Camilla smiles softly and then rests her head against my chest. "I like dancing with you. In your arms, I feel safe."

"Good, I want you to—"

"Hey, Isaac." She cuts me off, popping her head back up and breaking our contact. "Is that your marina... on fire?"

I glance out the window, seeing what she's talking about, as my phone rings in my pocket. "Isaac Petrosian," I answer, watching the red and orange flames seep from my goddamn warehouse.

"This is Atlas security. A fire has been reported at 2551 Marina Dr. The fire department is on their way. Is everyone safe or do we need to send an ambulance?"

"I have no fucking clue."

Seventeen

CAMILLA

NOT WANTING TO GET IN THE

way, I watch Isaac for hours handle the fire.

In the pit of my stomach I know who was responsible for

this—James. I warned Isaac not to mess with him, but he

didn't listen. I get it... he's bigger and badder than James.

He has more money and owns more property, but he

isn't crazy like him. I've seen what James is capable

of. I watched him and his father throw my father

under the bus without even blinking an eye. He

thinks—no, he knows he's above the law and he'll

stop at nothing to make sure he ends up on top.

And Isaac is currently in his way.

When the fire trucks, ambulance, and police

finally leave and Isaac doesn't come home, I head

down there to check on him. When I enter the

warehouse, it's stifling hot and smells like a bonfire gone bad. There's an area blocked off with yellow tape, so I walk around it in search of Isaac, finding him on the other side talking to someone.

"I want to know everything there is to know about him... Make it a priority." When he pauses and no one else speaks, I realize he must be on the phone. Not wanting to disturb him, I consider going home, but adrenaline is coursing through my veins. Isaac could've been in here, he could've been hurt or worse, killed. So, without thought, I step into the large room, where I find him on the phone and Noah standing next to him.

Isaac's eyes lock with mine, and he juts his chin, silently calling me to him. I cut across the open area and go straight into his arms, burrowing my face into his chest, while he finishes his call. He smells like his usual cedarwood, but it's mixed with soot, and the thought of him being caught in the fire forces a sob from my throat. When he hangs up, he glances down at me, tilting my chin up.

"What's wrong?"

"I just had to feel you," I tell him honestly. "You could've been in here..." I shake my head, unable to finish my thoughts out loud.

"The damage was minimal. I have fireproof walls and they

contained the fire to only one small area. Whoever started it, either didn't know, or was only trying to make a point. Nothing was damaged."

"Whoever?" I squeak. "You know who did this. James."

"Probably. The cameras only show a person in all black, with a hoodie covering his head and a mask over his face, so there's no proof. They gathered some fingerprints, but I doubt anything will pan out. He'd have to be in the system."

"So, what's our next move?" Noah asks, his voice filled with rage.

"No!" I step out of Isaac's hold. "No move. You don't do anything. You leave him alone, unless you want to end up blacklisted from the town like me, unable to get a job anywhere, or in prison like my dad. And let's not forget about his mother, who vanished off the face of the planet after she was caught cheating on his dad." I had always assumed she ran scared, but after watching the way they successfully framed my father, who knows what they're capable of.

Noah opens his mouth to argue, but Isaac raises his hand and shakes his head. "We'll talk tomorrow."

"When I'm not around," I finish for him. "Fine, go ahead. Go after him, retaliate. But I'm not going to be here while you do it." I sear my gaze into Isaac. "I already lost my dad because of them. I'm not going to lose you too."

"You're not going to lose me." He steps toward me, but I back up.

"You're right. Because I'm done." I raise my hands in the air, silently waving the white flag. "I'm moving out."

Noah groans and Isaac's eyes go wide in shock and confusion before his face morphs into what looks like fear. "Like hell you are."

"Yes, I am. I'm not going to sit by and watch while another person I care about either ends up in jail or six feet under." I turn on my heel and stomp away—fully aware I sound like a child, but not caring, because my heart can't handle losing another person, and I meant every word I just said. I won't stay and watch helplessly like I was forced to do with my mom and dad.

I'm barely out the door before Isaac scoops me up over his shoulder and carries me through the parking lot and into the building, all while I'm screaming and crying, kicking my feet and demanding he put me down. He doesn't listen, until we're inside the house and he sets me on the countertop in the bathroom.

"Let me go!" I yell through my tears. "You can't expect me to stay here and watch you put yourself at risk." I reach up and rub my chest, trying to calm my racing heart.

"I get you're emotional right now," he says, palming my cheeks that are tear-streaked. "But you're not going anywhere. Nothing is going to happen to me."

"You can't know that." I try to push him away, but he doesn't budge. "What you're doing is wrong," I cry. "You made me fall for you, and now you're going to leave me." I bang my fists against his chest, and he lets me. "I can't stay here. Please," I plead. "Let me go. I don't want to lose you too."

Isaac fists my hair and tugs my head up. "I promise you, baby. I'm not going anywhere." His mouth crashes against mine, and his tongue plummets into my mouth. With a swipe of his tongue and a caress of his lips, he coaxes the fight out of me.

When I've calmed down and my tears have dried, he softly kisses me one more time. "You're never going to lose me," he murmurs against my lips.

"You can't know that."

He sighs and nods, pressing his forehead to mine. "You're right, I can't. We can lose the people we love at any given moment." When he says this, his hands tighten on my face, and I know he's thinking about his parents and how he unexpectedly lost them. "But I promise you, I will do everything in my power to ensure that never happens to me."

"By poking the bear?"

Isaac chuckles. "Sweetheart, James is not a threat to me. I know he fucked over your dad, but I'm actually having it all looked into. Clint and his son are messing with the wrong person and they're going to learn, even if it's the hard way, not to mess with me."

"What do you mean you're looking into it?"

"At the time your dad was accused of those crimes, I didn't give a shit because it wasn't my problem. But now you're mine, which means it's my problem. I can't promise anything, but if Clint framed your dad, or is doing anything shady still, my guy will find out about it and I'll expose him."

My heart swells in my chest. I would never ask him to do that, or expect him to, and the fact he's doing it without me asking has me falling that much harder for him.

"Thank you, but please, *please* keep yourself safe."

He kisses the tip of my nose, then the corner of my mouth. He trails his lips down to my jawline and then tugs on my earlobe. "I'll always be safe, just like I will always keep you safe."

His declaration—his promise—warms my insides like the thickest, fluffiest blanket being draped around me on a chilly night. It's insane how quickly I've grown to care about Isaac. He's taken up residence inside of me and embedded himself in my heart, and I don't even want to imagine losing him. Just the thought of walking away almost had me crumpling to the ground in pain.

I push his suit jacket off his shoulders, then undo each of the buttons on his shirt, kissing my way down his muscular chest and torso, focusing on every divot, every freckle, wanting to memorize every part of him. It doesn't matter what he promises, nothing lasts forever. Our parents are examples of how quickly life can change. We're born and then we die, and in the middle, we live... but we have no say in how long we're here. How much time we get with the people we love, and when those same people will be taken from us.

When I get to his pants, I unbutton and unzip them, exposing his neatly trimmed pubic hair. He helps me, pushing his boxers and pants down his thighs and kicking them to the side. His dick, thick and long, and so perfect, springs up between us, and I grab a hold of it, loving the feel of the soft velvety smooth skin under my fingers.

Needing to taste him, I push forward and hop off the sink, dropping to my knees and taking him into my mouth, swallowing him as far as I can go.

"Jesus," he chokes out, looking down at me with lust-filled eyes. "The sight of my dick down your throat is enough to make me come." His fingers tangle in my hair, helping me to suck him down deeper, until my eyes are watering and I'm gagging on his dick. I don't know what's come over me. Maybe it's the realization of how much Isaac means to me, or the fact he called me his and is willing to try to help my dad—even if it's most likely too late. Or maybe it's because until I was with him, I had no idea how pleasurable and intimate and amazing sex could be, but my insides are tingling and I'm so turned on, I have no doubt my underwear is soaked. I want him, in me, all over me, hard and deep, rough and fast. I can't seem to get enough of him, and I don't know how to satisfy the hunger and need I feel toward him.

Isaac pulls my head back and I exhale a deep breath. "Fuck my mouth." His eyes light up, and my lady parts clench in anticipation. "Please."

With my hair fisted tightly in his hand, he pulls my face toward his dick. I open wide, making sure I'm ready for him, and latch my fingers around the backs of his thighs to steady myself. Once my mouth is filled with his entire shaft, I suction my cheeks.

"Fuck, yes," he groans, pushing all the way down my throat ever so slowly. "You're so goddamn beautiful." I expect him to fuck my mouth like I asked, but he doesn't. He's slow and deliberate, his eyes staying trained on mine. I didn't think it was possible, but as he pushes in and out of my throat, just deep enough to make my eyes water and saliva to drip down the corners of my lips, I realize he's not fucking my mouth but making love to it.

"Isaac," I growl around his dick, pulling back slightly, so he can understand what I'm saying. "Fuck my mouth. *Hard.*"

"You sure?"

"Yes."

He growls under his breath and thrusts his dick back into my mouth, this time with more force. Every time his head hits the back of my throat, I swear I get wetter and wetter. I consider reaching into my underwear and fingering myself, but I'm too focused on him, on the way he's now thrusting in and out of my mouth.

"Fuck, Cam. Your mouth. Those lips... Fuck!"

I assume he's going to come down my throat, but he shocks me by pulling out and lifting me to my feet. He rips my shirt off my head and yanks my jeans and underwear down my legs, then twists me around and pushes me up against the edge of the sink.

His eyes lock with mine in the mirror as he spreads my legs and then enters me in one slick thrust, filling me so deliciously.

"Holy shit, you're fucking wet." One hand goes back to fisting my hair and the other snakes around my front, finding the swollen nub between my legs. Even now, with him so close to losing it, he makes sure I'm taken care of. I'm quickly realizing it's who he is. With his gaze never leaving mine, he fucks me so damn good.

"Do you feel that?" he asks, his voice raw with emotion. "Do you feel how goddamned perfectly I fit inside you, stretching your tight cunt?" He thrusts in and out of me, hitting a spot deep within me, and my body shudders. Between his words and my clit already being primed, my orgasm builds higher and higher.

"You're mine," he growls, tightening his hold on my hair, his eyes never leaving mine. "Say it, tell me you're mine."

"I'm yours," I breathe, my walls tightening and my climax close to the precipice.

"Fuck yes, you are." He lets go of my hair and smacks my ass, and I damn near convulse. "That's it, baby. Come all over my dick." His thumb presses down on my clit and I explode around him. My walls clamp down on his shaft, and he groans out his own release, his warm seed filling me.

When we've both come down, he pulls out of me and spins me around. Before I can ask him what he's doing, his mouth crashes down on mine and his fingers delve inside my swollen and hypersensitive pussy. "You're mine," he murmurs against my lips. "And I'm yours." He thrusts his digits deep inside me, our combined orgasms making a squishing sound as some of it drips down the inside of my leg.

He pulls back and a sexy smirk quirks in the corner of his lips. "I love this." He scissors his fingers inside of me. "Knowing there's a chance every time I come in you, you might get pregnant. It turns me on. Makes me want to stay buried in you every second of every day."

This isn't the first time he's said this, and it should probably freak me the hell out. We're moving fast, probably too fast. But as I look at the way his eyes light up at the idea of getting me pregnant, I just don't have it in me to freak out. Because the truth is, I'm completely okay with anything he wants. He has me locked under his spell. It might sound crazy, but I know this man is my forever.

Eighteen

ISAAC

"YES, SIR, I'LL HAVE HIM CALL you as soon as he gets in." Camilla's heated gaze stays trained on me the entire time she speaks to whoever is on the other line, and I have to refrain from taking her right here on the desk. We've been working together all week, and after the second time Noah walked in on us, she made a no fucking in the office rule—one I have no intention of keeping long term.

"While I appreciate the offer, and I have no doubt you'd make a wonderful dinner companion..." Her eyes twinkle with mischief as my jaw clenches tight at her words. "I must tell you that I'm taken... Oh, trust me, he knows how lucky he is... Have a good weekend."

She hangs up the phone and walks around the

desk, wrapping her arms around my neck, and I immediately relax. "Who was that on the phone?"

"Victor Cooper," she says with a small, knowing smile.

I chuckle. Victor is the city commissioner, nearing his seventies and due to retire soon. His flirting with Camilla is *almost* completely innocent.

"Do I need to worry about him?" I joke, laying a kiss on her lips.

I wasn't sure how it would work with Camilla answering the phones and handling everything Elouise handles—especially since Elouise is still under the weather and hasn't been able to come in and formally train her—but she's risen to the challenge and has every damn man who calls under her spell. I'm trying like hell to keep it professional, but it's taking a miracle not to metaphorically lift my leg and piss on her so they all know she's mine.

"You don't need to worry about anyone," she says, kissing the corner of my mouth. "How was your breakfast meeting?"

"Productive." I grab the globes of her ass and tug her toward me, capturing her mouth with mine. She sighs into the kiss, threading her fingers through the back of my hair. The kiss quickly turns heated, and I force myself to pull away, knowing I'll have the entire weekend to get lost in Camilla.

"The phones have been slow this morning. Do you need me to do anything?"

"Yeah, shut down, so we can go home."

Her brows knit in confusion. "It's only ten in the morning."

"And we're starting our weekend early. Did you ask your friend if she can go?"

"She has to work all weekend and can't bail. I thought we weren't leaving until tomorrow. I have to go see my dad first..."

"We're leaving today instead, and we'll visit your dad on the way."

Her interest is piqued. "We?"

"Yeah. I got the approval expedited, so I'm on his visitor list."

Her eyes go wide. "You're going to visit my dad... with me?"

"I would like to." I tuck a wayward strand of hair behind her ear. "He's important to you, and you're important to me. Is that okay?"

"Of course. I just hate this is how you'll officially meet him as my boyfriend." Her lips curl down into a frown. "But I guess it's something I'm going to have to get used to."

"For now, yes, but you never know what will happen." My guy has already told me he's found tons of incriminating shit on Clint and James. And while that's good, and when the time is right, I plan to use it, he knows my ultimate goal is to find proof to overturn Daniel's conviction.

"So, after we visit my dad, we're leaving?" she asks, changing the subject.

"Yep. Go upstairs and pack and I'll meet you up there shortly."

"Is it just us going?"

"Noah's gonna tag along, but I doubt we'll see much of him once we're there. Is that okay?"

She nods. "Yeah, too bad Yasmin couldn't go. I bet they'd hit it off."

I chuckle. "You don't want him for her, trust me. Noah's my best friend and I love him like a brother, but he's a womanizer. He has no desire to settle down, ever."

Adorably, she scrunches her nose up in disgust. "Maybe he just hasn't met the right woman yet."

"Maybe." I kiss the tip of her nose. "I need to handle a couple things at the marina and then I'll meet you at home. We're going to go visit your dad then meet Noah at the airport."

"Sounds good."

I watch as she saunters away and then head into my office to finish up a few last-minute things, since I'll be out of the country for the next few days. Once I'm done, I shut everything down and lock up, turning on the alarm system. After what happened at the marina with the fire, I've upped my security and cameras. It needed to be done anyway.

When I get down to the marina, I head straight into the warehouse and to my office, where I find Noah and Adrian Burgrov, a business associate of mine, waiting.

"Isaac, how are you?" Adrian asks in his thick, Russian accent, extending his hand to shake my own.

"I'm well." I gesture for him to have a seat. "How are you? How's Patrice?"

"Spending my money as always," he says with a laugh, but the smile on his face tells me how much he loves his wife and is perfectly content with her spending however much she wants. I've only met her once in all the years we've been doing business, but it was clear how in love they are.

"Noah, here, tells me that you're off the market as well. I told him I won't believe it until I see it for myself."

I mentally roll my eyes at my best friend. Fucking asshole has to make sure everyone knows I'm no longer a bachelor.

"It's true. We'll have to make time for a double date at some point."

Noah groans under his breath, making Adrian chuckle. "That sounds like a wonderful idea. My Patrice will love that."

I pull out the folder I need and open it, pushing it toward Adrian, so we can switch into business mode. "Here's the details of what you requested and the prices."

He's already seen all of this, but I always show it to them before the transaction takes place, so they can double-check.

"That's perfect, my friend." He signs on the line and then pulls out his phone. A minute later, he says, "Funds have been wired."

I quickly log into my account to confirm—because I don't trust anyone completely—and once I see they're there, we head out to the equipment, where his order is waiting to be loaded into his vehicle.

I nod toward my men, giving them the okay, and they start loading as Adrian double-checks the merchandise, making sure everything is to his satisfaction.

Everything is about loaded into the vehicle, when there's a screeching sound from somewhere, and then the baritone voice of one of my men. Before I can go check it out, several of my men, as well as Adrian's, draw their weapons, preparing for whatever's to come.

A few seconds later, Camilla comes stalking toward me with Xavier, one of my guards, chasing after her. "You can't go in there," he barks, but she ignores him, her focus only on me.

Her eyes are red-rimmed and her cheeks are stained with tears. I'm so concerned about her, I forget what's happening behind me, until her gaze darts to the men with their weapons aimed at her.

"Oh my God!" She shrieks. "What's going on?" She raises her hands, her eyes filled with fear, and the men all stand down, putting their weapons away.

"Sir," Xavier says, no doubt about to explain how he let a woman half his size get past him and interrupt my meeting. We'll be having words later.

"Camilla, what's wrong?" I ask, walking over to her. "Why were you crying?" I lift my hand to wipe a tear that's resting on the top of her cheek, but she moves out of my touch, her eyes landing on the merchandise.

"Forget me," she says. "What's going on?" Her hands go to her hips, and she juts her chin out in defiance—if it weren't for her walking in on something she wasn't supposed to see, I would be laughing at how adorably stubborn she looks right now. "Are those all guns?"

There's a throat clearing and then Noah steps forward. "Let's go upstairs while Isaac finishes, and then he can speak to you afterward." His hand comes down on her shoulder, but she dodges him.

"No, tell me what's happening here." Her eyes dart back and forth between me and the vehicle that's housing a few dozen illegal firearms.

"I take it this is your girlfriend," Adrian says, breaking through the tension that's surrounding us.

"I am," she says slowly, turning her attention on him. "But if someone doesn't tell me what the hell is going on, that might be changing."

"Cam," I growl under my breath. She has no idea who she's speaking to like that.

Luckily, Adrian chuckles. "Go, my friend." He pats me on the shoulder. "I know a thing or two about a pissed off woman." He winks at me, and I sigh in relief that he's a married man. "Everything looks good. We will speak soon."

"Thank you." I shake his hand, then give Noah a quick look. He nods once, letting me know he'll finish up so I can speak to Camilla. Adrian is one of my biggest customers, and I'm always present for our exchanges. When someone spends millions of dollars a year with you, you make it a point to handle it personally—and you don't piss them off.

"Let's go," I say to Camilla, grabbing her hip hard enough that she understands I mean business, but not too hard that it hurts her. I guide us outside, glaring at my guard, who looks a mixture of pissed and scared. As he should be. Camilla is maybe one-thirty soaking wet. There's no reason she should've been able to get past him.

God knows what could've happened had I been with someone not as understanding as Adrian. I should've made it clear to her how my life works, but I've been too busy getting lost in her, in our own little bubble. She could've been seriously hurt, if not killed. Men in my world don't fuck around. They shoot first and deal with the fallout later.

By the time we get upstairs, I'm so worked up at Camilla for putting herself in harm's way, the moment we're through the door, I have her backed up against a wall with my body caging her in.

"Do you have any idea what could've happened?" Our bodies are close, but far enough away, I can look her in the eyes. "You could've been shot. I told you I would meet you when I was done."

"I'm sorry. I needed to talk to you." Her voice is small, filled with emotion and regret, and it hits me like a ton of bricks. This is my fault. I've never had someone serious in my life. Someone who needs to know everything. She might've put herself in harm's way, but it was only because she doesn't understand how my world works—because I've yet to open up to her about it.

"Xavier told you not to go into the warehouse," I say with a softer voice. "Next time, you need to listen." I close my eyes and burrow my face into the crook of her neck, inhaling her sweet scent, thankful she's okay and safe. If something had happened to her... fuck, I don't even want to think about that.

"Why were you giving that man all those guns?" she asks. "Is it true, then? Are you a criminal?"

My hackles rise at her accusation. "Where the hell did you hear that?"

"I asked you a question first." She pushes me back slightly and crosses her arms over her chest. "Are you a criminal?"

I sigh and take her hand, pulling her over to the couch. "Did someone tell you I'm a criminal?"

"It's been said in gossip, and when I told my dad about you, he said to be careful because you were involved in illegal activity and he didn't want me to get hurt."

I raise a brow. "And yet, you're still here."

"Because I didn't believe whatever you were doing would hurt someone else. But then I walk into your warehouse and have a dozen guns aimed at me, men are loading what looked like illegal weapons, and you're speaking to a man who I'm almost positive has a Russian accent. Are you like in the mafia or something? Aren't you Armenian? Is that the mob?"

I chuckle in amusement at her innocence. "That's a hell of a lot of stereotyping. Yes, my father was Armenian, and my mother was Brazilian, but no, I'm not in the mob or mafia, and neither is that *Russian* man you saw."

"Then tell me what I walked into."

"First, tell me why you were crying." I pull her into my lap. She's reluctant at first, but quickly gives in, because even when she's upset, she likes it when we're touching.

"My dad called and asked me not to come see him tomorrow. He said he won't be available. When I told him that's perfect because I'll actually be going to visit him today, he asked me not to come. He gave me some stupid reason and I knew something was wrong. I refused to accept his excuse and he finally gave in and told me he was beat up. He said he's okay, but his face is black and blue and he didn't want me to worry."

Fresh tears fill her eyes. "I didn't think stuff like that happened there. I mean, it has a golf course and a tennis court." A tear slides down her cheek and I catch it with my thumb.

"Anything can happen anywhere." The question is, who's responsible? That's what's important. Fights happen all the time in prison, but in a federal prison it's less, and they only happen for a reason. I don't mention that to her, though. I'm planning to speak to her father today anyway, so I'll ask him then.

"Did he say you can visit?"

"I am," she says. "He tried to argue, but I told him there's no way I'm not seeing for myself he's okay."

"Good. We'll leave soon. Have you packed?"

She backs up slightly, shooting daggers my way. "Don't think you're getting out of telling me what I walked in on. I'm so sick of everyone keeping me in the dark. You know that's a hard limit for me, especially after what happened with my dad. What's going to happen next? I'll come home one day and find out you're going to prison too?" She swipes several tears that are falling. "I can't do that. I can't be in the dark. Either we're together and I'm standing by your side, or we're not."

Fuck, this gorgeous, strong, stubborn woman.

"Of course we're together." I run the backs of my knuckles down her cheek. She means the world to me and I won't lose her over secrets. "How about this? Let's get on the road, so we can visit your dad and make our flight on time..." Technically we can leave whenever the hell we want. It's my company's plane. But I want to arrive on time, since our time is limited. "We can talk on the plane."

She looks like she wants to argue, but instead nods and climbs off me. "Fine, but don't think I don't notice you're pushing to have this conversation during our twelve-hour flight on our way to another country, where I can't escape." She quirks a single brow and glares before traipsing down the hall.

"ARE YOU SURE YOU'RE OKAY?" CAMILLA ASKS HER father for the dozenth time since we arrived and she saw the black eye and busted lip he's sporting. With only the patience of a father, he nods and tells her again that he's fine.

The guard announces we have ten minutes, and I place my hand on Camilla's leg to get her attention. "Can you do me a favor? Can you give your father and me a few minutes to talk alone?"

She huffs, glancing from me to her father and back to me again. "I don't like being in the dark."

"I know, but there's something I would like to speak to him privately about."

"That you can't say in front of me? No." She shakes her head. "Whatever you guys need to talk about, I want to hear."

"Cam..." I groan.

"No," she insists. "We're together."

I curse under my breath at her stubbornness. I both love

and hate it, and right now I really fucking hate it. But fuck it. She wants to know... fine.

"Okay." I turn my attention on her dad. "I'm in love with your daughter. I fell for her the first moment I saw her and I've been falling every day since. I know to some, it might seem like it's too soon, but she's the one for me, and I'd like your permission and blessing to ask Camilla to marry me."

Camilla gasps, her hands flying up to her mouth, and her dad snickers. "I-I didn't... know..." she stutters.

"No shit," I say dryly, mock glaring at Camilla. "That's how it works. The man asks permission *before* he proposes."

She groans, dropping her face into her hands, muttering something that sounds like, "Kill me now."

I reach for her face, not caring that we're in front of her father, and tip her chin up. "You can't die." I give her a chaste kiss on her lips. "I'd miss you too damn much. Even your stubbornness."

Daniel chuckles, and I turn my attention back on him. "It's clear from our short visit today how much you two love each other, and while I hate that this is being done from inside prison, I'm grateful my daughter has you to protect and love her." His eyes gloss over, and I feel for him. Having to watch his daughter from behind bars, only seeing her once a week for an hour. And all while knowing he doesn't deserve to be here. "You have my permission and blessing to marry my daughter."

"Dad," she chokes out, shaking her head. I pull her into my side and kiss her temple, vowing to make this shit right. "I can't do this..."

He reaches across the table and takes his daughter's hand in his own. "Yes, you can, Cam. It would break my heart for you to stop living your life because I can't live mine. I live for seeing you every week, hearing about your life, and it's been killing me inside to see you so unhappy and hurting and struggling. Last week, when you walked through the door, I could tell something was different, and when you told me you've met a man, I could tell it was love. The way your face lit up reminded me so much of your mother."

He smiles softly. "You have no idea how happy it makes me to know you're safe and protected and being loved." He looks at me. "Thank you."

The guard lets us know our time is up and Daniel envelops his daughter into a tight hug, telling her how much he loves her and to have a good birthday. When they're done, he extends his hand, then pulls me into a half hug. "Take care of her, please. James is—"

"I know," I tell him, not needing him to explain. "I got her."

I back up and look into his eyes, hoping to silently convey what I want to say to him but can't. I'll kill anyone who fucking tries to hurt her.

Nineteen

CAMILLA

ISAAC ASKED MY FATHER'S permission to marry me. He wants to *marry me*. In the visitor room of the federal prison, he told him he loves me. I've been in shock ever since, having no idea what to say or think or feel.

Isaac's been giving me space, focusing on his phone instead of me, and once we arrived at the airport and boarded his lavish company jet, he's been talking with Noah about work-related stuff. The entire time I keep replaying what happened in my head. It feels as though my life has become a whirlwind of emotions and I can't keep up.

He loves me. He wants to marry me. This shouldn't surprise me. I mean, he's flat out said I'm his and he has every intention of knocking me up.

But love...

Noah's phone rings, since apparently the plane has full service, and he excuses himself to take the call. The second he's out of earshot, and Isaac looks my way, I blurt the first thing that comes to mind.

"You can't possibly love me!"

He doesn't react to my outburst. He closes his laptop and sets it, along with his phone, on the table, then turns to face me, since we're sitting on the same couch.

"I do love you," he says matter-of-factly.

"You can't. It's too soon."

I was with James for months and neither of us ever spoke those words. And looking back, I now know why. It wasn't love. What we had was wrong and fake and so stupid.

But Isaac... He's right and perfect and—

"A heart doesn't know time," he says, pulling me into his lap like he always does, making me instantly relax. I don't know why, but when he's holding me or touching me, my entire body goes calm. "It knows what it feels." He places his palm against my chest, right over the area where my heart is. "I've felt it since I saw you coming out of that building, in that black dress, with your hair down around your shoulders, walking toward the limo. My heart clenched tighter, pumped harder, it beat faster, and I knew you were the woman I was going to spend my life with. I love you, Camilla Hutchinson, and I will show you how much every single day for the rest of our lives."

His words of admission have my head spinning, because what he described, I felt it too... I still do. Every kiss, every touch, I feel what he feels, but that can't mean... "I... I don't know..." I'm trying to form the right words, but they're not coming to me.

"Shh, it's okay." He presses two fingers to my mouth. "You don't need to say anything back. I'll be right here loving you until the day comes when your head catches up to what your heart already knows... that you love me too." He hits me with a lopsided grin that causes butterflies to explode in my belly, and I know what he's saying is true.

"My head has already caught up to my heart," I tell him, encircling my arms around his neck. "You love me... and I love you. And what we have is so rare, it's almost hard to believe. My feelings came on so fast and hard that you're right, sometimes I think this can't be real..."

"But it is," he says with conviction in his tone. "Our love is real. I love you."

"I love you too," I say back without thought, making him grin like a crazy person.

"Say it again."

"I love you."

His mouth attacks mine and my body goes warm, my insides tingling. I tighten my hold on him and am about to suggest we take this to the bedroom, when a door opens and I see Noah in my peripheral vision walking out.

I pull back, about to slide off Isaac, but he grips my hips tighter and lifts me. "I suggest you use noise canceling headphones," he calls out to Noah as he carries me toward the back of the plane. "My girl just told me she loves me, so it's about to get loud in here."

I half-groan, half-laugh at him in embarrassment, but I'm too happy, too in love to really care.

"THIS IS AMAZING." I INHALE THE SALTY SCENT OF THE Mediterranean Sea our terrace is overlooking and tilt my face toward the blazing sun that's shining down on us. After the twelve-hour flight, it feels good to be standing outside and stretching my limbs. After Isaac and I made love twice, I fell asleep for the rest of the flight, only waking once we landed. Technically it's two in the morning where we live, but with the time difference, it's eleven in the morning in Monaco. I'm rested and refreshed and ready to have some fun.

Isaac wraps his arms around me from behind and rests his chin on my shoulder. "Happy Birthday, *meu amor*," he murmurs into my ear. I have no clue what he just called me, but the sexy accent that came along with the word has me wanting him to talk only in whatever language that was.

"What does that mean?"

"Sweetheart." He places a soft kiss to the side of my neck. "My mom spoke Portuguese."

"I like it, and I like how you say it." I push back against him, indicating what I want, but he halts my actions, gripping the sides of my hips.

"Not now, baby."

I turn around in his arms and pout playfully. "Did you just turn me down?"

He chuckles. "I did, but only because we have reservations for lunch. After sleeping for damn near eight hours, I imagine you're hungry. I know I am."

"I am," I admit. "For you." I stand on my tiptoes and nip the corner of his jaw teasingly.

"Woman, don't tempt me," he says, unwinding my arms and stepping back. "Today's your birthday and I want to spoil you."

"And you totally can... in bed." I waggle my brows.

He shakes his head and pecks my lips. "Later."

We change into different clothes—him in a pair of khaki shorts, a powder blue collared shirt, and boat shoes, and me in a flowy palm print maxi dress and white strappy sandals Isaac bought me for the trip—then head down to the restaurant. We're on the same floor as Noah, but we have our own suite. The second we arrived, he wished me a happy birthday then disappeared.

We're seated at a table outside, under a gazebo that's sandwiched between the luxurious pool and the gorgeous blue sea. There are people lounging in daybeds, boats sailing in the water, and a few swimming in the pool. The entire scene looks like something straight off a website, and I realize that while my father made a good living and we never wanted for anything, Isaac's amount of wealth is on a whole different level. My parents did trips to ski resorts and once went to Paris, but Isaac flies on his private jet to an entirely different country for the weekend like it's no big deal.

He has so much to offer, while I bring nothing to the table.

"What are you thinking about?" he asks, snapping me from my thoughts.

"You and me." When he doesn't say anything, I further

explain. "I can't help but feel like we have a little bit of a *Pretty Woman* thing going on."

"A what?"

"*Pretty Woman*. Richard Gere and Julia Roberts. You've never seen the movie?"

"Can't say I have."

The waiter comes over and Isaac orders us a bottle of water as well as a bottle of white wine he swears is one of Monte Carlo's best. When he asks if I want an appetizer, I tell him to surprise me. So he orders a bunch of items from the menu and then turns his attention back on me.

"Now, tell me about this pretty woman, who I doubt could be compared to you."

I laugh at his flirting. "They meet by mistake. She's a poor prostitute and he's a gazillionaire businessman."

His brows dip in confusion. "That's nothing like us. One, you're not a prostitute. You were a fake escort for less than a second. And two, I'm not a gazillionaire. Not even close to a billionaire."

"You know what I mean." I roll my eyes. "He's rich and she's poor. He whisks her away from her shitty life and spoils her rotten, all while falling in love with her, and her with him."

"And that's a bad thing?"

"No... yes... I don't know." I sigh in frustration. "I love the movie. I've seen it a dozen times. It's romantic and sweet, and I'm sure most of the women who watched it wished for a man like him to save them... even if they weren't poor or a prostitute. But now that I'm in a similar situation I can't help but wonder how many people looked at her and thought she was weak and should've tried harder to save herself instead of letting him save her."

He nods in understanding. "I don't care what we look like to the outside world, and I sure as hell don't give a shit what anyone thinks or says. Yes, you were struggling when we met, but I guarantee had I not met you or asked you to move in, you would've found a way to survive. It's one of the things I love about you. You're strong as hell, Cam, and yeah, you had a bad hand dealt to you, but you were handling it. Playing that hand of cards the best you could.

"I haven't seen that movie, but I would bet, if you're comparing them to us, she was strong and beautiful and maybe even a little bit of a hot mess..." He winks playfully. "And he fell in love with her, just as she was. It wasn't about the money, it was about the moments, the chemistry. The way they knew how they felt about the other person."

"Well, when you put it like that..."

"I do," he insists, reaching over and threading his fingers through mine. "Yes, our situations are the reason why we met, but that's called fate. I've been going through life, barely living, definitely not loving, until you stepped out of that building." He swallows thickly and backs his chair up. I'm confused, thinking he's getting up, until he instead drops down... on one knee.

"I planned to do this later, over a romantic dinner, but right now feels like the perfect time. Kind of like us meeting. Life isn't about creating the perfect life. It's about living and seeing what it has in store. Not once in all the years Noah used that company did I ever use it, but the first time I did, I met you. And you didn't even work for them. It was just happenstance you took the job for your friend.

"Yes, I have money and the means to take care of you, and if you let me, I plan to do so every day for the rest of our lives. But it's not a one-way street. You reminded me about the most important part of this life: love. Maybe that guy in the movie helped her out of her shitty situation, the way I helped you, but you have helped me too. Every day since we've met, I've laughed and smiled and have gotten to experience what it's like to fall in love. And really, isn't that what life is about? Finding the person you want to fall in love with over and over again?"

Isaac pulls a ring box from his front pocket and pops it open, exposing a way too big and beautiful diamond ring. "Many would say what's happening between us is too soon, too fast, but I've never cared what anyone says and I'm not about to start now. I know in my heart you're it for me. I don't know what our future has in store for us, but I know you're the person I want my future to be with.

"What do you say, *meu amor*? Will you marry me and spend the rest of your life living with me?"

"Yes," I tell him, the only answer I can give him. "I will marry you and live with you. The good, the bad... whatever life sends our way, I will live it with you."

He slides the ring onto my finger and then lifts me into his arms, kissing the hell out of me. "Tell me you're mine," he murmurs against my lips.

"I'm yours."

"Damn right you are. Just like I'm yours."

We spend the weekend celebrating not only my birthday, but our engagement. Isaac does just as he promised and spoils me rotten. From the couples massages, to the gambling, to the hours of making love, we have the best time. We spend one of the mornings touring the city, and an afternoon sailing, and when it's time to go home, I wish we never had to leave. Of course, Isaac assures me we can come back any time we want.

Once we're back on the plane and taking off, I realize something... "We never discussed the guns."

Isaac nods once. "You're right, we didn't. But we need to. I was caught up in the moment, in you, but the truth is, we should've talked about this before I proposed. You should know what you're getting into by marrying me."

"So, it's true?" I ask, not for the first time. "You're a criminal?"

"No." He shakes his head. "I'm a vigilante."

"A what?"

"Vigilante," he repeats. "A group of people who undertake law enforcement because—"

"I know what a vigilante is... I watched *Arrow*."

He chuckles. "I'm not that kind of a vigilante. I have morals..."

"So, what, you're like Batman?"

Isaac snorts a laugh. "Hardly. I'm more like the middle man. Let me start from the beginning..." He pats his lap and I climb into it like I always do. We're seated on the comfy, extra-large couch, while Noah is sleeping off his hangover in the bedroom.

"When my mom was eighteen, she was walking home from a college party when a guy attacked her. She was raped and beaten and nearly left for dead." Isaac's fists tighten on my hips, but when I flinch from the pain, he loosens them, tilting the side of his lip up in an apology.

"She knew who did it. A guy from her college. They had flirted, but she left without sleeping with him. Apparently he was humiliated that she didn't give in and wanted to take what he felt was owed to him, while teaching her a lesson. My dad's the one who found her, and he swears, it was love at first sight. He picked her up and carried her to his house. He took care of her, and the next day they called the police. Since she knew who it was, it should've been an open and shut case."

His jaw ticks, and I have a feeling whatever he's about to say isn't good.

"Due to lack of evidence, among a list of other reasons, he walked free. The man who took my mother's virginity on the dirty ground behind some bushes, then beat her and left her for dead, walked away without anything happening to him."

"That's horrible."

"It happens all the time. The judicial system isn't perfect, nowhere near it. Innocent people are locked away, while guilty people are roaming the streets. So my dad took matters into his own hands. He knew someone who knew someone and that someone led him to a man who makes it his business to remove the filth off the streets. Jeffrey Stark, the man who raped my mom, was taken out of this world one year after he was found innocent."

I sigh in relief, even knowing how he was taken out.

"My father had just started up his importing business and in exchange for the guy taking out her rapist, he agreed to accept a shipment of illegal firearms from Japan. And that's how it started. We receive mining and construction equipment from Japan, and when they come in, inside are firearms I sell to private companies whose purpose is to free the world of trash like the man who raped my mother."

He brushes his thumb across my bottom lip. "I may not kill anyone like the guy from *Arrow*, but supplying them puts me in just as much danger. It was my dad's thing, and like his other business ventures, I wasn't interested in participating, but then they were killed and he left everything to me. And it felt like I owed it to him... to them."

"That's very selfless of you." I wrap my arms around him and snuggle into his front, inhaling his fresh scent and syphoning his warmth. "You and your father are protectors. It's why I feel so safe when I'm with you."

"But this world is dangerous," he murmurs, running a soothing hand down my back. "There are a lot of people who don't agree with what I do, what I'm a part of, and they would like nothing more than to bring me down. We haven't discussed it yet, but you being with me means by default you're a part of this."

"I don't care." I burrow myself deeper. "All I care about is being with you. I get some people have the 'Don't play God' mentality, but I'm not one of them. Not everything is black and white. Look at my father. He's in jail for fifteen years because the judicial system failed him."

Isaac sighs into my ear. "Thank you for understanding. I've been holding off because you've been home with me, in our little bubble where it's safe, but when we return, things are going to change a little bit. I need you to understand it's because of what I do."

I sit back and look at him. "What's going to change?"

"Your phone and card came in, for one. So you'll have access to the world and money. The phone has a tracker on it. It's not to spy on you, but—"

"I get it." I shake my head. "It's to keep me safe."

"Yeah. And your vehicle has arrived. Like my truck, it's bulletproof. Any time you go anywhere on your own, you need to either drive yourself or let my driver take you."

"Okay," I agree. "Whatever you think is best."

I kiss the corner of his mouth, expecting it to end there, but then Isaac kisses me back, harder, his tongue thrusting past my parted lips. "I can't believe how well you took all that," he murmurs against my lips. "I knew you were the one for me."

His growing erection grinds against me, and my core pulses with need for him. I'm about to rip my shirt off, when Noah walks out, grumbling about getting a room.

Isaac laughs and lifts me into his arms. "Now that you're out of my damn room, gladly."

Twenty

CAMILLA

"GIRL, IS THAT A MERCEDES I
saw you get out of?" Yasmin asks, enveloping
me in a hug.

"It is," I say, hugging her back. It's been several weeks
since I've seen her and I've missed her like crazy. Between
the whirlwind romance with Isaac, him taking me
away for my birthday, and me helping him at the
office—he insisted I take today off to meet up with
Yasmin—add in my weekly visits to see my dad,
which Isaac now accompanies me to, it feels like
the fast forward button has been pressed on my
life and time is flying by.

"The thing is a tank." I cringe, remembering
the first time I drove it. Having been used to small,
sporty cars, I ran over several curbs and Isaac damn

near lost his shit, declaring me the worst driver ever.

"A sexy as fuck tank," she sasses, as we walk over to the line to place our orders. I knew Isaac was getting me a bulletproof SUV, but what I didn't know was that the SUV was a black on black Mercedes-AMG G 63. I should be annoyed he bought me such an expensive, over the top vehicle, but the thing is seriously badass—even if I can't drive it.

"And who's the man?" she whispers, nodding toward the stuffy suit standing in the corner of the coffee shop, sticking out like a sore thumb.

"My bodyguard," I tell her truthfully.

Her eyes go wide. "So, it's true then? Isaac is into illegal shit?"

"It's a lot more complicated than that." And I can't talk about it. "Let's just say he's into shit and leave it at that."

She nods in understanding, and I'm thankful my friend doesn't push. We order our coffees and pastries, and I insist on buying since she's done so much for me the last several months when I had nobody else.

Once we sit, she snags my hand and admires my engagement ring. "Holy shit! It's gorgeous."

"You saw it in the picture I sent you." I pull my hand back and laugh.

"Yeah, but in person, it's bigger and prettier." Hearts dance in her eyes. "I'm so happy for you, Cam. You deserve to be happy and in love. Have you guys set a date yet?"

"Not yet, but I'm sure it won't be a long engagement. Isaac's already mentioned on several occasions he wants me to have his last name as soon as possible."

She giggles. "That guy has it bad for you."

"He does," I agree. "And I have it just as bad."

We take our coffees outside, so we can do some window shopping downtown while we catch up. I glance behind me and find Tony trailing behind us. It's the first time I've left without Isaac and I kind of feel bad that he's stuck following me around, but Isaac insisted this is what he does for a living and he's paid more than generously.

"How's work going?" I ask, changing the subject.

"Eh, it's okay." She shrugs, taking a sip of her coffee. "Dating wealthy old men is becoming kind of monotonous. But, I'm stowing away a shit ton of cash, so I can't really complain. It won't be forever. How about you? You said you're helping out Isaac, right?"

I give her a recap of Isaac's secretary retiring early—since he's convinced her to—then tell her how she's helped train me to take over.

"So, in other words, you guys are playing sexy secretary and dirty wealthy businessman all day?" She cackles, and I give her a playful shove.

"No! He works hard."

She side-eyes me. "You're telling me you haven't once been fucked over his desk?"

Heat blooms on my cheeks, and I look back at Tony to make sure he can't hear. If he can, he doesn't make it known.

"Of course I have," I whisper-yell. "The man is insatiable. He can't go a day without being inside me."

She giggles. "But is he good in bed?"

I bring my drink up to my lips and nod emphatically. "So damn good... like multiple orgasms every time good."

"Gah!" She shrieks. "I'm so freaking envious of you. A sexy, wealthy man, who's not only head over heels in love with you but is also amazing in the sack." She stops in her place and playfully brings her arms up and down, pretending to bow down to me.

"Oh my God! Stop!" I hiss, my eyes darting around.

"Have you figured out what you're doing about school?"

"I applied to the Fashion Institute of Washington and am waiting to hear back. It's only a thirty-minute drive. Isaac offered to hire someone else once school starts, but I'm sure

I can make both work." When I told him I was applying, but would only go if they approve me for a loan, he insisted we would pay for it. I wanted to argue, but the way he said *we*, because we're in this together, stopped me from doing so.

We spend the next couple hours shopping. I buy a sexy dress that I texted a picture of me in to Isaac—who insisted I'm wearing it out to dinner tonight—as well as a pair of cufflinks I saw that made me think of Isaac.

We stop at a bistro for lunch and are about to walk in, when my name is called. When I look to see who's calling me, I stop in my place, as James stalks toward me.

"You fucking whore!" he slurs. He doesn't make it anywhere near me because Tony steps in his way, preventing him from getting closer. "You tell your piece of shit boyfriend he's going to get what's coming to him!" he yells as Tony holds him in place, refusing to let him move.

"James, go away," I hiss as he continues to spew harsh words my way.

"The only person who's going to be going away is that meddling asshole when I end him." His threat makes my hackles rise because unlike most people who are all talk when they're mad, I know firsthand how serious James's and his father's threats are.

"Miss Hutchinson," Tony says. "Please go inside and enjoy your meal. I'll handle this guy and be in to get you when I'm done."

Yasmin takes my hand and pulls me into the bistro, James's screams fading as the door closes behind us. The entire meal I try to remain in the present and not let what James said affect me, but it's pointless because his words do affect me.

As I'm signing the check, wondering if Tony is okay since he hasn't come in yet, Isaac strolls in, locking eyes with me. "*Meu amor*," he murmurs softly, kissing my cheek, and my entire body sags in relief.

"Did Tony call you?" I ask, standing.

"He did. That's why I'm here. He had something he had to handle, so I thought I would come and accompany you home." He glances at Yasmin, who's practically drooling at the sight of him. I don't blame her, though. She's only met him once, and she was drunk and said she barely remembers him, aside from him being hot as hell.

Isaac is dressed in one of his sexy *I'm taking over the world today* suits and his hair is messy in that just fucked way it always is, with several days of stubble donning his face. He needs a haircut and a shave, but I love him like this, so I won't mention that to him.

"Isaac, this is Yasmin."

"We've met," he says, raising a brow.

"Yeah, but she was a bit... inebriated the first time, so this is your official introduction."

He laughs, deep and throaty, and I have to refrain from jumping his bones. "It's nice to officially meet you," he tells her, extending his hand and shaking hers. "Do you need a ride home?"

"I walked, but it's not too far..."

"Nonsense, we can drop you off on the way." He turns to me. "Tony will pick up your vehicle later." He takes my bags out of my hands and puts a strong, comforting palm on the small of my back, kissing the side of my temple.

"Don't you have to go back to work?" I ask Isaac, when he types in the code and presses the third floor button instead of the second that leads to his office.

"Trying to get rid of me?" he jokes. "I'm starting my weekend early. I made reservations for tonight, so I can show you off in that sexy dress before I rip it off of you later." He waggles his brows, making me laugh.

"You're such a caveman."

"Hey, a caveman wouldn't feed you before ripping the dress off."

"HOLY SHIT," ISAAC SAYS WHEN I SAUNTER DOWN THE hall in the champagne-colored maxi dress and gold sky-high stilettos. The dress is by far the sexiest thing I've ever worn, and I must admit because of its revealing qualities—plunging V-line and completely backless, with high slits running all the way to my hip bones—I was a bit worried about wearing it out of the dressing room. But as Isaac drinks me in, his eyes filled with heated lust, I'm happy I bought the dress. I would give anything for him to look at me like he is now for the rest of our lives. I've never felt so wanted as I do with him.

When he steps over to me and his hand glides down my bare back, landing on the swell of my ass, he stills. "Are you wearing anything under this dress?" he asks lowly.

I shake my head, and he groans, moving his hand to the slit and sliding it inside. He cups my bare ass and tugs me into him. "I take it back. There's no way I'm feeding you before I rip this dress off."

His mouth crashes against mine as he slides his other hand under my dress and lifts me, forcing me against the wall. He devours me, his tongue coaxing, his lips gliding against my own. And then he moves to my neck, nipping and sucking on my heated flesh. With his body flush against mine, his fingers massage the globes of my ass.

"Fuck," he groans, meeting my eyes. "I want you so damn badly."

"You saw me in the dress earlier," I say cheekily.

"It's not the same thing." He backs up slightly and gently sets me back on my feet. "Seeing you like this in front of me… I can't control myself." I assume, since he's put me down, we're going to leave for dinner, but then he drops to his knees and lifts my floor-length dress over his head, disappearing underneath.

I gasp in shock and then moan in need when he spreads my thighs and lips and his wet tongue licks a line straight up my slit.

Holy shit! I can't see him, but I can *feel* everything. He ravishes my pussy, his fingers pumping in and out of me, while his tongue does the most amazing things to my clit. It doesn't take long for my orgasm to rise and my body to detonate. My hands grip his shoulders from under my dress, as he laps at the juices between my legs.

When he's finally had enough, he lifts the material and stands. His lips are shiny from my climax, and it makes me wonder what I taste like.

"Now that I've had my appetizer, I guess we can go eat,"

he says, his eyes alight with humor. "But when we get home, I'll be spreading you out on the bed and enjoying my dessert." He darts his tongue across the seam of his lips, and I pull him toward me for a hard kiss, tasting myself on him.

"I vote for dessert now," I murmur against his lips. I turn around, my hands slapping against the wall and my ass jutting out.

Isaac growls, "Fuck yes," under his breath, then rips the dress clean off my body, leaving me naked and in only my heels. His hands slide around to my breasts, tweaking and plucking my taut nipples, while he grinds his front against my ass, raining kisses along the top of my shoulders.

"Isaac..." I spread my legs and push my ass out farther. "Please fuck me now."

He moves away from my body, taking his warmth with him, but a few seconds later, he's back. I glance around in time to watch as he takes his hard, thick cock and moves it along the center of my pussy, up to the crack of my ass. When he gets to the puckered hole, he swirls the smooth head around the tight rim, rubbing the juices from my pussy onto my ass, and I damn near combust.

"Fuck, I love your ass," he mutters, palming it with his other hand. "I swear to God, every part of you was made just for me."

I'm about to beg him to fuck me, when he slides his dick between my legs and enters me in one fluid motion, not stopping until he's balls deep and filling me to the hilt. One hand fists my mane and the other digs into my hip. He fucks me like he's a starved man and I'm his meal, hitting me in the perfect spot over and over again. My climax hits me hard and fast, white stars flashing behind my lids as I come completely undone, my arousal coating his dick.

Isaac's hold on my hair tightens, as he fucks me with complete abandon. His hand comes around and finds my clit, massaging circles along it, and within seconds, another orgasm hits me, nearly taking me to my knees. He pins me against the wall, and with a few more deep thrusts, spills his warm seed inside me.

With both of our bodies humming with adrenaline, he pulls out and lifts me into his arms, carrying me to our room. My body is limp from the three mind-blowing orgasms, and my eyes close in exhaustion. When they open, we're in our bathroom and I'm sitting on the counter, with Isaac staring at me.

"What?" I ask.

"Marry me."

"What?" I repeat with a laugh, lifting my hand up. "I think

we already established that."

"I know, but I mean now. I don't want to wait. I want you to be mine in every way possible, including legally."

"How soon? Like tomorrow?" I half joke.

His eyes widen. "You'd do that?"

I shrug. "You're the person I want to spend my life with. Today, tomorrow, next week. I don't care when we marry. It's not like we're going to have some big wedding anyway."

His brows dip. "What do you mean?"

"Well, I always imagined having this beautiful extravagant wedding. We would marry in the church my parents married in. Then, afterward, we would have the reception at the country club."

"Then that's what we'll do," he says, framing my face. "I want you to have your dream wedding. I can wait."

I swallow past the ball of emotion lodged in my throat. "What's the point? My mom is dead, my dad's in jail. I have no friends left aside from Yasmin. Your parents aren't alive... There's no point in having a wedding."

"The point is that we make the day special and memorable."

"I thought you wanted to get married tomorrow."

"I do, but I want you to have your perfect wedding more, and I'd bet, even though your dad can't be there, he'd want that too. I don't give a shit if it's only me, you, Noah, and Yasmin. I want you to walk down that aisle in your white dress and for us to stand before God, giving ourselves over to each other. I want to dance with you and at the end of the night make love to you as my wife. Then I want to take you on the honeymoon of your dreams so I can get lost in you for days."

A smile spreads across my face as I imagine it all... the wedding, the honeymoon... I hate that my dad can't be there, but Isaac's right. My dad would still want me to have the wedding I always imagined. "I like the sound of that."

"Then that's what we'll do," he says. "How about at the end of the summer? So we're back before you start school."

I wrap my arms around his neck and kiss him, loving that he remembered my wanting to go to school. "That sounds perfect."

Twenty One

ISAAC

"YOU KNOW I HAVE TO ADVISE against this," Frank says, sliding the papers I've requested across the desk.

"And you know I've already made my decision," I tell him, flipping through the pages to verify he's included everything I've requested. "In less than three weeks, Camilla will become my wife and I want to ensure, if anything happens to me, she's taken care of."

"I understand, but that doesn't mean you can't create a prenuptial agreement. What if one of you wants a divor—"

I snap my head up from the papers and glare at Frank. "Nobody is getting a fucking divorce. She's it for me. And if she wanted to divorce me, she can have whatever the hell she wants."

"What can who have?" Noah asks, walking into the doorway of my office. My door is open, since Camilla is at her orientation for school today. She found out a couple weeks ago she was accepted into the fashion institute she applied to and will be starting in the fall as she hoped.

"Camilla... and everything," I say, signing the papers. "I had a will drawn up, so if something were to happen to me, Camilla is taken care of." I look up at Noah quickly, then glance back down, flipping to the next page and signing. "I also made sure to include in there, if something happens, your job is secure. She won't know how to run the business on her own, so she'd need your help."

"You're leaving her the business?" Noah asks.

"I'm leaving her everything that's mine." I sign the last page and pass the stack over to Frank. "Thank you for handling this so quickly." I stand and shake his hand. "I'll see you out."

As we walk to the door, I stop since Noah is still standing in the doorway. "Is there something you needed to talk to me about?"

"No," he says. "I've got it handled."

"HOW'D IT GO?" I ASK, WHEN CAMILLA WALKS through the door with a bright smile on her face. She's been like this every day since her orientation. Between planning our wedding and preparing for school, she's on cloud nine and I fucking love it. All I ever want is for her to be happy.

Today, she left work early to meet with her advisor. She was nervous about her transcripts being sent over, but based on the look on her face, it all got worked out.

"Really good. All my classes are picked out, and because I was going more than full-time before, based on my course load, I can still graduate in May." Juggling two boxes in her hands, she comes over and sits next to me. "I stopped by the deli and picked us up dinner and dessert."

"I'd rather eat you," I say, pulling her into my arms once she's set the boxes down. She squeals when I nip at her jaw playfully.

"Later! We have a decision to make."

"About what?"

She opens the first box. "First, we eat dinner." She hands me a wrapped sub and takes her own. While we eat, she tells me more about school and the classes she's registered for. I'm so proud of her for getting back on the horse. This year has been hard on her, but she's not letting it keep her down. She has plans and dreams and I can't wait to watch her achieve them.

Camilla was meant to soar, and I'll make sure she does.

"Okay, now it's decision time," she says once we've devoured our food. She takes the box and opens it up, showcasing an array of little cake squares. "Every part of our wedding is planned, except for the cake. I went by to order it on my way home and the baker gave me these to try. She said I can call her with the flavor we choose."

We've decided on a small church wedding with just us and our close friends. The pastor will marry us, and then we'll go to Christianson's, Camilla's favorite restaurant, and have dinner. It's not the way she originally envisioned it, but it's intimate and fits our situation. I've rented out the backroom, so it's private, and I've made plans with the manager to ensure we have music so we can have our first dance.

Since the restaurant is located in the hotel, I've booked the Presidential suite for the night. The following morning we'll head out on our week-long honeymoon—destination is a surprise.

"This is German chocolate," she says, lifting the square to my lips. I take a bite and it's delicious. Flavorful with a tinge of bitter-sweetness. She takes her own bite and moans, her eyes rolling backward. I'm about to tell her if she moans like that again, I'm going to be eating her, when my phone rings. It's a call I've been waiting for.

"Give me a second." I kiss her forehead and accept the call, walking to my office. "Hello."

"Hello, Mr. Petrosian. You asked me to let you know when the place was clean and ready to be shown. I'll have the keys sent over to you immediately."

"Perfect. Thank you, Gloria." Gloria is one of the commercial real estate agents I have on staff. She handles several of my properties that I buy, sell, and lease. One of my storefronts has become available and I think it would be perfect for Camilla to open her boutique. I know she wants to finish school, and she still can, but I don't see why she can't work on opening her boutique now. If she's not ready, it will be there for when she is. I just want her to know I believe in her and support her one hundred percent.

As I'm walking back out to Camilla, my phone rings again with a number I don't recognize. "Hello."

"Hello, this is Atlas Security. We're calling to let you know the fire alarm has been triggered at Chester Creek Commons. We've dispatched emergency."

Are you fucking kidding me? I swear to God if this is James's doing, we're going to have a problem. I thought after the hefty fines he was served and the beating he took after going after

Camilla, he'd learned his lesson. He's been quiet these last several weeks, so I figured he's smartened up. Guess not.

"Cam, I need to go check on something," I tell her when I get out to the living room.

"What's wrong?" she asks, instantly on alert.

"I'm not sure yet." I kiss her quickly. "I shouldn't be long. We'll finish the cakes when I get back." I kiss her one more time. "And then I plan to eat you for dessert." I suck on her bottom lip and she giggles.

"The cakes are the dessert."

"Fuck no, they're not. Your sweet pussy is my real dessert." I laugh when spots of pink tinge her cheeks. "I'll be back as soon as I can. Love you, *meu amor.*"

"Love you more."

Twenty Two

CAMILLA

I'M TAKING A BITE OF THE
vanilla cream cake when it feels as though
the building has shaken. *Are we having an earthquake?*
is my first thought. Until the fire alarm goes off in the
building.

I jump up, unsure what's going on, and call Isaac.
He left several minutes ago, but maybe he's still here.
It goes straight to voicemail, so I try again, but it
does it again.

With the fire alarm blaring in my ears, I grab
my phone off the table and exit the building,
taking the stairs in case there really is a fire. When
I get down to the first floor and step outside, the
overwhelming scent of smoke hits my senses. I
rush farther out, trying to see where the source is. It

looks like it's coming from the parking garage. I call Isaac again, but it doesn't ring, going straight to voicemail once again.

The weirdest feeling in my gut hits me, and suddenly I'm nervous. This isn't the first fire that's been set. Was this on purpose? Is Isaac okay?

I'm about to head for where the fire is to check it out, when a loud explosion rocks the ground I'm standing on. Red and orange flames, along with black smoke, billow out of the parking garage, and I gasp in horror as several explosions occur in quick succession.

With trembling hands, I call Noah, and thankfully he picks up. "Where are you?" I rush out.

"At home."

"There's a fire at the marina. I think it's coming from the parking garage. I can't get ahold of Isaac. He left a little while ago. It looks like it's spreading to the main building."

"Is the fire department on their way?"

"I don't hear anybody…" The last time the warehouse caught on fire, they came immediately. "Should I call them?" I had assumed they would get the message from the alarm going off and show up like they did last time.

"Yeah, I'm on my way."

"Do you know where Isaac is?" I ask, starting to panic as the flames grow higher, the heat intensifying. I'm standing several feet away from the garage, but I can feel the heat from here. Even if I wanted to go check it out, I would be burned trying to get past the flames.

"No, call the fire department." He hangs up and I call, explaining what's happened the best I can, since I don't really even know what's happened, and they assure me they're sending trucks right away.

A few minutes later, they arrive, and I still can't get a hold of Isaac. My nerves are on edge and tears of frustration are leaking from my lids. Noah shows up shortly after and stays with me while we watch the fire department put the fire out.

I try Isaac over and over again, but he doesn't answer. It just goes straight to his voicemail every single time.

"He said he had something to take care of," I tell Noah. "Do you know where he was going?"

He glances up from his phone. "According to the security company, a fire alarm in Chester Creek Commons went off. False alarm. He must've gone to check it out."

"Then where the hell is he?" I hiss, my eyes going to the firefighters who are still working on containing and putting out the fire.

When the police arrive, they disappear behind the parking

garage and a few minutes later, several all black vehicles arrive. I still can't get ahold of Isaac and nobody will tell us anything. Noah holds me while I cry, scared and assuming the worst, while praying Isaac is far away and his phone is just dead. But something in me, the deep, dark part of me, has a horrible feeling.

"Are you the person who called nine-one-one?" a police officer asks when he walks over what feels like hours later.

"I am. I'm Camilla Hutchinson." His eyes quickly go wide, revealing he recognizes my name, but I ignore it, not giving a shit about what he thinks of me or my family's name. "And this is Noah Reynolds. I live in the building and he works with my fiancé, Isaac Petrosian, here."

The officer nods. "We're still trying to piece together what happened, but the explosion was so strong it cracked the infrastructure, and the heat seeped inside. We don't know what damage has been done, but you won't be able to go inside until it's checked out."

"What happened?" I ask, my voice shaky.

"From what forensics is gathering, a bomb went off. It was most likely attached to a vehicle, and because it was in an enclosed area, after it went off, the heat of the car on fire caused an additional explosion. I'm not sure how many vehicles were down there, but they're all totaled. Do you know anyone who would want to blow up your parking garage?"

His words cause a shiver to race up my spine, and before he can stop me, I'm running to the parking garage. It's no longer on fire, but it's stifling hot and, because of the debris, it's hard to breathe.

"Ma'am, this is a crime scene," one of the men says when he spots me standing on the edge of the garage.

"How many vehicles are in there?" I ask, doing the math in my head. Isaac has a truck, two sports cars, and then there's my SUV. Noah wasn't visiting, so his vehicle is parked down the street, and the employees would've already left for the day, since it's well after five o'clock. That's...

"Four total," he says, and my heart stutters in my chest.

No. No. No. This can't be right. "Count again!" I bark out, stomping on the bits and pieces of glass and metal. Luckily, I had the foresight to put on flip-flops before I left the condo.

"Ma'am, you can't be in here. This is a crime scene and the area is under investigation."

"I don't care!" I yell, sprinting toward the wreckage. The area is black and covered in ash and smells like gasoline mixed with fire. The vehicles are all melted and damaged and you can barely make out which is which, but they're in their assigned spots.

"Which vehicle was blown up?" I ask, even though I already know. The truck. It's the least recognizable. Nothing more than white-covered rubbish.

When he points to the area, I drop to my knees, but before I hit the ground, someone catches me. Tears of emotion fill my lids and my head spins. I hear people talking, but I can't make out what they're saying. My heart is pounding behind my ribcage and my body feels as though it's having an out of world experience. My senses are all blurred. I can't hear, I can't see. I'm numb. It's hard to breathe.

I gasp for air, trying to fill my lungs with oxygen. But it's not working. I think someone is murmuring something into my ear, but my head and ears are now ringing. My hand wraps around my throat as I gasp for air. But it's too late. I'm too far gone.

And the world around me goes black.

I PRY MY EYES OPEN AND MY TEMPLES THROB. I glance around, and for a second, I forget what's happened. I'm confused, unsure where I am. Unlike the view of the marina from my bedroom window, there are trees and shrubbery. I take in the beige walls instead of the gray and the cream sheets instead of our silver and white ones. When I roll over, I find Noah sitting in a chair looking at me, and it all comes back to me. The explosion. Isaac not answering his phone. The police saying it's a crime scene.

"Where are we?" I croak out, locking eyes with Noah.

"My house." He brings me over a bottle of water. I accept it and drink it all, the cold water feeling good as it runs down my parched throat.

"Have you heard from Isaac?" I ask once I've finished the bottle and set it on the nightstand.

"No. Listen, Camilla..." His eyes fill with sympathy and I look away, not wanting to see it.

I snatch my phone from the nightstand and swipe up, checking for any missed calls or messages from Isaac, but there's nothing. Only a string of them from Yasmin demanding I call her back. News of the explosion and fire must've gotten out.

"He's alive." I pull the covers off me and swing my legs over the side of the bed. The room feels slightly dizzy, so I close my eyes, giving my head and body a chance to catch up with each other. This started a couple weeks ago, so I know it's not because of my panic attack last night.

"Did you not see the aftermath from the explosion? Nobody could've survived that." His voice is soft, bleeding sympathy, and I hate it because I don't need him to feel sorry for me. "His truck was there, along with all his vehicles. Unless he walked wherever he was going…"

"Maybe he did!"

"Then where is he now?"

"I don't know, but I'm going to find him." I jut my chin out in defiance, and he sighs, shaking his head.

Like a woman on a mission, I quickly use the restroom, ignoring the queasiness in my stomach, slip on my flip-flops, then head out of the room and down the hall, taking note of the rustic feel Noah's house has. It's more like a cabin, all wood beams and walls, brown leather sofas and different colored wood furniture. When I get outside, I glance around and see nothing but lush greenery for what looks like miles every which way. His home is in the middle of the woods, and it hits me, how the hell am I getting anywhere?

"Where are we going?" he asks, twirling his keys around his finger.

"We?" I'm going to need him to give me a ride, since I have no purse or money and my car is permanently out of commission, but from the way he sounds, he's already confirmed Isaac's dead and has attended the funeral, which makes me wonder…

"Why aren't you more upset?"

"Excuse me?" He raises a single brow.

"Isaac is like a brother to you, and you think he's dead, so why aren't you more upset?"

His jaw ticks, and his eyes dart away from me, ignoring my question by asking one of his own. "Do you want a ride or not?"

"Do you believe he's alive?" I push. "Is that why you're not crying?" It's why I'm not crying. Because I know Isaac is alive. I just have to find him.

Once again he ignores my questions, stalking toward his car and opening the door for me. I get in and he rounds the front, sliding in. His muscle car is loud and growly and I welcome it. The ride to town takes about twenty minutes, most of the road dirt and deserted.

When he arrives at a shopping plaza, I look at him confused. "This is Chester Creek Commons," he explains. "He was supposed to come here to check out the fire alarm that went off, but he never showed up."

I swing open the door and start walking in one direction, my eyes darting around like I'm looking for a missing dog or child. The farther I walk, finding nothing but shoppers, talking and laughing, ignorantly going through life, the more worked up I get.

I don't see him anywhere, not sitting on the benches, not walking down the sidewalks... He's not here. I know he's not because if he were, he would be with me.

"Maybe he's hurt," I blurt out. "The docks, his yacht, is the closest thing to the building. Let's go there. Maybe he's hurt and doesn't have his phone and needs help."

Noah nods wordlessly.

His yacht is empty. The warehouse, the parking garage, every other boat that's docked are all empty. When I try to open the door to the building, Noah stops me. "It's locked. The damage is too bad. The heat destroyed everything. The office, the condo, the destruction the fire caused is beyond repair.

"What?" I tug on the door, needing to get inside, but it doesn't budge. "What about our things? Our clothes? What if Isaac is in there?" I scream, losing my cool.

"They checked everywhere and confirmed it's empty."

"This can't be right!" I glance around, unsure where to go, where to look. "He has to be somewhere," I cry, tears filling my lids. "He can't just be gone!" A gut-wrenching sob tears through my chest, making it hard to catch my breath. "He has to be somewhere!" I repeat. "Isaac!" I yell, banging on the mirrored glass door. "Isaac!"

When nobody answers, I twirl around. "Where is he?" I demand as tears gush down my cheeks. "Noah..."

I stumble forward, having no clue where to go, what to do. My heart is straining to the point that it feels like I'm having a heart attack. Noah catches me, pulls me into his arms, and holds me tight as my grief pours out in a flood of uncontrolled tears. I cry in his arms, begging for God to take me. I can't imagine a world without Isaac in it. How is this fair? We only just got started. We were supposed to have more time together. Get married, have babies.

I think about the last time we spoke, when he told me he loved me before he walked out the door. My cries get harder. We've only written one chapter, maybe two... It's not time for it to end yet.

At some point, Noah and I end up on the floor in front of the building, with me in his lap while I sob into his chest, cursing the world and God and everything in between.

When it feels as though I've cried myself sick, Noah picks me up and carries me to his car, depositing me in the front seat. I barely recall him putting my seat belt on and driving me back to his place. He must carry me into his house and lay me in his bed, and I must pass out at some point because the next thing I know, I'm waking up in his bed again, staring out at the trees.

I'm checking my phone and finding nothing from Isaac *again*. It's like the worst case of Groundhog Day imaginable.

Only this time I don't bother asking Noah if he's heard from him, because I know he hasn't. Because there's no way if Isaac were alive, he wouldn't be right here, holding me and telling me how much he loves me. Which means only one thing... Isaac is dead. I've lost him forever.

With that realization, my stomach roils and I jump out of bed, running to the bathroom to spill the entire contents of my stomach into the toilet. I hear footsteps and then a cool washcloth is placed on the back of my neck. Noah doesn't say anything, just stays behind me while I empty my stomach over and over again, until there's nothing left.

Then he turns the shower on for me, places a towel on top of the sink, and leaves me alone so I can rinse off. The shower is lonely without Isaac, so I wash my hair and body quickly, then get out. I find a shirt and sweats—most likely Noah's—on the counter, and I put them on. I towel dry my hair and then pad back to the bed, pulling the sheets over me and closing my eyes.

Maybe tomorrow when I wake up this will all be a horrible dream.

Twenty Three

CAMILLA

"WE HAVE TO TALK."

"I'm sleeping," I mutter from under the sheets. Between the queasiness and my heart feeling as though it's been yanked out of my chest cavity, thrown onto the ground, and stomped on repeatedly, I haven't had the energy to move from the bed unless necessary. Noah's been really sweet, bringing me my meals several times a day, forcing me to shower, and holding my hair back when I actually eat and a little while later end up hugging the porcelain bowl.

"I spoke to Frank and he's organized the funeral for the day after tomorrow."

This gets my attention. I throw the blanket off me and sit up. "Excuse me? I don't think I heard you correctly because it sounded like you said Frank,

Isaac's attorney, is planning a funeral for my fiancé, and that can't be right since he's not dead."

"Cam..."

"No, there's no proof he's dead. There's no body."

"You know why... The police said—"

"I don't give a fuck what the police said!" I bark, climbing out of bed. My stomach roils, and I close my eyes, willing myself not to upchuck right now. "I can feel it in here." I stab myself in the chest. "He's alive."

"Then why hasn't he shown his face?"

"Maybe he's in trouble. What if he was taken?" And then a thought occurs to me. One I haven't thought of before. "I need to go somewhere." I throw my drawers open, where the few outfits Noah purchased for me since I have no clothes, reside, and change out of my pajamas, not caring that I'm in my bra and underwear in front of him. Once I'm dressed, I throw on a pair of Chucks he also bought me and grab my phone. When I check to see if there are any messages or missed calls, I notice it says no service.

Weird.

I try to dial out, but nothing happens. When I try to send a text message, it pops up as unsent.

"What's wrong?" Noah asks.

"My phone doesn't work. I don't get it. The bill..." And then it hits me. The bill was in Isaac's name. I drop onto the bed, a fresh wave of emotion hitting me like a tidal wave. "It's on Isaac's account."

"Everything in Isaac's name has been frozen or cancelled because he's been declared dead." Noah takes the phone from me. "I'll get it taken care of."

"I don't have any money," I whisper as hot liquid slides down my cheeks.

"Hey," he says softly, kneeling in front of me. "If you let me, I'd like to be here for you."

I'm already shaking my head. It was one thing for Isaac to take care of me. He was my other half, my soul mate. It's the only reason I allowed myself to be vulnerable to him. I knew he wasn't doing it out of pity, it was out of love. "I'll figure it out. I'm not your responsibility."

"No, but Isaac was my friend, and he loved you. And whether you like it or not, I'm in a position to help." He takes my hand in his and I want to shove it away, but I don't want to offend him, so instead I leave it be. "Camilla, have you thought about why you've been throwing up?"

His question has my mangled heart picking up speed because I have thought about it, but I didn't want to admit it to myself. "I can't go there right now," I tell him, taking my hand back and standing. "I need to find someone."

His brows furrow. "Who?"

"James."

"Pruitt?"

"Yeah. The last time I saw him, he was threatening Isaac. What if he's the reason Isaac has disappeared? Maybe he has him somewhere. It would make sense. He wanted him to pay."

Noah sighs, clearly not agreeing, but I don't care. I refuse to believe Isaac is dead. It might sound crazy, but I feel like if he were, I would feel it. When my mom died, I felt it, like she took a piece of my heart with her when she left this earth. Isaac and me... our hearts and souls are connected on a deeper level and if he were gone, I'd feel it, like a piece of me left with him.

"All right," he finally says, giving in. "We'll go pay James and Clint a visit, but you have to promise me something."

"What?"

"If we don't find him... if there isn't any proof of foul play, you need to start the process of accepting that Isaac is gone."

I'll never accept it, but I nod anyway, since it's what he needs from me.

"Say the words."

"I'll accept... that he's gone."

It's Saturday and highly unlikely James is in the office, so I have Noah take me straight to James's house since he won't be expecting me.

When we pull up to the gate, since I know the code, having lived in the same community before my dad went to prison and lost our house, I type it in and the gate opens.

"Park around the corner," I instruct. "I don't want him knowing I'm here."

Noah arches a brow. "You don't honestly think he's keeping Isaac here, in this house, do you?"

"Got a better idea?"

"If he's holding him, it would be somewhere people wouldn't look, like at a warehouse. Not in broad daylight, in a neighborhood in the suburbs."

That makes sense... "Okay, I'm going to get out and sneak around, peek into the windows, just to make sure. See if he's home and if he's doing anything that looks shady. I won't let him know I'm here unless I see reason to. If everything looks normal, we'll go check out his other properties."

I put my hand on the door handle, about to get out, when Noah clicks the lock. "You're staying right here."

"What?"

"I'll go check. You might want to be in denial of the changes that are happening to your body, but I'm not going to risk you getting hurt, knowing the truth you don't want to admit to."

I nod once, unable to verbally admit that he's right. Mentally, I just can't go there... not yet. First, I need to find Isaac, then once I have him back and all is right with the world again, I can focus on that.

He gets out and jogs along the sidewalk, disappearing through the thicket of bushes. He's gone for several minutes, during which time a few cars pass by—none of them James— and I hold my breath, praying he finds Isaac. When he finally returns, alone and with a frown marring his features, my stomach churns.

"He's not home. I checked in all the windows and didn't find anyone or anything that looks out of the ordinary."

"Okay. Where to next?" I ask, refusing to give up.

"He owns a shit ton of properties."

"Then we better get moving."

Noah nods, looking like he wants to argue, but thankfully doesn't. We spend the entire day checking out every property James owns, asking tenants if they've seen anything fishy. I show them a picture of Isaac off his company website, hoping maybe someone will know something, but nobody has seen or heard anything.

When the day turns to night and I'm out of places to look, I almost consider facing the facts that Isaac is gone, until I think about something. "You said James wasn't at home, right?"

"Yeah."

"Well, he wasn't anywhere we looked either. So, where the hell is he?"

"I don't know. Maybe we've missed him... or he's at the country club or bar. He could be out of town."

"I want to talk to him," I say, well aware of how desperate I sound but not giving a shit.

Wordlessly, Noah drives back into town. He pulls into the country club, and I immediately spot James's ostentatious vehicle valet parked. "I'm going in," I tell him, jumping out before he can stop me.

"Cam!" he yells, following after. "Think about this..."

I ignore him, my eyes darting every which way, until they land on the man I've been looking for. He's sitting at the bar with a blonde, whispering into her ear. She throws her head back with a laugh, and I know she's faking it because James isn't the least bit funny.

"We need to talk," I demand, tapping him on the shoulder.

He turns around, opening his mouth like he's about to tell whoever is interrupting him to get lost, but when he sees it's

me, he closes his mouth and stands. "Cheri, give me a moment."
The woman nods, then glares my way.

James reaches out to steer me away, but I shake him off.
"We can talk right here."

"Okay…"

"You threatened Isaac, said you would, and I quote, 'End
him,' and now he's gone. Where are you holding him?"

"I didn't do shit to him," he flat-out says.

"I don't believe you. Tell me where he is."

He looks around like he's waiting for someone to do
something, but everyone is now quiet, watching our exchange
since my words, spoken loud enough for everybody to hear, has
gotten everyone's attention.

"It's no secret you hated him. And you told me the last time
I saw you that you were going to end him, so I want to know
where he is. It's not too late. You can let him go and I'll make
sure he doesn't press charges or retaliate."

"Camilla…" he says softly, sounding so unlike himself.
"Listen to me." He steps closer and the look of sympathy mixed
with pity has me stepping back, tears burning my lids. "You're
right. I didn't like Isaac. We're rivals in business, but I didn't
do anything to him." I expected him to scream and shout, tell
me to go fuck myself, but the way he's speaking to me, like he

almost cares, is even worse. Because it has me almost believing what he's saying, until I remember what he did to my father.

"You're lying," I hiss. "Just like you lied about my father. You're lying now!" With every word I spit, my voice rises several octaves. "You took my dad from me, and now you took the father of my baby!" Liquid devastation races down my cheeks as I realize what I've just said. "I need him back!" I yell through my sobs. "I don't understand what I did to you to make you do this to me. I cared about you. I was faithful to you even though you cheated on me and treated me like shit. It was bad enough you took my dad, but then you had to take the man I love. Please," I beg, cutting the distance between us. "Please give him back to me." My fists pound against James's chest, taking every emotion I feel out on him.

And he just stands there, staring at me with pity, until Noah pulls me back and lifts me into his arms, hauling me away as I kick and scream and beg James to give me Isaac back. When we get to the car, I'm crying so hard, it's difficult to catch my breath. White spots dot my vision, and I have no doubt I'm about to black out. Sure enough, seconds later, everything goes dark, and rather than being scared, I welcome it, almost wishing I'd never wake up.

When I open my eyes, I'm back in bed, the covers over me,

and an older woman is sitting beside me. "Welcome back."

I startle, confused, and find Noah sitting in the chair in the corner of the room. "This is Dr. Parker. She's an OB/GYN. I asked her to come check on you."

"Your blood pressure is high," she says. "I understand you're going through something hard, but you can't put your body through stress like that."

I close my eyes, remembering everything that transpired before I blacked out. The way I worked myself up yelling at James, then crying until I passed out. I wanted so badly to believe he was responsible for Isaac disappearing, but the fact is, if he's the one who wired his truck with a bomb, he'd never admit to it. Isaac told me himself he has enemies and it could be anyone who did this. He could be alive, somewhere, but I have no idea where to look, and like Noah said, if he were able to get to me, he would've. It's been almost a week since the explosion and it's time to face the facts. Isaac is gone and more than likely never coming back.

"Cam," Noah says, snapping me from my thoughts. "I think you need to have your pregnancy confirmed."

I nod once and the doctor pulls out a small instrument. "Do you have any idea how far along you might be?"

"No," I choke out. "We never used protection."

"Can you recall when your last period was?"

I think back, trying to remember, but my brain is fuzzy. My cycle has never been regular, and I know I haven't had my period since I met Isaac. We were only together for a short time... I count back to when I first met him. "We were together for about two months."

She stills her hand. "Then we should probably use the probe." She glances back at Noah. "Can you give us a few minutes? Camilla's going to have to get undressed."

He jumps up. "Yeah. If you need anything..."

"Thanks," I whisper.

Once he's gone, Dr. Parker hands me a paper cover up, so I can take my pants off. "This is a portable ultrasound machine, so it's not going to be as clear as the newer ones in the office, but it'll tell us what we need to know."

She rolls a condom on the wand and drops some lube on the head. As she pushes it inside of me, I wince at the intrusion. "Sorry, it's normal for it to hurt a little."

As she moves it around, I stare at the screen, unsure what I want to see. There are only two options in this situation: I'm either pregnant or I'm not, and I'm too lost in my grief to know which is the better option—until the screen fills with a gray circle and inside that circle is a smaller oval. She clicks a button and the room fills with a faint whooshing sound.

"That's the heartbeat. Strong and steady. I can't measure on here, but based on the size, I would say you're between six and eight weeks."

I block out everything else she says, allowing my mind to go numb, until she's gone and I'm left in the room by myself. Robotically, I climb out of bed and go straight to the bathroom. I pull my shirt over my head and step into the shower, turning it on hot. As the water runs down my body, it all hits me at once.

I'm pregnant with Isaac's baby and he's gone. I choke on a sob at the realization he'll never meet the baby we created through our love. He'll never hold him, kiss him, hug him. He won't be here to experience my pregnancy with me, or to witness his first steps, or first day of kindergarten. But as I cry over everything we'll never have together, finally accepting he's gone, my hand goes to my belly and I can't help but be thankful that in this horrible, tragic nightmare, he's left me with the most precious little miracle. A piece of himself. And even though I'll never see him again, a part of him will always be with me.

When the shower goes cold, I get out and get dressed, feeling better than I've felt since the day of the explosion.

"You okay?" Noah asks, when I walk out to the living room and find him sitting on the couch, typing on his laptop. "The doctor said..."

"I'm pregnant." I sit across from him on the love seat and tuck my legs under me. "Am I okay? No, but for the baby, I need to be." I cradle my still-flat belly, vowing to protect this little guy at all costs. He's all I have left of Isaac. He wanted this so badly, and it wasn't until I heard the heartbeat that I realized how much I did too. It didn't matter that we were only together a short time. We loved each other, and through this baby, our love will live on.

"I'm sorry," Noah says softly.

"It's not your fault." I wrap my arms around my body and Noah gets up and drapes a blanket over me. "So, the funeral? It's on Monday?"

"Yeah. Frank took care of everything. The service is being held at the same church his parents' service was held."

I snort humorlessly at the irony of it. His parents died in a car accident, their bodies burned from it exploding, and twelve years later, Isaac died in a similar manner. No bodies, no closure for any of them. They can never be laid to rest. No ashes. Nothing. It's as if they never even existed.

Twenty Four

CAMILLA

ATTENDING ISAAC'S FUNERAL

was harder than I imagined. I might've accepted that he's gone, but stepping into the church and being surrounded by people who are there to say goodbye to him was not easy at all. When the first person walked up to me and introduced himself as an associate and friend of Isaac's, and I didn't know who he was, nor had I ever heard his name mentioned, it hit me how much I still had to learn about the man I loved—and I would never have the opportunity to do so. What we had... those short, beautiful months, were all we would ever have.

When Noah saw I was close to losing it, he swooped in and saved me. He sat next to me in the front row of the church and held me while I cried silently as the priest spoke of love and loss and whatever the hell else he said that wouldn't change the fact that Isaac was gone.

By the end of the service, I was such a mess, Noah insisted on taking me back to his house instead of attending the post funeral reception. It's not like I know anybody there, and nobody, aside from Noah and Yasmin—who sat in a different row, since the first row was only supposed to be for family—which was pretty damn depressing since it was only Noah, me, and some other guy I've never met before—knows me.

"You need to eat," Noah says, bringing a tray of food over and setting it on the nightstand next to me. I'm not hungry, but for the sake of the baby, I thank him and pick at the sandwich and soup he made for me. When I've had enough to fill my stomach, I lie back under the covers and close my eyes, wondering if the pain in my heart will ever lessen. I know it's only been a short time since Isaac's death, but I can't imagine how anyone lives through the day to day pain. My heart literally feels like it's constantly being squeezed by a barbed wire every second of every day. Maybe it's because I lost my mom at such a young age, but I don't remember it hurting this badly. Some mornings, I wake up and find my pillow stained with my tears. Apparently I can't even escape my heartbreak in my sleep.

The days move forward, and I remain holed up in Noah's

guestroom. He offers to take me away, but I don't want to go anywhere. He brings me books, tries to get me to watch television with him, but I can't find it in me to do anything other than sleep and eat and think about Isaac.

I'm not sure what day or month or hell, even year, it is, until Noah drags me to the doctor for my checkup and the doctor tells me how far along I am.

"Based on the measurements, you're fifteen weeks along. Your due date is February 20."

"Fifteen weeks?" I go to sit up but quickly stop myself, remembering she's giving me an ultrasound. "I thought I was like... eight weeks."

Dr. Parker stops and glances at me, her lips curving into a concerned frown. "Camilla, you were eight weeks at our last appointment. You were supposed to make one to see me at twelve weeks, but you forgot. I called Noah to check on you and he scheduled one. It's been almost two months since I've seen you."

Two months... It's been over two months since Isaac died and I found out I'm going to be a mom. I thought I was doing okay, getting through it, but apparently not because I have no idea where the hell the last two months have gone.

"You can't feel it yet," she continues, "but your baby is

squirming in there." She points to the screen and my eyes follow, landing on the tiny little baby. Oh my God! It's a baby. There's a head and little limbs and a heartbeat fluttering in his tiny chest.

Tears spring from my lids and Noah is instantly at my side. I didn't realize he was in here. "Are you okay?" he asks, wiping a tear that's trailing down the side of my face.

"Yeah," I breathe. "I just..." I can't take my eyes off the screen, off the little baby moving. "I'm pregnant. I'm having a baby," I choke out.

"You are," Dr. Parker says with a hesitant smile. "How do you feel about that?"

A myriad of emotions run through me: scared, lonely, sad, angry, but more than anything... "I'm happy." I never imagined saying those words, but it's the truth. I'm scared shitless of doing this without Isaac. I'm lonely without his comforting love. I'm sad he's not here with me, and I'm angry as hell that someone took him from me. But I'm also happy that inside of me is a beautiful piece of us.

"Sometimes it's too early to tell the sex, but I was able to get a glimpse. Would you like to know if you're having a boy or a girl?"

"Umm..." I could wait for it to be a surprise, but right now,

I kind of feel like if I know the sex it will help me connect with the baby. "Yes, I would."

"Congratulations, you're having a boy."

"A boy..." I'm having a boy. I can already picture him with Isaac's messy brown hair and devilishly handsome smile. I wonder if he'll have my green eyes or his light brown.

"Everything looks good," Dr. Parker says, handing me a couple of tissues. "Before you leave, make your twenty-week checkup." She eyes me sternly before she walks out, but she doesn't have to worry. I'll be here for sure. This baby only has me and I'm going to make sure I give him everything he needs, just like my parents did for me.

My parents... My dad... Oh my God, I haven't spoken to my dad. I haven't gone by to see him, but it's not like him not to call me. And then I remember my phone. It was turned off because it was on Isaac's account. Noah said he would take care of it, but I've been so lost in my grieving, I haven't thought about anything else.

"Do you have my phone?"

Noah's brow furrows. "No. You haven't asked about it. I forgot."

"I need to go see my dad. I haven't spoken to him. I'm sure because of the news, he's heard about Isaac's death, but he doesn't know that I'm pregnant." I wipe the gunk off my belly, pull my shirt down, and sit up, on a mission. It's like I've been sleeping these last couple months and I've finally woken up.

"Can you take me to see my dad, please?"

"Yeah, but it's already late and I have some work to do. Why don't we go home and we can go in the morning?"

His words sound reasonable, but something about the way he says them leaves me feeling uneasy, but I push it aside. "Okay, thanks."

I hop off the table, and after scheduling my next appointment, and Noah paying for this one since I don't have insurance, we head out.

"I'm going to need to look for a job," I say, once we're in the car.

"For what?" Noah asks, glancing at me before averting his gaze back onto the road.

"To make money..." A million thoughts plink around in my head as the reality of my situation hits me. "I have a baby on the way, nowhere to live, no way to feed or clothe him." I was barely surviving when I met Isaac. I was homeless and penniless and now I'm back in the same situation, only I have a baby that will be here in a little over five months.

The rest of the ride back to his place is done in silence.

I excuse myself to shower, and when I come out, I find him sitting in the reading chair waiting for me.

"We need to talk."

"Okay…" I sit on the middle of the bed, facing him. "What's up?"

"I think we should get married."

It takes a second for my head to wrap around what he's just said, but once it does, I'm not sure I heard him correctly. "Come again?"

"I think we should get married." Okay, yeah. I guess I heard him correctly.

"I…" I don't even know what to say. "I'm so grateful for everything you've done for me. Taking me in, giving me a bed and a room to sleep in. Being there for me while I mourned Isaac…" Not that I'm done mourning him, but after seeing the baby on the screen today, it finally feels like I'm past the darkness and can see a shred of light.

Noah moves to the bed and cups my face in his big palm. We're so close, I can smell his cologne. It's not masculine and woodsy like Isaac's, instead it's more citrusy and sweet. And I wonder if there's a way I can find out what Isaac wore. I never paid attention, but now I wish I had.

"I care about you and your baby," Noah says, taking me

from my thoughts. "Marry me and I'll take care of you..." He rests his other hand on my stomach. "Both of you."

"Noah," I breathe, dizzy by the sudden turn of events. "I can't marry you. I'm in love with Isaac..."

"He's not here," he says harshly, making me sit back slightly to break our connection.

"I know he's gone, but that doesn't change how I feel. He was"—I clear my throat—"*is* the love of my life. My other half. He owns my soul and I can't just marry someone else."

"Give me a break," he scoffs. "You knew him for a damn minute."

The brashness of his statement has me climbing off the bed. "Fuck you." I don't know who this guy is, but this isn't the same man who's been here for me these last several weeks... Or maybe it is and I've just been too lost in my own head to notice.

"Look," I say calmly, trying to diffuse the situation. "I appreciate what you're offering, but I can't marry you. I think maybe it would be best if I go..." I'm not sure where the hell I'm going to go, but suddenly it feels like I can't be here.

I go to step around Noah, but before I can, his arm comes out and swings the door closed. "You're not going anywhere," he says, blocking the only exit. "I tried to be nice... patient. I catered to your every fucking whim while you cried over him..."

Oh my God, what the hell is going on? "You and I *are* going to get married. You'll live here, and we'll raise the kid together like a perfect little fucking family."

"No, we're *not*." I shake my head to emphasize my point, backing up in fear of the stranger standing in front of me. "I don't know what's gotten into you, but in case you've forgotten, Isaac was like a brother to you."

Noah throws his head back as the most maniacal cackle fills the air, sending chills racing up my spine. "Isaac's nothing more than the past. But you, my sweet Camilla, are my future."

He stalks toward me, and I back up, only I have nowhere to go, so my back hits the hard wall. He reaches out and I release a shriek, assuming he's going to slap me, but instead he fists my mane, bringing my face close to his. "In three days, you and I are getting married. I suggest you get with the program, or I'll be forced to take matters into my own hands."

And with those final words, he turns on his heel and exits the room, leaving me alone and confused, and so fucking scared.

The second the door shuts, I run to it, only the doorknob doesn't turn, and it's then I realize I'm locked in. What the fuck? He locked me in. How did I never notice the lock is on the outside? Or did he recently do this?

"Noah!" I yell, banging on the door. "Let me out!"

When he doesn't answer, I go to the window, only to find it's been screwed shut.

"Damn it!" I slap my hand against the glass.

I look around, trying to find something I can break the window with, but there's nothing aside from a bed, a dresser, nightstands, and a chair, all too big and heavy for me to throw. I race to the bathroom, scouring the cabinets and linen closet. Nothing. I go to the closet, but aside from a few items of clothing and some shoes, there's nothing. I go back to the door, wiggling it again, praying this is some kind of joke or dream.

As I slide down the door, it hits me—I'm locked in here, with no phone, and nobody even knows to look for me. What the hell am I going to do?

Twenty Five

CAMILLA

"TODAY'S THE DAY," NOAH SAYS as he strolls into the room like he isn't holding me freaking captive and forcing me to marry him. He lays a white knee-length dress on the bed along with a pair of heels and turns to me. "You need to get ready. The officiant will be here this afternoon."

"You hired an officiant?" I spit out in disgust. "How did you even get a marriage license?"

Noah snorts. "I'm Isaac's right-hand man. Did you forget he owned the city? I forged your name and applied for one." He walks over to me and gets in my face. "And the officiant has already been paid off, so if you think you can cry help to him, you're wrong."

"You're fucking crazy!" I hiss, which only makes

him laugh, proving my point.

"I blame it on my daddy issues." He shrugs before stalking out and slamming the door behind him.

Swatting the clothes and shoes away, I climb onto the bed and snuggle into the blankets. There's no way I'm going to wear that shit or go willingly. If he wants to hold me here and force me to marry him, he's going to have to drag me out of this bed kicking and screaming.

Ready for my afternoon nap—and the escape being asleep brings—I close my eyes and let sleep overtake me.

A SOUND OF SOME SORT JOSTLES ME OUT OF MY slumber, and for a second, I assume it's Noah, coming to collect me for our fake marriage. But before I can turn to find out, I'm being lifted out of my bed. My eyes fly open and land on the most beautiful set of brown eyes, and I smile in pure happiness, realizing I'm dreaming. He's come to me so many times in my sleep, but it's never been this vivid. I can smell his signature earthy, cedar scent, and I lean into his hold, inhaling it deeply, hoping to store the smell in my brain for later.

He glances down at me as he carries me out of the room

and through the house and I can't help the tears that fill my lids. His hair is longer and his scruff is now a full beard, but he's still my Isaac. The man I love more than life itself.

"I've missed you so much," I murmur, not caring that I'm talking to a fake man in my dream. I bring my hand up to his face and run it along his cheek, relishing in how real this all feels. When I wake up, I'll feel the emptiness in my chest, but for right now, it's like that hole is temporarily plugged, giving me a moment of reprieve.

I expect Isaac to tell me he's missed me too, since this is *my* dream after all, so I'm a bit taken aback when instead, he glares at me, not saying a word. When we get outside, the bright sun that I haven't seen in a few days nearly blinds me, forcing me to close my eyes and nestle my face into his chest. *God, I've missed the safety and comfort of him.*

A few seconds later, we're sliding into a vehicle, and when I open my eyes and look around, I see it's the inside of a limo. Isaac is still holding me, staring down at me with a mixture of what looks like awe and hurt in his features. I blink several times as I take him in. He looks so... *real.* I run a finger down the center of his nose and his brows furrow together.

"Say something," I murmur, needing to hear his voice. I have no clue how long this dream is going to last and I need to hear him say something, anything.

"We'll talk soon." The coldness in his words has me doing a double take. I scramble up, trying to figure out what's going on, but Isaac holds on to me, so I'm straddling his lap.

"Is this a dream?" I ask, lifting my hands to his head and running my fingers through his hair. He feels so real... so lifelike.

"More like a nightmare," he mutters, making me flinch.

I glance around again, taking everything in—the vehicle, Isaac, his driver, the outside breezing by us—and then reach over and pinch my arm. *Ow!*

"Isaac..." I say slowly, scared to hear his answer. "Is this a dream?"

His brows pinch together. "What are you talking about?"

"Am I sleeping?" This can't be real. He can't be alive. I can't really be sitting in the car with him, in his lap.

"Cam, are you okay?" His hard features morph into concern, showing me *my Isaac*, and my heart clenches in my chest.

"You're alive," I breathe, pressing my hands to the sides of his face. "I'm not dreaming. You're really alive." I lean forward and kiss him softly on the lips.

I can feel him.

Taste him.

Needing to test my theory again, I kiss his scratchy cheek

and then the other one. Then I kiss his neck, inhaling his scent. "Oh my God! You're alive," I shriek.

"You sound like you care," he mumbles.

I'm about to ask him why the hell I wouldn't care that he's alive, when the vehicle comes to a stop and Isaac swings the door open, edging out of the limo with me in his arms. When he steps outside, he tries to set me down, but I wrap my legs around his waist, locking my ankles, and cling to him like a koala bear. A million different thoughts are invading my brain. I've either died and joined Isaac in heaven, I'm having the most real dream ever, or Isaac is alive. No matter which one is reality, I'm not letting go of him any time soon.

He thanks his driver and tells him he won't be needing him anymore today, then starts walking up the drive with me attached to him. I twist my head to see where we are, but I don't recognize the place. It's a two-story home with colonial-style pillars that hold up the second floor wraparound porch. It's beautiful, but looks like it's been neglected for a while. The grass is on the tall side, needing to be mowed, flowerbeds that probably once housed pretty flowers are filled with weeds, and the walls of the house are a bit dirty.

"Where are we?" I ask, my body shaking in shock, as he shifts me slightly to unlock the door.

"My family home."

He walks us inside and the interior is gorgeous. Marble floors throughout, a spiraling staircase leading upstairs. A fountain—yes, a freaking fountain—is in the center of the foyer.

He takes us straight through to the living room, sitting us on one of the couches. There's a stunning fireplace and over it is a large painting of what looks to be a younger Isaac and...

"Those are your parents," I say, pointing out the obvious.

"Yeah. The picture was taken the day of my high school graduation and my dad had it painted for my mom as a gift."

He settles us on the couch, and when he goes to move me to sit next to him, I refuse. "Stop trying to push me away." I pout. "I haven't felt you in months."

"Sorry, I just assumed your *fiancé* wouldn't be happy about it." He glares down at me pointedly and I gasp, reality smacking me in the face. He knows about Noah and me? But how?

"I..." I shake my head, trying to find the words, but before I can, he speaks again.

"Just tell me this. Did you ever really love me? Because I can't imagine you dying and within days finding someone else to replace you that easily. I mean, fuck, Cam, you moved on like I meant nothing to you."

His question... his *accusation*... hits me like a bitch slap to my face, and I clamber off him, scrambling to my feet, as the last few months come back to me.

"Where the hell have you been? Everyone thought you died in an explosion months ago."

"I've been here," he says coldly. "Now, answer me."

"I don't know what you're talking about. I *never* moved on. I meant what I said when I told you, you're my forever." I try like hell not to cry, but my emotions get the best of me and sobs rack my body, as I remember the day that changed everything. How can Isaac believe I could ever move on from him, and so easily at that?

"I saw the marriage license!" he barks, making me jump back. "I know you and Noah are planning to get married. I loved you and you moved on like what we had meant shit to you."

He grips the side of the coffee table and flips it over. It crashes against the marble, the candles that were resting on top smashing into several pieces.

Is he fucking serious right now? "That's not what happened." As I'm about to explain the truth of the situation, a sharp pain slices through my side and I double over, my hands going to my belly.

Isaac is at my side in an instant. "What's wrong?"

"My stomach... I think it's the baby." I sit on the love seat and take a few calming breaths, until the pain dissipates slightly.

"You're pregnant?" Isaac blanches, and it feels as though my heart is being ripped out of my chest all over again. I dreamed of the day I would wake up and his death would be nothing more than a bad dream, but in my head, our reunion always went differently.

"I'm almost sixteen weeks."

He's quiet for several seconds and then he asks a question that, if I weren't already sitting, would knock me on my ass. "Is the baby mine?"

"Of course it's yours!" I hiss. "I can't believe you would even ask me that." I drop my face into my hands, wondering how everything got to be so messed up.

"You can't blame me after learning about you and Noah."

"Speaking of which, why are you giving me the third degree and not him? Where is he anyway?"

"I took you while he was gone because I wasn't about to let you marry him. I'm pissed as fuck at him as well, but I can't blame him for falling for you. I sure as hell couldn't stop myself. But you? You supposedly loved me, and just like that..." He snaps his fingers. "You moved on with my best friend, with the man who is like a brother to me."

"Let's get one thing straight. Your *best friend* is a psychopath, and I wouldn't touch him if he were the last man on Earth."

Isaac shakes his head in confusion. "Cam, you were about to marry him... I saw the license—"

"Only because he locked me in his guestroom and wouldn't let me out!"

"He what?" he barks, standing. "What did you just say?"

"I was locked in his guestroom. When you came and got me from his house, how did you open the door?"

"There was a key in..." His eyes go wide. "*Fuck*." He tugs on the ends of his hair. "I wasn't even thinking. I saw him leave, and I was so hell-bent on getting to you so I could confront you, I didn't even think about it." He sits back down, and his thigh rubs against my own. "You're going to need to start from the beginning. Tell me everything."

"I don't know where to start. Where's the beginning? When you *died*?" I back away from him slightly, breaking the connection. "Why are you only just now coming to me? Why have I been mourning you for months, thinking you were dead, when you weren't? The license was only filed a few days ago. I think *you* need to start from the beginning."

Twenty Six

ISAAC

THE DAY OF THE EXPLOSION

AS I RIDE DOWN TO THE PARKING
garage, I can't get my mind off of Camilla and those fucking
cakes that I should be eating off of her, instead of having to
go check out the fire alarm going off because more than
likely James is pissed and wants to play more games.
At some point, I'm going to have to put a stop to
this shit. Camilla asked me not to retaliate, but it's
too late to sit this game out. My only option at
this point is to play harder and beat James.

The elevator dings and I step off it, entering
the garage. I press the key fob to unlock my
truck and am about to open the door, when a
man, dressed in all black, appears from around the
corner.

"Horatio? What the hell are you doing here?" I've been supplying his company for years with weapons, but we're not due for another shipment until next month.

"Isaac, I need you to come with me."

I glance at the all-black BMW, confused as fuck. "You're going to have to explain what's going on." Sure, I've known this guy for years, but I learned a long time ago to never trust anyone completely.

"I will, but time is of the essence. This is a matter of life and death."

I follow him to his car and get in, and as we're driving out, he says, "Hand me your keys and phone."

I do as he says, and he presses the button on his window and chucks my phone across the garage. It smashes against the side of my truck, then hits the ground.

"What the hell?" I'm about to get out and go grab it, when he presses the button that automatically starts my vehicle—it's great for those cold as hell mornings when I want my truck to be nice and hot when I get in it. Before I can ask him what he's doing, he throws the keys at my truck as well and then takes off out of the garage. A second later, an explosion rattles the vehicle, and I whip my head around as flames lick the walls of the garage.

"What the fuck!" We're already down the road, but I'm still looking back in shock. "Was that my truck?"

"That was your entire garage, and most likely, part of your building, depending on how long it takes for the fire department to arrive and put it out."

My first thought is Cam. "My fiancée is in the building."

"She'll be fine. The cameras have all been shut down, and your security system has been blocked, but the alarm will still sound and she'll have plenty of time to get out before the fire catches."

"You want to tell me what the hell is going on and why you just blew up several million dollars' worth of vehicles and property?"

"Two weeks ago, my company was hired to take you out. The request was anonymous and for the price they paid, I normally wouldn't ask questions. But when the information came in, and I saw it was you, the game changed. I considered turning down the job and telling you, but for someone to pay that much money, I imagine they'd find someone else."

Holy shit. It's like my parents' assassination all over again, only I'm still alive.

"As you know, your father and I go way back. I owed him a lot before he was killed, so consider this repayment."

"Thank you. Mind if I ask where we're going?"

"I'm going to take you back to my headquarters so we can debrief properly."

When we arrive, I'm told the specifics on the order to take me out. The only person I can imagine that would do this is James, but I have no proof, and I'm not sure he has that kind of money to spend. When I mention needing to call Camilla to let her know what's going on, Horatio shakes his head.

"Whoever wanted you dead meant business. As of now, he, or she, thinks you're dead. If you show up right now, you won't be any closer to finding out who's responsible and they can try again. Your fiancée was never mentioned, which tells me whoever wanted you dead, wasn't going after her. With you dead, she's safer than if you show up right now."

"So, what do you suggest I do?"

PRESENT

"**AFTER GOING OVER THE PLAN WITH HORATIO, HE** called Frank. I explained what happened and for him to go through the motions as if I died. He didn't actually file a death certificate, but he handled the funeral and reading of the will.

Everyone would think I was dead while I worked to figure out who put a hit out on me."

Camilla's sitting across from me, frozen in her spot and glaring at me. "So, let me get this straight. You let me believe for months you were dead, and this entire time you were alive."

She stands and starts pacing the floor. "I cried... for days... weeks... for fucking months! I lost myself in grief." Her eyes, now glassy with emotion, meet mine. "Do you have any idea what I went through? Our home, everything I owned... I lost it all on top of losing you. I found out I was pregnant... without you!" She releases a harsh breath, and I go to her, wanting to hold her, to comfort her. Finding out she's pregnant should be a happy moment, but it's been tainted because of what's happened.

She backs up and raises her hand. "No, don't you try to comfort me now!" she shouts as tears fill her beautiful green eyes, making them appear brighter. "You took my control from me and left me to fend for myself. I had no money, you shut down the accounts, and I didn't even have a phone! You left me with that psycho."

"That's not how it was supposed to go down," I hiss, pissed off at the series of events that followed. "Frank couldn't find you." I bridge the gap between us and thankfully, this time she lets me. "He's had guys scouring everywhere in search of you. He even put a call in to your dad."

"I haven't seen or talked to him," she admits with a shake of her head. "I was so out of it, I lost my grip on reality. And then, when I finally started to come around, I realized my phone was shut off and Noah said he would take care of it, but he never did. I've been with him this entire time."

"Yeah, I know," I growl, pissed at the world for fucking me over.

Her eyes go wide and she takes a step back. "Don't you dare go there. You did this. You chose to keep me on the outside. You knew how much it hurt when my parents hid my mom's cancer, and when my dad got arrested, I was blindsided."

She shoves my chest and stalks around me. "You promised, Isaac!" she cries and her broken voice damn near breaks my heart. "Noah locked me in the room and was going to force me to marry him," she says softly through her tears. "And this whole time you've been living here safe and sound!"

"*Meu amor...*"

"No! Don't you '*Meu amor*' me! If you hadn't gotten me today, I'd be Camilla fucking Reynolds!"

"That was never going to happen," I bark, the thought of that fucker staking any kind of claim on Camilla making me see red. "Why do you think I came to get you? One of Frank's contacts tipped him off that Noah and you applied for a marriage license a few days ago. He told me to let him handle it, but I wasn't letting it happen. I know you're upset, but I did what I did to protect you."

"Yeah, like leaving me for months with your psycho friend?"

I lean back against the cushion and sigh, mentally drained. "I don't understand what's gotten into him. We've been friends for *years*. I want to ask him what the fuck he was thinking"— and then ring his neck with my bare hands for what he's put Camilla through—"but I still have someone out there who's after me, so I can't make it known I'm alive. Everyone needs to think I'm still dead, including Noah."

Mentioning my fake death was probably a mistake because as soon as I do, Cam's entire body tenses and her eyes go hard.

"Cam..."

"Damn it, Isaac. I'm so freaking happy and relieved you're alive, and I know I shouldn't be mad and hurt, but I am. In the beginning, every time Noah said you were dead, I argued with him. I searched everywhere for you. I even went to the country club and attacked James. When I found out I was pregnant, all I could think about was that this baby we created together was never going to know his father." Her words crack and she has to take a calming breath before she can continue.

Fresh tears well in her eyes and my hands twitch to hold her. "Baby, please, I know you're mad and hurt, and you have every right to be, but aside from carrying you out of that house, I haven't held you in my arms in months, so can you please just let me hold you?"

She looks at me, struggling with whether or not to give in, and I wait with bated breath to see which she decides. When she nods once, my entire body deflates, and before she can change her mind, I pull her gently into my arms and onto my lap, taking a moment to smell her sweet scent.

"I'm sorry for keeping you in the dark, and for thinking you moved on quickly after my death. I misread the situation. When I found out you and Noah were getting married only a few months after my death, yeah, I jumped to that conclusion. I was thinking with my head instead of my heart. Or maybe it was my heart... Fuck! I don't know. In my world, everything revolves around money. And since I left you everything in my will—"

"You left me what?" she asks, her brows furrowing in confusion.

"Noah didn't tell you?" This doesn't make sense.

"Tell me what?"

"I had my will redone so you were my sole beneficiary. Aside from my life insurance policy, which you couldn't file because I wasn't really dead and it would be illegal, you were supposed to have access to all my accounts. Frank said he tried to approach you at the funeral, but Noah told him you were grieving and he would speak to you."

"Noah knew you left me everything?" she asks slowly.

"Yeah. He walked in when I was having my will redone. I planned to tell you about my change of will, but it slipped my mind. But he knew. He knew that's why Frank was looking for you, but he acted like he didn't know where you disappeared to. When I found out you were with him the entire time, at his house, I thought you were just hiding your relationship."

"He never told me," she breathes. "I didn't know anything."

"Everything had to look like I was dead, but I never would've left you without making sure you were taken care of."

"Oh my God!" She gasps. "Now it all makes sense."

"What?"

"Noah wanting to marry me. He knew I was left everything..."

Holy shit, I didn't see it. I was too blinded by the rage I felt over them getting married, thinking she could so easily move on and leave me behind.

"He said he wanted to take care of the baby and me and

he could do that by me marrying him. When I refused, he snapped. Like, he turned freaking psycho. He went from sweet and caring, to crazy."

"He was hiding you from Frank so you wouldn't learn that you were a very wealthy woman. If you knew, you would have no reason to marry him." Motherfucker! When I get my hands on him, he's a dead man.

Camilla threads her fingers through my hair and I revel in her touch. Fuck, I've missed her so much. "Even broke, with nowhere to live, no one to turn to, I told him no. I told him you were the love of my life and I could never marry anyone but you." She shakes her head and I fear what she's about to say because I know I fucked up. I jumped to the wrong conclusions. "While I was mourning you, trying to figure out how to pick up the pieces and somehow live this life without you, you were hiding. I gave you my heart and soul, and even after you died, you had it, but—"

"No... Don't say it," I beg, knowing deep in my gut what's coming next. "Please, baby..."

She slides off my lap, and as much as I want to hold her to me, I let her go because I deserve what's to come. She pulls a ring from her pocket—the ring I gave her—and places it on my lap. "I had to take it off, so Noah wouldn't find it, but I kept it in my pocket, so it was always close to me. I believed in us, Isaac. You were... *are* everything to me. But when shit got rough, you not only pushed me away instead of pulling me closer, but you thought my love for you wasn't real... wasn't enough. You thought I could turn to another man only days after losing you."

"No." I shake my head. "Cam, please. I fucked up."

"Yeah, you did. And I could forgive you for faking your death to keep me safe, but what I can't get past is that when you came to get me today, it wasn't to save me, it was because you believed the worst in me."

She backs up and I stand to go after her, but she puts her hands up. "I need some space. I'm not going anywhere until we know you're safe, but I need some space."

As she walks away, taking my heart with her, I want to beg her to come back, but I know I have to let her go, because I did this. I hurt her, and now I have to figure out how to fix it.

I sit here for several minutes, thinking about everything Camilla said. Noah not telling her about the will, trying to force her to marry him. Something isn't adding up. And then it hits me, the day he walked in, when I told him about leaving her everything, he looked pissed. I assumed it was about something else, when he told me he was handling it.

Handling it... I swallow thickly as all the pieces of the puzzle shift closer toward each other. Noah has millions of dollars, access to Horatio... But what the hell were his motives? He's been working with me for years. Why try to take me out now? Something tells me once I figure out the missing piece, everything will click together.

My phone vibrates in my pocket, and since only one person knows this number, I answer it without bothering to look at the caller ID.

"Find anything out?" Frank asks.

"Yeah, we need to find Noah. I have a feeling he might've had something to do with my death."

"Oh, shit. All right, I'm on it."

Twenty Seven

NOAH

"HONEY, I'M HOME," I CALL OUT with a chuckle as I walk through the door of my house with a wedding cake in my hand. Camilla's been acting stubborn about this whole marriage thing, so I'm hoping something sweet will cheer her up. She is acting like her love for Isaac is all she's capable of, but I'll show her I can be a just as good, if not better husband to her. She might be upset now, but over time she'll grow to love me. And if she doesn't... well, I don't really give a shit. Her dad will be in prison for the next fifteen years, and aside from him, nobody gives a fuck about where Camilla is. The one man who did has been blown to smithereens.

I tried to be nice. I took care of her while she mourned over Isaac. Was the shoulder she could cry on. I remained patient and understanding while she cried every fucking day. And when I found out she was pregnant, I didn't even flip my shit even though I never wanted to have kids. And how does she repay me? By refusing to even give us a chance. She should be happy I'm going to take care of her and her baby instead of her being alone with no help from anyone. I didn't want to have to force her hand, but her stubbornness has left me no choice.

I set the cake on the counter and head down the hall to check on my bride-to-be, when I notice the door to my guestroom is open. Sprinting the rest of the way, I swing it open and call out her name. How the fuck did she get out? I search for her everywhere, but she's gone. What the fuck! The door hasn't been broken, which means someone let her out. But who?

I open my laptop in my office and click on the security footage so I can rewind it to see who the fuck I'm going to kill, only everything is black. Someone's messed with my shit. I check every camera. All fucking black.

"Damn it!" I swipe everything off my desk and stand, punching a hole into the drywall. "Where the fuck are you, Camilla?" The officiant is due here soon and without the bride, there can't be a damn wedding!

Think, Noah... Who could've done this? Nobody knows

where I live. I've never even had anyone over before. When I fuck women, I get a hotel room.

Could I have left the door unlocked? I double-check the house again and then run out to my car. If I left the door unlocked, she'd have to walk, unless she found someone with a phone—but that doesn't explain how the hell my cameras went offline.

I drive back down the street slowly, checking for Camilla. There are tons of woods out here, and I can't possibly check them all. Eventually she'll have to come out... Jesus!

When I get back to the city, I do another drive through to my house and back out again. Nothing. No goddamned Camilla.

This time, when I get back to the city, I go by her friend Yasmin's place to see if she's there. I'm not sure which unit she lives in, since I've only been here once to drop her off after the funeral so she wouldn't have to grab a cab. I ask around and after several tries, find someone who knows her and where she lives. I could knock on the door, but if Camilla is here, that will only give her time to hide or skip out the window to the fire escape. So instead I kick the door in and stalk inside. There's an older woman sitting on the couch and she screams, but when I point my gun at her, she shuts up real quick.

"Is Camilla here?"

"No! She hasn't been around in months." She sounds like she's telling the truth, but I'm not about to take her word for it, so instead I search the place, finding Yasmin in her room, listening to her headphones and typing away on her computer.

When she looks up and sees me, her eyes bulge open. "What are you doing here? Is Cam here?"

Guess I have my answer. "Have you seen Camilla?" I ask, pointing the gun at her.

"No! What the hell is wrong with you?" Yasmin shrieks.

"Write down my number. If you see her, you need to call me. She's in trouble and I need to find her." It's a lie, obviously, but if I tell her the truth, she isn't going to tell me shit.

After I give her my number, I leave, unsure where the hell to check next. I'm driving around, checking some of the areas I think she might go to, like the marina, where she might feel close to Isaac. Then I remember she still has her dad, so I drive up there. Only the asshole manning security won't let me through since I'm not an approved visitor.

"Is there a way I can call the man I need to speak to?"

"No, only inmates can call out."

I search the area to see if Camilla is around, but when I don't see her, I head back home. I have no fucking clue where she is, and when I still haven't found her, I'm forced to cancel the wedding ceremony.

One thing's for sure, when I find this bitch, I'm going to handcuff her to the damn bed.

Twenty Eight

CAMILLA

RING. RING. RING. RING.

The sound of a phone ringing jerks me out of my deep sleep and has me glancing around to see where the noise is coming from. When I spot the device on the nightstand, I grab it and find a note that reads: answer me.

"Hello?" I mutter, sitting up and wiping the sleep from my eyes.

"Cam..." At the sound of my dad's voice, my eyes open all the way.

"Dad?" I breathe.

"Hey, sweetie, yeah, it's me. I've been so worried about you." His words, matched with his concerned toned, have me tearing up. "Where are you? I just got a note that told me to call you at this number."

"Oh, Dad, I've missed you so much," I choke out.

"What's going on, Cam? I tried calling you when you didn't come to visit me, but your phone was turned off, and then I learned Isaac died in an explosion. I've been worried sick in here."

"I'm so sorry. Isaac is alive. Someone tried to kill him and he faked his death while he tries to figure out who did it." Isaac mentioned the other day, Noah is now a suspect, and it makes perfect sense since he has the means and clearly, for whatever reason, wants his money. If he was willing to hold me captive and force me into marriage, who's to say he's not capable of setting up Isaac to be killed.

"So, he's okay? That's good. How are you?"

Keeping it short, since our time is limited, I give him a brief recap about what's happened with me. How I leaned on Noah, thinking he was being a friend, until the second I refused to cooperate and his switch flipped, turning him into a psycho, who was holding me captive and demanding I marry him against my will.

"Jesus, Cam. Thank God Isaac was able to find you," Dad says, horror in his voice. "Damn it, I hate being locked in here."

"Isaac didn't save me," I mutter. "He saw pictures of Noah comforting me at the funeral and when he was told we applied for a marriage license and learned we were living together, he assumed I had moved on. I just don't get it. It's like he doesn't even know how much I love him. How could he believe I would move on that fast?"

"Oh, Cam. I don't believe that. I've seen you two together. He knows how much you love him, but sometimes love has a way of making us stupid." He chuckles under his breath, and for the first time I find myself cracking a smile. "The harder we love, the harder we hurt and we expect the worst, waiting for the other shoe to drop, because in our world, that shoe almost always drops. Maybe, instead of being mad at him for assuming the worst, you can show him why it's okay to believe in your love. I know you fell hard and fast, but this is all still new. You both have a lot of growing up to do... together."

His words, his wisdom, wrap around my heart like a vine, squeezing it just enough to remind me it's still inside me and beating. He's right. Our love might be strong, but it's still new and fragile. And neither of us is perfect. We're going to make mistakes. I asked him to pull me closer, yet as soon as I got upset, I pushed him away as well.

"Cam, you there?" Dad asks softly.

"Yeah, thank you, Dad. I needed to hear that."

"I'm always here for you, sweetie. Now tell me something

good. I don't want our conversation to end on a bad note."

"I'm pregnant," I blurt out, remembering the rainbow during the storm.

"What? I'm going to be a grandpa?" he asks, his voice filled with emotion.

"Yep. I'm due in February."

"Congratulations. You're going to make a wonderful mother."

"Thank you."

The guard announces our time is up, so we reluctantly say goodbye with me promising to see him as soon as I can and for him to call me when he can.

We hang up, and I sit in bed for several minutes staring at the phone, that's no doubt thanks to Isaac. It's been a week since I found out Isaac was alive, and every day, he's made it a point to spoil me rotten, while I've stubbornly ignored him.

The day after I arrived, a brand-new wardrobe appeared—all maternity clothes, complete with cute bathing suits to use in the pool. The next day, I woke up to an iPad on the nightstand with an Amazon account filled with money to purchase e-books. The fourth day, I found an assortment of sweets on the counter with a note that read, "In case you're having any cravings." There was also my favorite ice cream in the freezer and more snacks in the fridge. Two days ago, a maternity box appeared. It was for pregnant women in their second trimester and included items like lotion, relaxing herbal tea, comfy socks, and a plush robe. Yesterday, another box appeared filled with a pregnancy journal and polaroid camera to document every milestone. On top of all that, he's made me breakfast, lunch, and dinner every day, which I've accepted but refused to eat with him.

But him finding a way to make sure my dad and I could talk is my breaking point. Yes, I'm upset he hid shit from me. No, he never should've kept me in the dark. But what my dad said makes a lot of sense. Sometimes love makes us stupid. Our love is new, and instead of pushing each other away, we need to be holding each other close. We've already missed out on months together...

Throwing the phone on the bed, I run out of my room in search of Isaac. I check the master bedroom, where he's been sleeping, the bathroom, then the kitchen, but he's not in any of those places. I look outside, but he's not there either. So, I head out to the garage, only to find it empty. I'm starting to get worried something's happened to him, when I spot a set of stairs I hadn't noticed before. I climb up them, wondering what's on the third floor. When I get to the top, I open the door and find it's an attic, only a really big one.

"Isaac, are you in here?" I yell out.

"Yeah." He steps into view. "Is everything okay?"

I walk closer to him. "I was looking for you. What are you..." And that's when I see an older, yet gorgeous wooden circular bassinet.

"This was mine," he says with a small shrug. "My mom liked to keep everything. It's old but in perfect condition, so I thought I could restore it. I just finished sanding it down and was trying to decide what color to paint it, but since we don't know the sex—"

"A boy," I choke out over the ball of emotion lodged in my throat. "We're having a little boy."

"A boy?" he repeats, his voice full of wonder. "Yeah?"

"Yeah. I found out at my last appointment and all I could think about was if he'd look like you. I was devastated to not have you there, but I was also happy that through that devastation I would always have a piece of you."

Isaac drops his chin to his chest and shakes his head. "I'm so fucking sorry, Cam. All I wanted to do was protect you." He looks back up at me with glossy eyes. "What if Horatio didn't save my life and you got into that truck with me? What if I showed my face and the next time he blew up our home or another vehicle? I love you so damn much, baby. I didn't consider how badly you would be hurting, only that you would be safe... Fuck!" He slams the tool in his hand against the wall. "I didn't even manage that! You were living with, being held captive by the fucking bastard who probably tried to kill me. I hid, and by doing so, I sent you straight into the lion's den. If he hadn't filed for the marriage license..."

He's about to throw something else, but before he can, I rush toward him, wrapping myself around his body, my arms around his neck. His arms envelop me tightly, his face nuzzling into my neck. "Fuck, Cam," he mumbles. "I'm so damn sorry. I know I fucked up..." Each of his words come out mixed with hurt and fear and apology, and I know as upset as I was at him, he was even madder at himself.

"Shh," I say. "It's okay. You did what you thought was the best thing for me. Just like my parents did." I might not agree with any of their choices, but I can see now they didn't do it to hurt me. They did it to protect me, because they love me. I've only been pregnant for a few months, and I already know I would do everything in my power to protect my baby.

"You could've been hurt. He could've hurt you."

"I'm fine. I'm alive and well, and so are you. We're going to get through this together. Just remember in the future that we're stronger together than apart. Okay?" I pull back and our eyes meet.

"I love you so much. I promise. From now on, we're in this together." He leans down and presses a feather-like kiss to my lips, and I sigh in contentment.

"I can't believe you're really here," I murmur, running my hands up his chest over his thin Henley. "I dreamed of this every night. Wished and hoped and prayed..." Grabbing the hem of his shirt, I lift it over his head, exposing his tight muscular pecs and six-pack abs. Somehow, they're even more defined than they were months ago. "I knew you were alive. I felt it in here." I place my palm over his heart, and he releases a harsh breath.

"I was so hell-bent on protecting you, I didn't think about the stress it would cause you." He lifts my hand and brings it up to his mouth, kissing the inside of my wrist. "I made a mistake, a shit decision..."

"It's okay. All that matters is that we're here now." I snake my arms around Isaac's neck at the same time he lifts me. My legs wrap around his waist and he carries me out of the attic and down the stairs, to the master bedroom.

He lays me out on the center of the bed and removes my clothes, piece by piece, until I'm in only a small pair of cheeky maternity underwear he bought for me.

"Your turn," I demand, nodding toward his pants. He

reaches into his pocket and drags out his phone and keys, setting them on the nightstand before he unbuttons and unzips his jeans, pushing them down his muscular thighs and leaving him in only his boxers.

He turns his attention back to me, and his heated gaze rakes down my body, stopping on my newly protruding belly. I'm not big by any means, but there's a visible bump that's popped out in the last couple weeks, bringing me from slightly bloated to pregnant status.

A soft smile splays across his face as he dips down and places several kisses to the center of my belly. As I watch him kiss every inch of my flesh that's housing our growing baby, I reach for his phone and snap a couple pictures for the journal he bought me.

Once he's done giving my belly attention, he crawls up my body and his mouth connects with mine in a slow yet passionate kiss. One of his hands holds him up, while the other skates down my body, tweaking my nipple, massaging my side, and landing between my legs. Our kiss heats up, as his fingers push into me slowly.

"Your body knows my touch," he murmurs against my lips. "The second I touch you, it reacts. You feel how wet you are..." He thrusts his fingers into me harder, deeper, before he pulls them out, bringing them up to my mouth, dragging them across the seam of my lips so I can taste myself. I dart my tongue out, licking his finger, and his eyes light up.

He crashes his mouth back against mine, and after pushing his boxers down and hooking my leg around his torso, he enters me in one fluid motion, deliciously filling me up. My fingers grip his shoulders and my back arches slightly.

Isaac makes love to me slowly, methodically, as if every thrust of his hips, every swipe of his tongue, every bite to my lips is a silent apology, begging me to forgive him. And in response, I hold him tighter, squeeze my thighs harder, kiss him deeper, wordlessly conveying how much I love him and need him and forgive him.

When we've both found our release, Isaac pulls out and picks me up, carrying me to the bathroom so we can get cleaned up. Once we're done, he carries me back to bed and wraps me up in his strong, comforting arms, spooning me from behind. "I'm never letting you out of my sight again," he murmurs softly. "Not you or our baby."

With his hand protectively over my belly, we both fall asleep, and for the first time in months, it feels like I actually do sleep.

Twenty Nine

ISAAC

"HEY, ISAAC. DIDN'T YOU SAY you're an only child?" Camilla glances at me from behind a box of shit in the attic with a confused look on her face. We've spent the morning going through the stuff in the attic after Camilla noticed a few baby items in a box. It's been mostly sentimental items from my childhood and Camilla has even found a few pieces of clothing I wore as a baby she plans to wash so the baby can wear them as well. After my parents died, I boarded up the place and never returned until I needed a place to hide that nobody knew about. Since everyone thought I sold it years ago, it was the perfect place to disappear to.

"I am." I set the box down I was looking through and walk over to where she is.

"Not according to this birth certificate." She hands me a document and I skim over it. It's an older looking birth certificate. The name on it is Ian Perry and the parents listed are Ophelia Perry and Samuel Petrosian. I read through all the information in shock.

"Have you ever heard of that name before?" Camilla asks.

"No, but whoever this is, was born after my parents met. I can't believe my dad knew about another child and had nothing to do with him. Growing up, he was such a hands-on dad."

"Maybe something happened to him, like he died, and it was too hard for your dad to talk about."

"Maybe." I pull my phone out and dial Frank. He answers on the first ring.

"Everything okay?"

"I'm not sure. Do you know an Ian Perry?" The silence on the other end tells me he does. "Frank..."

"Before your mom came along, your dad played the field. He was young and having fun. He met Ophelia and they had a fling. When he met your mom, he cut it off because he only had eyes for your mom. Ophelia took the breakup hard and to punish him, didn't tell him he had a son. It wasn't until years later, when she was sick, she decided to tell him."

What the fuck... "Are you telling me I have a half-brother

out there somewhere I've never known about?"

"When she approached your dad, your mom was also sick. She had cancer and was going through chemo. Your dad was pissed this information was kept from him for years, but he didn't want to upset your mom when she was in such a fragile state, so he made the decision to keep the past in the past."

I blow out a harsh breath, dropping onto a tub. "I can understand why he would want to protect my mom, but damn, to deny his son? I'm not sure how I feel about that."

"He was doing what he felt was best. Was he right or wrong? I'm not going to judge him. We all have to make decisions in our life we hope are the right ones, and live with the ones that aren't."

"Can you find out about Ian for me? Where he lives, what he's doing with his life. Maybe after all this shit is over I can reach out to him. He's the only blood family I have left."

"Yeah, I'll look into it. How're you holding up? How's Camilla?"

I glance at her sitting on the floor, rubbing her belly. In the last few weeks since we've been here her bump has grown significantly. She's begun to feel the baby fluttering inside, but I'm not able to feel it on the outside yet. While we're worried about the fact that nobody can seem to find Noah, we've spent the time together making up for lost time.

"We're good. Any news?"

"No. Aside from him asking about Camilla when she first disappeared, he's been silent. We searched his house, but he hasn't been there. I'll let you know if I hear anything. And I'll have Ian Perry looked into as well."

"Thanks, Frank."

We hang up, and I tell Camilla what Frank told me, and of course, she agrees with him about my dad. "He's not alive, so you can't ask him what happened, but you knew your father. Do you believe he would just ignore his own child without reason?"

"No, I don't." My dad was a tough man, but he was also a family man. I don't believe he would deny his son without a good reason. I don't know why he never reached out to Ian after my mom was better, but there had to have been a reason.

"I'm starving," Camilla says, changing the subject. "What do you say we take a break and eat lunch and go for a swim?"

"Sounds perfect." I help her up and we head downstairs. She's been on a chili kick lately, so I heat some up for us, while she toasts a few pieces of bread and slices up some fruit. Then we take our food out onto the patio since it's a beautiful fall afternoon. All too soon winter will be in full swing, so we've been soaking up the sunshine while we can.

While we eat, she flips through her pregnancy journal, so she can tell me what's happening with the baby today. For every day, it gives you a tidbit on the baby's growth. "Today, I'm twenty weeks," she begins, then stops, her eyes going wide. "Oh no! I'm twenty weeks."

I immediately go on alert, unsure what the hell that means, aside from it being halfway to her due date. "What's wrong? What do you need?"

"Oh, nothing is wrong. I had a doctor's appointment scheduled..." Her face twists into a grimace. "With the OB/GYN Noah found for me."

I sigh in relief. "Jesus, woman. You scared me half to death."

"Sorry." She blanches. "But I do need to see a doctor. I can't believe it's already been over a month since my last appointment." She glances around and smiles. "I was thinking... Since the building where we used to live in was ruined, and we're going to need somewhere to live and raise our baby... What about staying here?"

The idea of being here used to make me sad. It was hard to walk around, knowing my parents would never be in this home again. But a lot of time has passed and since I've been here, it's felt like I'm a little closer to them. "You want to make this our home?"

"Yeah." Her smile widens. "I love how peaceful it is out here, and it's safe for a child to run around and play. We could remodel it to our liking, since it needs some updates, but it's a beautiful home that's meant to be lived in." She shrugs. "It's just an idea."

"I love it." I drag her chair toward me and kiss her. "And I love you."

After we finish eating, I call Frank and explain we need to get Camilla's records from her old doctor and have them sent to a new one. He already knows everything needs to be kept under wraps. A few hours later, he texts me with the new doctor's name and appointment information.

"Dr. Tobias will be here tomorrow morning at nine o'clock. She's aware of the need for discretion and has agreed to be driven here."

"That was fast."

"Money talks."

"THANK YOU FOR COMING ON SUCH SHORT NOTICE."

I shake Dr. Tobias's hand, welcoming her inside, as her assistant carries the equipment needed for the appointment.

"It's no trouble." She turns her attention on Camilla. "And you must be the patient." She winks sweetly, and Camilla sags in relief. She was worried she wouldn't like the doctor the same way she liked her other one. I can tell she's been nervous, and I hate her being even more stressed.

"I am. Thank you for coming all the way out here."

"I'm going to have Josie take your blood. It's standard procedure. When the results come back, if there's any cause for concern, I'll give you a call."

After her blood's been taken, we make our way to the guestroom, so Camilla can lie down. The doctor has her change into a gown she brought so she can check her internally, while the nurse sets up the ultrasound machine.

She warns us that because it's a traveling machine, it won't be as clear as the newer ones, but she'll be able to get the measurements and check everything she needs to check.

Wanting to see everything, I carry a chair over to sit next to Camilla's head, while the doctor gets situated and the nurse takes Camilla's blood pressure. Camilla's hand finds mine, and she squeezes it softly. When I glance down at her, she mouths, "I love you," and I lean over to kiss her forehead.

"Love you, *meu amor*." With the transducer on Camilla's

stomach, the doctor clicks on the screen. It takes a few seconds, but then a loud *whoosh, whoosh, whoosh* fills the silence, and Camilla giggles.

"That's the heartbeat," she gushes. "Isn't it the most beautiful sound in the world?"

"Yeah, it is," I agree, my gaze locked on the gray and white screen, showcasing the outline of our baby. Holy shit, we're having a baby. A tiny little human who's going to be part of this world in a few months. Who I'm going to need to protect and keep safe. Meanwhile, Noah is hiding, and he may or may not be the person who put a hit out on me. I have a brother somewhere I know nothing about, and Camilla and I are hiding while the world thinks I'm dead.

"Hey, you okay?" Camilla asks, shaking me from my thoughts.

"Yeah, just thinking about everything we need to do before this little guy gets here."

The doctor walks us through the measurements and other technical stuff, concluding the baby is measuring perfectly with his due date, weighing in at eleven ounces and seven inches long.

After we schedule the next appointment, we see her out and are heading back inside, when my phone buzzes in my pocket with a text from Frank.

Frank: Dr. Parker, Camilla's previous doctor, called and said her file has been stolen from her office. It had Dr. Tobias's information in it. I'm calling Dr. Tobias now.

Motherfucker.

"Hey, Cam, have you ever shot a gun before?"

She blanches at my question. "What? Did something happen?"

"No, baby." I pull her into my arms, ready to lie before I remember my promise to her. "Actually, yes. Someone broke into Dr. Parker's office and stole your file containing your information and now knows who your new doctor is."

Her face turns white in fear. "It has to have been Noah. What if he comes here?"

"The chances of that happening are slim, since the doctor was picked up from her home and driven here, but you asked me to be honest, so I'm telling you what happened. I want you to be prepared in case anything happens." I walk us over to the foyer table and pull the small drawer open, exposing the gun I placed there months ago.

"Isaac," she gasps, but stays rooted in her spot.

"If something happens and you need to protect yourself, you shoot first and ask questions later. This is the safety." I place the gun into her hand and she accepts it reluctantly. "In order to shoot, you have to release the safety." I show her how it's done. "Now you try." I flip the safety back on and let go, so she can try it herself.

She mimics what I did, then looks up at me for approval. "Good. I have a gun in this drawer." I place it back in the drawer and close it. "Another one in the kitchen drawer to the left of the sink, and there's one in my nightstand drawer."

I cup her face in my hands and kiss her softly. "Hopefully you never have to use it, but I don't know what Noah is capable of."

"I get it," she says with a steady voice. "What happens when your guys who are searching for him find him?"

"I don't know," I admit truthfully. "But if it's between him and us, I'm always going to choose us."

***

"OH MY GOD! DID YOU FEEL THAT?" CAMILLA'S FACE lights up, her eyes filled with such love and happiness, my heart damn near stutters in my chest.

"Feel what?" I joke, making her slap my shoulder. We're lying in bed in post coital bliss and Camilla is trying to get me to feel the baby kicking. The last few weeks the baby has been getting more active and she's dying for me to feel what she's feeling. Dr. Tobias came over this morning for her twenty-four-week checkup and everything looks good. Camilla's bloodwork is perfect and she took some glucose test that made her feel a bit sick, but the doctor said is important.

I can tell Camilla is starting to get antsy here. She's missing her dad, and with the holidays right around the corner, she's mentioned wanting to visit him so he's not alone for Thanksgiving. It will be their first holiday without each other. She also feels bad that Yasmin has no idea if she's dead or alive, since she can't speak to anyone until we find Noah and get this shit sorted.

I've told myself that if my guys haven't found him by Thanksgiving, I would step back out into the spotlight because I can't keep Camilla locked up here forever, even if I love having her all to myself twenty-four-seven. She's already missing a semester of college and won't be able to start back until January, putting her behind. On top of that, the baby is due in February.

"Put your hand... right... here," she says, her eyes locking with mine as she places my hand against her bump. We lie in silence for several seconds, and I'm about to roll over on top of her and kiss the hell out of her, when I feel it. A nudge against my hand.

"Holy shit," I breathe. "That's..."

"Our baby."

"Do it again."

She throws her head back, laughing. "I can't do it again. It's the baby, not me."

"I'm going to keep my hand on you until he does it again," I tell her, mesmerized by the feel of my son's tiny body connecting with mine in some way.

"That could be hours!" she says through another laugh.

"I don't care."

"Well, I do because I need to go pee and shower." She scoots up into a sitting position. "Wanna join me?" She waggles her brows. "You can clean me up since you were the one who dirtied me."

I'm about to tell her it's on, when the sound of my phone rings out through the house. "Shit, I must've left it downstairs. Get the water running and I'll meet you in there."

I peck her lips and climb off the bed, throwing on my sweats before I sprint down the hall and stairs to find my ringing phone. It stops momentarily and then the sound indicating there's a text chimes. I swipe it off the counter where I left it, click on the text, and am reading it, when a throat clearing from behind me draws my attention.

"I couldn't figure out how the fuck the bitch got away. I was searching everywhere for her, and then when I realized something fishy was going on, I disappeared to stay under the radar. Good job hiding." Noah slowly claps as I turn around to face him. "And bonus points for faking your death." His shitty smirk confirms what I already knew. He was responsible for trying to have me killed.

"I never would've thought to come here," he says, pulling a gun out and pointing it directly at me. He clicks the safety off. "All these years and you never once mentioned keeping this place."

"Apparently I wasn't the only one hiding shit," I say in response to the text I just read. "*Brother*."

Noah laughs, full on crazy fucking laughs. "So, you figured it out, huh?"

"That you're Ian Perry and my half-brother... yeah. But what I want to know is, why you didn't tell me. All these years, I thought we were friends." It doesn't make any sense, for him to go over a decade of knowing me without saying a word.

"I was your friend," he barks. "Until you chose that bitch over me, the same way our father chose your mother over me and my mom." His words have the hair on my nape standing at attention, as everything suddenly clicks into place. My truck being bombed... My father's vehicle blowing up... There's no way... It can't be.

"Did you... kill my parents?"

"Do you have any idea what it's like to wonder how you're going to get your next meal?" he asks. "My mom busted her ass every day to take care of me, but when she got sick, when her body and her brain started to work against her, she was fired from her job and nobody would hire her. For years we struggled to make ends meet, and the whole time... The whole fucking time!" he yells, his entire body vibrating with anger. "Your family was living it up in mansions and on yachts!"

I keep my mouth shut, not wanting to piss Noah off more. There's nothing I can say that's going to make this better, and by keeping him on me, he's staying the hell away from Camilla.

"I went to him," he says softly, after a long beat. "When shit got really bad and my mom needed medical help we couldn't afford, I went to Samuel. I told him I was his son, and you know what he did? He dismissed me. Fucking dismissed me! Told me his wife was sick and once she was better, he would reach out."

"And did he?" I ask, needing to know. "Did he reach out

after she was better?"

"He tried, but it was too late. I'm not some afterthought," he hisses.

A small movement in the corner of my eye tells me Camilla has made her way down here and I will her not to come any closer, not to make her presence known. To keep Noah's attention on me, I speak up.

"I didn't know about you. He never said anything."

"I know. I asked you about your family when we first met and it was clear you were never told about me, which is why, after my mom died and I killed our father, I left you alive."

Motherfucker. I knew it. Deep in my gut, when I found out Ian was Noah, I put the pieces together, but I was hoping I was wrong. Because that means for the last decade I let the man who killed my parents into my life. He's lived off the money my dad made because he ended his life. The thought makes me sick to my stomach.

Camilla moves closer, but I don't look at her, not wanting Noah to catch sight of her. "Why spare my life? You already killed my parents."

"Because I realized you weren't our dad. He might've put a woman above his son, but you weren't him. Until you were..." With the gun in his hand, he swipes at a jar on the counter, knocking it to the floor, so it smashes everywhere. "From the day we met, you put me first! And then you met that bitch. And just like your dad chose your mom over me and my mom, you threw me to the side for her!"

He steps forward with his gun aimed straight at me, and with a manic look in his eyes, I have no doubt he's going to shoot to kill.

When he takes another step, I inhale a sharp breath, preparing for the blow that's to come, sending up a silent prayer that Camilla runs for her life and saves herself and our son.

With my eyes on Noah, I tell him the only thing I can say. "I'm sorry."

"Not fucking good—"

Bam! A bullet pierces through his body and his gun flies out of his hand, falling to the ground. I'm not sure where he's been shot, but I don't take the time to care. Quickly grabbing the gun from the ground, I point and shoot to kill, refusing to chance him coming after Camilla.

As the bullet enters his chest, his empty eyes meet mine. "I loved you like a brother," I tell him, needing him to know. "But you're right, I will always choose Camilla."

Epilogue

CAMILLA

THIRTEEN MONTHS LATER

"ARE YOU NERVOUS?" YASMIN ASKS AS I stare at my reflection in the mirror. I'm dressed in a floor-length, long-sleeved wedding gown, and with its plunging illusion bodice and sparkling sequin lace, it's the perfect mix of sexy meets fairy-tale princess. My makeup is done, but not too much, and my hair is down in beach waves, pinned slightly back with a beautiful diamond headband.

"No," I tell her, turning around and extending my arms. "Now give me my precious baby."

Sam—also known as Samuel Isaac Petrosian—squirms in Yasmin's lap, reaching his chubby arms out as he giggles and babbles for me. But before I can grab him, she pulls him back slightly.

"Do you really want to risk him throwing up on your gorgeous wedding dress? He just ate." I consider it for a moment and decide I don't care because anytime I can hold him, I'm going to. As he gets older and more independent, now crawling and walking along furniture, the less he actually wants to be held—unless he's tired of course.

Scooping him up into my arms, I hold him tight, twirling us around, while I kiss the top of his head, inhaling his fresh baby scent. He's dressed in an adorable black tux with a cute pink bowtie that matches the beading of my dress. He laughs and smiles so carefree, my heart feels as though it's leaping from my chest. All the women who come into my boutique love him because he's such a happy baby, always smiling and laughing when they talk to him. Such a flirt, just like his daddy.

I close my eyes and momentarily get lost in my son, until Yasmin says my name.

"Cam, seriously, are you okay?"

"Yeah," I choke out. "I'm about to marry the love of my life, I have a beautiful, healthy little boy..."

"But..."

"But I wish my dad were here," I admit. "He's just missed so much. Our housewarming party after we finished renovating the house, the birth of Sam, our engagement party, his christening, my graduation, the opening of my store."

"I'm sorry, sweetie," she says, wrapping her arms around me and Sam, who squeals in delight, thinking she's playing a game. "I wish there was something I could do."

"I know and I appreciate that." I take a deep breath, kiss Sam on the forehead, and hand him back to Yasmin. Since we decided on an intimate wedding with only Isaac and me, Yasmin and Frank—who are serving as our witnesses—and Sam, we didn't do a bridal party, keeping it simple. Yasmin will hold Sam, while I walk myself down the aisle and once we've said our vows, she'll give him back to me. Afterward, we're going to go to dinner to celebrate, and then Yasmin is taking Sam for the night, so Isaac and I can enjoy our wedding night, before we take off, with Sam, on our honeymoon—destination is a secret—where we'll be spending the holidays.

Yasmin heads out with Sam, and I wait for the wedding march to begin so I can walk out. The photographer Isaac hired to capture the day stays back with a camera in her hand. After a few minutes, when the music still hasn't started, I'm about to head out, thinking maybe I misunderstood, when the door opens and my heart drops into my stomach.

This can't be... I must be seeing things...

"Dad," I breathe.

"God, you look beautiful." He smiles softly. "I heard you're in need of someone to walk you down the aisle."

Raw emotion clogs my throat as I run into my dad's arms. "Oh, Dad! I can't believe you're here." We hold each other for several minutes before I glance up at him and he smiles warmly down at me.

"Don't cry, sweetie, it'll ruin your makeup."

"How is this possible?" I ask, stepping back and swiping under my eyes. Luckily, the makeup artist I went to insisted on water-proof makeup.

"You have one determined husband. My conviction has been overturned."

"What?" I gasp. "You're out for good? I had no idea."

He chuckles lightly. "Isaac asked me not to say anything. He didn't want to get your hopes up. I actually got out a little over a week ago, which was why I asked you not to visit. I had some things I had to deal with. Clint and James have been charged with fraud, on top of money laundering and tax evasion."

"I can't believe this. How?"

"Isaac... He hired people to investigate and didn't stop until they found everything Clint and his son were hiding. You have a good man, Cam."

"Yes, he is." I hug him again, needing to feel him.

After I quickly clean up my face, my dad hooks his arm in with mine and the music starts. We walk together to the top of the aisle, where I find my sexy soon-to-be husband standing at the altar with our son in his arms.

"Mama!" Sam yells, making us all laugh.

I step forward, ready to sprint down the aisle to get to my boys, but my dad halts me in place. "Go slow, Cam. Take it all in. I can still remember the day I married your mother."

With his words, I release a calming breath, and we step forward together. The walk to the front feels like it takes forever, but I do as my dad said and soak in all the details. Isaac in his tux, holding our son in his strong arms as he watches me move toward them. When we reach the front, Isaac hands Sam to Yasmin, who continues to shriek in excitement, wanting me.

Dad kisses my cheek as he releases my hand and places it into Isaac's. "Thank you for loving her and making her happy," Dad says to Isaac, who nods once, his eyes never leaving mine.

"Thank you for making today perfect," I whisper to my soon-to-be husband as we step up to the altar.

The officiant speaks about love and life and happiness and once he's done, we say our vows, promising, in front of God and our family and friends to love each other, until death do us part.

"You may now kiss the bride," he says after I've placed Isaac's wedding band on his finger. He steps closer and, cradling my face in his hands, softly and passionately kisses me.

"You're finally mine," he says against my lips.

"Officially," I murmur, "but we both know I've been yours since the day we met."

"Yeah, you have," he agrees. "Just like I've always been yours."

About the Author

Reading is like breathing in, writing is like breathing out. – Pam Allyn

Nikki Ash resides in South Florida where she is an English teacher by day and a writer by night. When she's not writing, you can find her with a book in her hand. From the Boxcar Children, to Wuthering Heights, to the latest single parent romance, she has lived and breathed every type of book. While reading and writing are her passions, her two children are her entire world. You can probably find them at a Disney park before you would find them at home on the weekends!

Printed in Great Britain
by Amazon

10605612R00208